I0564133

Montag Press Team:
Editor – Mara Hodges
Cover Illustration – Dwight Clark
Cover Design and Ebook – Sean Barnes
Book Design and Layout – Badger McInnes
Managing Director – Charlie Franco

A Montag Press Book
www.montagpress.com
1066 47th Ave Unit #9
Oakland CA 94601

Montag Press, the burning book with the hatchet cover, the skewed word mark and the portrayal of the long-suffering fireman mascot are trademarks of Montag Press.

Printed & Digitally Originated in the United States of America
10 9 8 7 6 5 4 3 2 1

THE GONAYMNE WEAPON

NIGEL ANTHONY SELLARS

MONTAG

DEDICATION

This one is for absent friends and lost loves, all of whom believed
in me even when I couldn't.

GLOSSARY FOR THE
GONAYMNE WEAPON

General Terms and Askanderian Terms

The "purely" Askanderian words are either twisted versions of English words or the literal pronunciation of an acronym. Other terms are derived from Arabic, while a couple are complete inventions. While written Arabic is virtually the same for all Arabic countries, the pronunciation can vary considerably, so much so that Arabic speakers can identify from where another speaker comes by the dialect and pronunciation of some words. For example, the Arabic **kh** is pronounced like the **ch** as in Scots **loch** or German **Bach**. The Gaelic terms are Scots Gaelic, from the Highlands, and are pronounced pretty much as written in Roman letters, with a few unique variations, such as **bh** being pronounced like the letter **v** in English.

Ajnabi: *(Ahj-nobby)*; From Arabic: Literally, stranger, or alien.

Araki: *(ah-ROC-kee)*; Arabic for brandy, though specifically it refers to anise-flavored, unsweetened, clear, distilled alcoholic drink, similar to Greek ouzo or Scandinavian akvavit.

Arcology: *(AR-call-ogee)*; a combination of the terms "architecture" and "ecology," an arcology is a hyperstructure building designed for very densely populated habitats. A single arcology would contain a variety of residential, commercial, and agricultural facilities and essentially operate as an independent entity. Arcologies were meant to minimize individual human impact on the environment. The term itself was coined by Italian architect Paolo Soleri (1919 – 2013.) Another name for an arcology is an *urban monad –*"single city structure," a term coined by science fiction writer Robert Silverberg.

Baraka l'aufic: *(barakah loffik)*; Arabic: "Blessings upon you." On Askander, the blessing would be from the Hidden Hand.

Bhagavad Gita: *(Bog-o-VOD Geetah)*; a 700-verse section of the long Hindu epic Mahabharata. Basically a dialogue between Prince Arjuna and the god-king Krishna concerning duties, attitudes, and methods of attaining enlightenment. At one point, Krishna takes on the incarnation of Shiva, the deity of death and destruction.

Chador: *(CHA-dor)*; Persian, derived from the Sanskrit for "cloak." A full, body-length semi-circle of fabric open down the front. Tossed over the woman's head, the chador has no hand openings or any buttons or clasps. It is held closed in the front by the wearer's hands or tucked under her arms. It does **not** cover the face.

Cittern: (sit-TURN); A stringed instrument of 4 to 6 double courses, like a lute, mandolin or bouzouki. It dates from the Renaissance, although it has roots in the medieval period. It was more a popular culture instrument like the modern guitar than it was an orchestral instrument.

Czardas: (ZAR-dos); A traditional Hungarian folk dance. The name derives from csárda, an old Hungarian word for a tavern. Oddly, it apparently developed from the 18th century Hungarian verbunkos, a recruiting dance of the Hungarian army.

Dacha: (Dack-uh); From Russian for a small summer house in the countryside.

Databug (aka a plug-in): Cyber data device, which can be inserted (plugged in) to a wired-in socket just behind the ear.

Dhirek: (deer-EK); Askanderian: director.

Einstein-Rosen bridge: An Einstein-Rosen bridge is another name for a **wormhole**, a topological feature of spacetime that would act as a "shortcut" through spacetime. Like a tunnel, the bridge has two ends, each in separate points in spacetime.

Estampie: (EH-stam-pee); French: a slow, stamping, round dance originating the Provençal region of France. The dance was popular in Europe from the 12th to 15th centuries.

Fredaris: (Free-dar-ees); a drug similar to hashish and made from the resin of an unnamed Askanderian plant. When smoked, the drug heightens the senses and increases paranoia slightly, all for the purpose of keeping the user from being swindled.

Gall Oglaigh: (Gal O-glah); Scots Gaelic. Often Anglicized as "gallowglass." Historically, they were mercenaries of Scots and Norse ancestry from the Scottish Highlands who worked for Irish, and later Norman Irish, lords. The Tuatha version are genetically engineered elite troops akin to Nazi Germany's Waffen SS.

Gesellschaft: (GEH-zel-shaft); German: corporation.

Gonaymne: (GAN-ime); Term for the Nameless Ones, the aliens who built the hyper-portals. From the Irish "gan aimn," meaning "without a name."

Great Leap Outward: Term for the diaspora of different human groups to the stars following the Third Zaibatsu War (early 22nd century OCE).

Hamami: *(Hah-MAM-ee);* A dove, from Arabic.

Hausfatah: *(hous-fah-TAH);* "house father"—head of a family who controls a city-state/corporation.

Hedgehog: A tracked mobile rocket launcher.

Hyperspace Portal: The devices built around an artificial black hole to create Einstein-Rosen bridges for use in interstellar travel. Built by the Gonaymne thousands of years before human civilization emerged.

Isaak: A name for small, handheld computer or a computer tablet. Named for Isaac Newton. A play on the name of Apple Computer's early message pad, the "Newton."

Istar'far: *(istar-FAR);* Arabic, roughly "please forgive me" or "my sincere apologies."

Jherek: *(Jer-REK); Askanderian:* Junior executive.

Kaffiya: *(ka-FEE-yah);* A traditional Middle Eastern headdress made from a square cotton scarf with a distinctive checkered pattern. In arid regions it provides protection from sun, dust and sand.

Keriha wardi: *(KER-ee-ha WAHR-dee);* Stink flower, turd flower. Askanderian flora. A rose-like flower of numerous colors possessing a very unpleasant, strong fecal scent. Name is adapted from Arabic.

Kruskal pathway (aka Kruskal–Szekeres coordinates): Kruskal–Szekeres coordinates refer to the system for the Schwarzschild geometry describing the spacetime geometry of empty space surrounding any spherical mass such as a black hole. While the geometry was developed by mathematician Karl Schwarzschild, those specifically for a black hole are named after Martin David Kruskal, American mathematician and physicist (1925-2006) and Hungarian–Australian mathematician George Szekeres (1911—2005).

Kyoketsu shogi: *(key-oh-KET-soo SHO-gee);* Japanese: A weapon featuring a double edged blade, with a smaller, curved blade attached a 45-60 degree angle above the hilt. This is attached to a 3.5 to 5.5 meter (12-18 feet) length of rope, chain, or braided hair that has a large metal ring attached at the opposite end. Used almost exclusively by the ninja.

La souffrance: *(LAH SOO-frans);* The Suffering, from French. It refers to a secular meditation discipline developed in the mid-twenty-first century.

Larkinites: Tuatha radicals who tried to stop Alba Nuadh from selling its young people as mercenaries. Less than a century before the novel begins, they were arrested, tried and executed for treason. Their name derives from Irish labor leader and political radical James Larkin.

Manag: *(MAN-awj);* Askanderian: manager.

Midnight lace: slang for an illicit drug that is a synthetic combination opiate and hallucinogen.

Mirjan'zhur: *(mur-jan-ZHOOR);* Coral flower. It describes a flower of mostly reddish brown color that resembles coral from Earth. (Askanderian flora) Name is adapted from Arabic.

Misbaha: *(miz-BUH-ha);* Worry beads (from Arabic).

Mostazafin: *(mu-STAH-zuh-fin);* Workers (from Arabic).

Mukhalafi: *(moo-ka-la-FEE);* Resistance (from Arabic).

Mutui: *(moo-TO-ee);* pouch for carrying smoking materials, such as *fredaris.*

Nafs: *(navz);* Soul, spirit (from Arabic).

Nebid: *(NEH-bid);* Wine (Arabic).

Ox: *(Ahks);* A Tuatha battle-machine that "walks" on four legs like a bovine, hence the name.

Pavane: *(PUH-van);* A sedate and dignified couple's dance, common in Europe during the Renaissance. In duple meter (2/2) rhythm.

Pinocheted: *(pee-no-SHET-ed);* The mass killing of hundreds or thousands of people in a public venue, like a stadium or theater. Derived from Chilean dictator Augusto *Pinochet* and his slaughter of 1,200 to 3,200 dissidents in a Santiago stadium in 1973 OCE (Old Common Era).

Plasticrete: *(plas-ti-CREET);* Concrete analogy made of synthetic compounds rather than natural materials.

Plasteel: *(pla-STEEL);* Synthetic compound resembling steel but containing no metals.

Rebab: *(reh-BAB);* Type of a bowed string instrument dating from at least the 8th Century C.E. Arabic traders carried it to North Africa, the Middle East, parts of Europe, and the Far East. Some versions have a spike at the bottom to rest it on the ground. Another version, with a pear-shaped body like a lute, reached western Europe in the 11th century C.E., and became the rebec, a forerunner of the violin.

Reconstructionist Movement: Planetary colonization movement trying to restore what some believed were ancient or historical ethnic or religious cultures, most of which never existed except in the minds of the Reconstructionists themselves.

Rupush: *(roo-PUSH)*; a loose-fitting dress, worn with a chador.

Saighdear, pl. Saighdearan: *(SAY-der: SAY-der-ahn)*; Foot-soldiers. From Scots Gaelic.

Samki: *(SOM-key)*; Arabic: fish.

Sebsi: *(seb-SEE)*; Arabic, a smoking pipe.

Séo: *(SAY-oh)*; Askanderian pronunciation of the acronym for CEO, or Chief executive officer. The head of a corporate city-state.

Santour: *(SAN-toor)*; A Persian version of the trapezoid-shaped hammered dulcimer, often made of walnut or different exotic woods. The classic santour has 72 strings, although versions with 100 strings are not uncommon.

Shawm: *(SHA-um)*; A double-reed woodwind instrument from the Medieval Period and the Renaissance. It probably originated in the East as its name resembles that used for nearly identical instruments from Arabia, Turkey, Persia, China, and India, although its roots are probably ancient. The forerunner of the modern oboe, the shawm has finger holes instead of keys and is significantly louder than its descendant. The shawm was traditionally made from a single piece of wood with a conical internal bore. It ended in a flared bell similar to a trumpet. It was made in several sizes, including a large bass one that is the ancestor of the bassoon. Besides the oboe and bassoon, the shawm's descendants include the bombard of Brittany, which is loud enough to compete with bagpipes in marching bands.

Sidi: *(SEE-dee)*; From Arabic for "my master," although more similar to conventional English "sir" or "mister."

Skean dubh: *(Skeen-doov)*; From Scots Highland Gaelic. Literally "black (dubh) knife (skean)" or "hidden knife." A small, single-edged knife (Scots Gaelic *sgian*) originally worn as part of traditional Scottish Highland dress. It was normally worn on the leg, but which leg depended on whether the wearer was right or left-handed. The knife is usually under 11 inches long, including the black-colored hilt. The primary meaning of *dubh* is "black" but it has the secondary meaning of "hidden."

Souk: *(sook)*; Arabic for a market or bazaar.

Suma: *(SOO-mah)*; Consumer—anyone not an executive.

Tawarik: *(ta-WAHR-eek)*; An Ajnabi Bard, historian, tale-teller.

Tourdion: *(toor-dee-on);* A 15th and 16th century lively Burgundian dance in triple meter whose name comes from the French verb "tordre" (to twist).

Tuatha: *(too-AITHA);* Celto-Aryan Mercenaries, name comes from the mythical Irish "Tuatha De Dannan," or "tribe of the goddess Danu."

Uisge beatha: *(whisk beeth);* Whiskey. Scots Gaelic for "water of life."

Voder: *(VO-dhur);* Universal translator.

Volapük: *(Vo-la-pook);* An artificial language based on English, French, German, Latin, etc, invented by Johann Schleyer (1831-1912) in 1880. Briefly used in Austro-Hungarian Empire to overcome German/Magyar language issues. The name translates as "World Speak."

Yadd la yuhish minnak: May the Hidden Hand bless you (from Arabic).

Yadd-khabba: *(YAD kabuh);* Hidden Hand (from Arabic).

Ynglas: *(eeng-GLAS);* Askanderian: Dwarf pseudo-coniferous "tree" native to Askander. Similar to a pine, cedar, or fir (Askanderian flora).

Zaibatsu: *(zie-BOT-su);* Japanese term for corporations.

Iimarae Terms

The Iimarae terms are invented words meant to sound a bit like bird calls. The Iimarae proper names are actually anagrams based on the last names of some friends.

Fah'gid'sla: *(Fuh-GED-slaw);* An outcast, not part of the Flock, or one banished or shunned by the Flock.

Hree'Rchee: *(Hu-REE-ri-chee);* Proper name of a Great Hen, roughly akin to "She Who Must Be Obeyed."

Ki'ind'rou: *(KEE-ind-roo);* Iimarae meditation state in which the elders psychically merge with their group and seek out improper thoughts, mainly seditious or rebellious ideas. The elder can then kill the dissident by telekinetically stopping its heart and squeezing its lungs empty.

Ryf'Tael: *(RIFF-tale);* Proper name meaning "Lowly Messenger."

Se'bes'vos: *(see-BEZ-voos);* Dominant matriarch in a group of elders. Usually the *se'bes'vos* is destined to become a Great Hen—a queen—whose superior genes are passed on to the Flock as a whole.

Shin'kmiqt: *(sheen-KIM-eekt);* An insult aimed at males—roughly means "worm" or "turd."

Ajnabi names

Ishan: *(Ee-shun).*

Hakyka: *(Ha-kick-uh).*

Fadyli: *(Fah-dhy-lee).*

Place Names

Alba Nuadh: *(AL-bah NOO-ad);* New Alba, the Tuatha homeworld (from Gaelic). Alba was the historical name for Scotland. The Latin equivalent is "Nova Scotia."

Ciudad Rand *(See-oo-dad Rand);* Friedmanville; Von Misestown: The three largest and most powerful of more than twenty major arcologies on Askander.

Coase Mare: *(Cos Mah-REE);* The ocean that encompasses five-sixths of Askander's surface. Named for Chicago School neo-classical economist Ronald Coase (1910-2013 OCE) and the Latin, *mare,* for ocean.

Dravidia, Dravidians: *(DRUH-vid-ee-uh; DRUH-vid-ee-uns,);* Colonists of a planet orbiting Tau Ceti. It was settled by people of Dravidian ancestry seeking to restore an early, non-Hindu Indian sub-continent society from the Indus Valley (modern Pakistan), and one of the earliest human civilizations. Mostly from Southern and Eastern India, Dravidian languages are not Indo-European, and therefore not derived from Sanskrit. Dravidian languages include Tamil, Malayalam, Telugu, Kannada, and Gondi. In this universe, Dravidia was part of the Reconstructionist movement.

Fama: *(FAH-ma);* Small continent off the south coast of Stiglera. Named for neo-classical economist Eugene Fama (b. 1939).

Feltsvurld: *(FELTZ-wurld);* The fifth planet of the star Wolf 154, it was settled as Reconstructionist religious colony, but became an authoritarian theocracy.

Fogelland: *(FOE-gull-lund);* Small continent to the north and east of Stiglera.

It is the closest land-mass to Askander's polar ice cap. Named for neo-classical economist Robert Fogel (1926–2013).

Jabal Shiti: *(JA-bal SHee-tee);* Rainy Mountain.

Nahr Sakhr: *(NAR-Sack-HAR);* Stone River. The largest river and most significant waterway, the Nahr Sakhr flows past the foot of Ciudad Rand and cuts a valley through the mountainous area down to a sea.

Ramal: *(RA-mol);* Planet orbiting Barnard's Star. A Reconstructionist colony that collapsed into a brutal autocracy. Its capital is Dareshab.

Rothbard Mountains: The major mountain range of Askander. Ciudad Rand is built on a plateau in the range. Named for Austrian School economist Murray Rothbard (1926–1995).

Shaul Khala: *(shal HA-la);* Great Desert; this dominates most of the land area of Askander.

Stiglera: *(STEEG-lur-uh);* The major continent of Askander, named for Chicago School neo-classical economist George Stigler (1911–1991).

Treason's Tooth: Name of the huge volcanic mesa into which Ciudad Rand is built.

Planetary League starships (PLS) and starship classes

PLS Ferdinand Lassalle: Named for Ferdinand Johann Gottlieb Lassalle, a nineteenth century (1825-1864) German jurist, philosopher, and international-style socialist political activist.

PLS William D. Haywood: Named for William Dudley Haywood, an American labor leader and socialist (1869 -1928). Haywood was a hard rock miner who became a leader of the Western Federation of Miners and in 1905 helped found and later led the radical Industrial Workers of the World (IWW).

Kautsky-class: Heavy, military starship type named for Karl Kautsky (1854 –1938) Czech-German philosopher, journalist, and Marxist theoretician. From the death of Friedrich Engels in 1895 to the start of World War I, Kautsky— nicknamed the "Pope of Marxism"—was a leading advocate of orthodox Marxism. After World War I, Kautsky was an outspoken left-wing critic of the Bolshevik Revolution.

PROLOGUE

"By now the story is old, but it should never be forgotten. Humanity had somehow survived the first two Zaibatsu Wars in the Twenty-First and Twenty-Second centuries of the Old Common Era. The privatized wars between the great multinationals for markets and consumers produced great suffering, but neither came as close to destroying humanity once and for all as did the horrific Third War. That war carried far into space, with conflict over Mars and the Jovian and Saturnine moons. Then, in one of the greatest and paradoxical incidents in human history, a North American Free Trade Zone war vessel searched for a Greater Asian Co-Prosperity Sphere ship hiding among the comets in the Oort Cloud at the farthest reaches of the solar system. Instead of finding the enemy, however, the North American ship stumbled upon the first of the mysterious Hyperspace Portals. The system for interstellar travel, built eons ago by unknown beings,

initially offered hope of new resources that could stabilize the world's economies and bring the wars to an end. That naïve hope went unfulfilled.

'Instead, the Portals became the means for both the desperate and the wealthy to abandon the Earth for other worlds."

—Wilhelm von Mansker, Humanity Looks Back and Ahead, 3rd edition, London, 849 New Common Era

CHAPTER ONE

"As the destructive Third Zaibatsu War neared its final, deadly stage, the Hyperspace Portals became a means to escape Earth. The Chinese, either without irony or failing to understand the irony, called the diaspora the Great Leap Outward. Many who abandoned Earth sought to reconstruct what they believed were mythic Golden Ages of the Past. Some hoped to recreate the corporate society now collapsing on Earth. More idealistic or, rather, more adolescent propertarians planned free market 'utopias' that always proved short-lived or disastrous and usually both."

—Victoria J. Riddick, The Zaibatsu Wars and After: A History, New York, 223 NCE.

The scream of the land-skimmer's turbine engines shattered the still, calm and chilly air of the mountains. Riding on a thin cushion of forced air, the vehicle rocketed down the poorly maintained excuse for a road that cut through the mountains. The road quality was deficient because the corporate cities that ruled the planet of Askander preferred not to spend money on infrastructure that they themselves rarely used. The elite, who rarely traveled, preferred airborne vehicles, such as the helicopter-like veetols, or hypersonic sub-orbital shuttles. Land travel was only for cargo, or for poor, desperate migrants traveling between the arcologies in search of work. Why spend profits on maintaining that?

That lack of concern by the planet's oligarchs would prove costly.

Barely an hour earlier, the skimmer and its two-person crew had left von Misestown with cargo for Ciudad Rand. Their cargo seemed incredibly mundane. It was a small, locked satchel made of a carbon-fiber fabric. The satchel itself sat inside a composite and titanium alloy strong box. The importance of the satchel was that if anyone tried to open it without the proper access codes, he would trigger the release of caustic compounds that would dissolve the contents.

Neither of the pilots knew what item the satchel contained, other than that it was important and secret. Had they known just how important, or how dangerous, that information was, they might have refused to transport it or demanded more in payment. The pilots, however, knew that refusal or demands for higher payment could possibly cost them their livelihood, if not their lives. They learned long ago that not asking questions proved more profitable and much safer.

This time, however, they would have done better to ask about a few things. That was their mistake.

They had elected to drive their skimmer through the mountains rather than take the easier, but far longer, and much less secure, route across the desert that lay between the two urban monad city-states. It was a calculated risk. The curving mountain roads offered dangers, but mostly for the careless pilot who took turns too tightly or pushed the skimmer a bit faster than necessary on those roads. Those hazards actually kept a pilot more alert and aware, unlike being lulled into mind-numbing stupor by the endless, unchanging desert sands. Equally critical, the mountain route also provided cleaner, particulate-free, air for the turbines.

In addition, the mountains, for all their dangers, were actually more secure, or so they thought. Few bandits or brigands favored the mountains when the pickings were easier on the road running through the open, broiling desert sands.

Bandits and brigands, however, were the last things on the minds of the pilots as their skimmer crested the highest point of the mountain road and began the descent toward the canyon of the Nahr Sakhr, the Stone River. There they would cross the Kantara Bridge and enter the brief plateau and the shorter foothills that surrounded the stark, solitary mesa of Treason's Tooth, into which Ciudad Rand had been built. The crew had no idea they would never see that monad.

The concussion explosive detonated as the skimmer came around a tight turn on a narrow ledge that barely deserved to be called a road. Although meant to simply disable the skimmer, the explosion instead pushed the vehicle sideways and into the road surface. Its supporting air cushion disrupted, the skimmer's nose crushed itself against the ground. That caused the vehicle to tumble end over end. It vaulted a decrepit guardrail that could barely hold spit back from the edge. The skimmer slammed into the small outcroppings of rock along the rugged mountain slope, rolled sideways a half-dozen times, and finally came to rest against the trunks of a small stand of bizarre twisted plants called ynglas that served as trees on Askander.

The wreckage did not appear to be on fire, but that was difficult to tell as the methanol and other compounds the skimmer used as fuel all burned with a faint blue flame. Aflame or not, the scent of hot methanol vapor soon saturated the air.

In the moments after the explosion, a small squad

of armed individuals emerged from hiding places in the cliff face and worked their way toward the wreck. One man, however, stood on the edge near the guardrail and watched the others as they reached the blaze.

He was a large, barrel-chested man dressed in a light khaki uniform, black nylon boots and a red-and-white checkered headscarf called a kaffiya. His face was broad and well tanned, although his cheeks and chin were hidden behind a thick salt-and-pepper beard. On either side of a bulbous nose, the man's dark brown eyes locked on to the guerillas who were examining the wreckage.

"Anyone survive?" he shouted, his deep voice echoing off the cliffs. His spoke with some pain from the broken jaw he had suffered years ago at the hands of Tuatha mercenaries. The pain was one reason he rarely smiled, but another reason was the line of missing and broken teeth from the same injury. Even years later, he remained self-conscious about that injury. Sometimes he hid his mouth behind an upraised right hand, hoping the twisted fingers would hide his teeth, or at least distract attention from them.

"The crew are dead!" one of the men below replied.

"Damn," he muttered. "What were they carrying?"

"Only this strongbox!" another man answered. Although a muscular athletic type, the man still struggled as he climbed up the mountainside. He awkwardly sought handholds with one hand while the other carried the strongbox. As he reached the roadway, he looked up to see the larger man reach down to help him up. He grabbed the larger man's wrist and clambered up the last few remaining steps to the roadway.

"Thank you, Al-Sabah," the man said, out of breath. He handed the strongbox to Al-Sabah, who had no difficulty opening the container.

"Cheap locks," Al-Sabah said with a slight grin. "Probably gave way from the impact." He lifted the lid of the strong box and pulled out the pouch. "This is odd," he said, dropping the strongbox to the ground. "All they were carrying was a diplomatic pouch."

"That's all we found in the skimmer," the other man said. "Seems a waste of time and fuel for such a small thing."

"Yes, if what it contained is a small thing," Al-Sabah replied. "But I do not think the contents are tiny or unimportant." He looked the pouch over, noting a hard object just below the access panel at the top of the pouch. He knew it was a security device of some kind, probably set to destroy the contents should it fall into the wrong hands. Wrong hands just like Al-Sabah's.

"Rahal, hold this for me, with the top pointing away from your body and toward me."

Rahal took the pouch and followed Al-Sabah's instructions. Al-Sabah tugged at the rim of a large ring he wore and unwound a coil of monomolecular line. It took no more than a heartbeat for him to pull the line across the pouch, just below the destruction device.

The sealing mechanism and its device tumbled to the roadway, landing with a dull thud. A bubbling, caustic liquid spilled out from the security mechanism and onto the road. Both men carefully stepped away from the liquid, which was already burning a spot in the road surface.

Returning the line to his ring, Al-Sabah grasped the sides of the pouch and pulled them apart. The inside revealed something he had not expected. There was no data crystal, no flash knob. Instead, there were only three folded sheets of what seemed to be paper. He removed them from the pouch and carefully unfolded them. On the sheets, which were made from assorted synthetic fibers, was a lengthy message written in the skilled hand of an expert calligrapher. Such skill was rare in a society that relied completely on electronics. He also saw the writing was in black ink, no less. Whoever had wanted this message written this way had paid a considerable sum to have it done. That could only mean a séo had this done. Something terrible is afoot, Al Saba thought.

"Is that paper?" Rahal asked in amazement.

Al-Saba nodded.

"I have never seen paper before, "Rahal said.

"That is because it's so expensive to obtain," Al Saba explained.

"So why then would anyone use it to convey a message?"

"Secrecy, my friend," Al-Sabah answered. During the darkest days of the Zaibatsu Wars, he explained, it was ironically much more secure to send messages written on paper rather than try to send them electronically. All the bandwidths were monitored by the corporations, and even secure connections remained safe only for a short time. Encrypting an electronic message was useless too, as the zaibatsu's quantum computers could easily decode them. So notes on paper became the best means to send messages. On Earth, paper was plentiful and easily obtained. The messages written on paper could not be hacked, could be secreted anywhere on the body, and, if one feared imminent capture, the messenger merely had to swallow the note to effectively destroy it

"So what does this message say?"

"That, my dear Rahal, I don't know, for certain, but I would venture to guess that someone — probably a powerful séo — is making big plans and is going to extraordinary lengths to be sure the fewest number of eyes see this. And it is written as cryptograph, probably a unique one."

"Code? But why? Couldn't the quantum-computers decode it?"

"Perhaps, but one would have to enter it in the computer first, and a unique code and symbols complicate matters. This code doesn't seem to be human, however, although I suspect the key is buried in the message itself," Al Sabah said. "I would say the intended recipient already has the key and probably would have it decoded long before anyone else could even begin to do so."

"You said the code seems non-human?"

Al-Sabah nodded. He didn't dare tell Rahal that the symbols appeared to be Iimarae. If indeed they were Iimarae symbols, then whatever the message contained much worse than he could imagine.

"I know who could decode it, if it is alien," he said. He refolded the sheets of paper and stuck them into the breast pocket of his field jacket. "There is a League legation visiting Ciudad Rand. We must get this to them. If it is alien code, they'll know how to decipher it. Whatever plot is in these notes, and whoever wrote them, I can't tell just yet. But I know deep down that it is evil and undoubtedly threatens not just Askander, but all the human colonies."

"So what must we do?" Rahal asked, a hint of fear in his voice.

"We must get this to our operatives in Ciudad Rand so they can contact the League and get it decoded," Al-Sabah paused a moment. "Then we hope for the best, but prepare for the worst. As we always do."

The rest of the squad, after having buried the pilots' bodies, now returned to the roadway.

"My friends, we must scatter for now, and meet back at the caves of Rainy Mountain," Al-Sabah said. "For I fear war is in the air, and far too soon we will be unable to breathe the air as free men."

The troopers dispersed so quickly and completely that in the space of a few minutes only the shattered skeleton of the dead skimmer gave mute witness that anything had ever happened along that stretch of cold and lonely road.

CHAPTER TWO

Somewhere near, in the inky night of deep space, a thousand million voices chirruped as one — a song of war, a song of victory to come.

Long had the hand of the Others held back the Iimarae. But the Flock required new resources to grow, to breed. It needed living room. What it was not given freely, it would take — as was its right. A hundred races had already been subjected to the Iimarae's needs. They toiled in the vast engines of industry that provided the Flock with the goods it needed for survival. A hundred more now fed the Iimarae's hungry fledglings.

Just as the blind forces of time and environment and natural evolution had shaped humans, so too had they shaped the Iimarae. But those unthinking forces formed a very different creature than the one shaped from humanity's ape forebears. Evolution formed in humans an animal quite plastic in nature: intelligent and instinctual, gentle and brutal in nature, but always flexible, fluid, malleable, and infinitely adaptable. Unspecialized for any particular ecological niche, humans found means to fight their way into and adjust to any number of niches. The genome generally held little sway over humanity's behavior, except in granting greater or lesser degrees in adapting to a situation. Even so, the environment itself molded that adaptive ability. Humans became creatures whose existence was interplay of internal and external factors, forces that continually shifted, unfettered by rigid instinctual boundaries, trapped only by social barriers of their own making.

Nature, however, played a different game with the Iimarae.

In their earliest incarnations, the Iimarae's raptor-like ancestors rode the rising air currents of their homeworld, from which they scanned for meals. But as they evolved, the Iimarae matriarchy used this skill to surveil and control their own lower orders and the alien races that they has subdued and enslaved. It was known that the Iimarae treated many of their conquests as livestock. They rarely mated indiscriminately, but they were known to mate with virtually any living thing, although they generally killed and consumed their non-Iimarae sex partners. Those races that had encountered the Iimarae and had survived saw them as unscrupulous and deceitful at best. Those that had not survived their encounter clearly had nothing to say, although their fate spoke volumes.

All the Iimarae had sooty black plumage, although they had white markings resembling a pattern of eight-pointed stars at the wingtips. Their black heads were bald and featherless, a legacy of their carrion-eating ancestors whose naked heads could feast on festering corpses without trapping deadly microbes on their own bodies. The Iimarae's frightening hooked beaks were their most impressive characteristic. Each beak was distinctly colored and uniquely marked, as individual as a human's fingerprint. Their lifespan was unknown, but some evidence suggested they lived well beyond a century in human years.

A clear sexual dimorphism, however, made it easy to identify which were female and which were male. The lanky Iimarae females stood over two meters high, with a robust upper body distinguished by large, powerful pectoral muscles attached to their broad wings. On the other hand, their short tail feathers gave them a rather teetering flight form, which explained their preference to ride the thermals. Even at rest, an Iimarae female posed an intimidating figure.

The Iimarae also had two nearly vestigial small arms, rather like a tyrannosaurus rex from earth. Unlike the tyrant lizard's puny limbs, the Iimarae's arms were agile and adept, ending in small taloned fingers that could easily hold a weapon or manipulate tools. Only males displayed their arms, as they did all the manual labor. The females preferred to keep their arms at their sides, which gave them a rather imperious appearance, especially when they also had their wings folded close to their torsos.

The males were also more compact and quite a bit smaller. They rarely stood more than one hundred sixty centimeters tall, or roughly two heads shorter than adult humans.

The Iimarae were highly social beings, and their matriarchy possessed a fierce family loyalty, if one could determine what their families actually were. Supposedly their relationships were monogamous, but few male Iimarae were encountered. Females, however, showed great affection among themselves. They shared food with relatives and fed their young for months after they had fledged. The males assisted in incubating the eggs and caring for the chicks, regardless of who fathered them. Males even regurgitated food for the chicks from a special pouch in their throats.

In some ways, the Flock — as humans called it — was more like a planet-wide ant or termite colony. Males were kept only for breeding and menial tasks. On the other hand, the males possessed a surprising linguistic ability that the females exploited in their diplomatic connections with aliens, whom the Iimarae viewed as "unclean."

While humans were plastic, adaptable, syncretic, and flexible, bound only by their self-created cultural borders, the Iimarae were rigid, inflexible, driven by instinctual urges to smash borders, go beyond limits, and destroy what did not fit, did not belong, or could not be used. Environment, culture, and religion played games with humans. The genome was the game for Iimarae: The twisting fragments of DNA in their chromosomes dictated the Iimarae's social structures and hierarchies, their individual specialized abilities, and so much more.

For the Iimarae, all was the Flock and everything was for the Nest. All workers must submit, for the glory of the egg-mothers and their children, especially for egg-mothers to be. All worked for the greater glory of the Great-Mother Hen who had laid the egg that birthed the cosmos and from which the first Iimarae had hatched.

The environment only rarely changed the conservative Iimarae. Instead, the Flock was programmed to change their environment. Change too often came only through mutation, accident, or the seemingly logical end product of instinctual festivity. Even then, change had to filter through the Flock's collective consciousness. If the change appeared to strengthen the Flock, then the Iimarae embraced it as a preserving, conserving force and assimilated it at all levels. If it did not preserve the Flock, did not strengthen it, or if it threatened the Iimarae, it was not simply rejected. All vestiges of it had to be hunted down and destroyed.

Then the enemies came. At first the powerful Nameless Ones, the Gonaymne, held back the Iimarae as it had thousands of other species wanting to conquer new worlds. The Nameless Ones had broken the Flock's relentless will, driving the Iimarae from their hard-earned colonies and forcing a retreat to the Iimarae homeworld. Fear gripped the Flock, for it knew the Nameless Ones could destroy entire star systems without a second thought. Then, the Gonaymne vanished as swiftly and as mysteriously as they had appeared. They had, however, left behind technology of wondrous sorts that the Iimarae could utilize. When they discovered the Gonaymne's mind-controlling bands, the Iimarae enthusiastically adopted them. After all, the bands preserved the Flock and held it together. The bands also established greater order within the Flock, and they gave the Great Hens, the matriarchal elders called *se'bes'vos* who ruled the Nests, absolute power over the Flock. This was good change, change that did not change things at all.

Now free of the restive power of the Gonaymne, instinct drove the Iimarae to expand. The fertile egg-mothers, the Great Hens, brought forth many eggs. When the fledglings hatched, they were raised only for the survival of their nests and for the expansion of the Flock. The morality and logic of empire and of showing justice toward conquered races lacked meaning for the Iimarae. Only the Flock's inborn drive for conquest mattered. Unlike humans, who could find all kinds of moral and religious and political reasons to assuage their inherent discomfort with empires, the Iimarae cared little for understanding or justifying their conquests. Was there not enough food for the hatchlings? Then take it where it could be found. Did this world offer technology and weapons the Flock could adopt? Then seize it. Nothing was to restrict the Flock and the growth of the Flock. To survive, they had to obey the instinct to expand. The Iimarae never thought about why they did anything; they simply did it.

Expand the Iimarae had, rapidly subjugating and enslaving the flocks of other species on their home world. They conquered their own stellar system before once more making the leap into interstellar space. The Iimarae, after all, were creatures of habit and habit was the hardest thing to change, especially when the results proved so satisfying.

The Iimarae found little resistance to their urges at first. After all, most worlds' native flora and fauna lacked intelligence and were readily overwhelmed. Should they encounter a native species that actually displayed even a hint of intelligence, the Iimarae drove them into extinction.

Extinction had no meaning for the Iimarae. Opponents were mere obstacles to be crushed and destroyed if they stood in the way of the Flock. It was the Flock that had to expand, to grow, and to locate and consume the resources necessary to maintain survival. Other species were just disposable nuisances.

The Iimarae and its Nests had prospered unhindered on their seemingly irresistible course of empire until the Others appeared.

Soft-skinned they were, naked but for thin amounts of hair, like the vermin Iimarae speared with their beaks and fed to their children. These vermin, who called themselves humans, were quick and large and intelligent. Though loyal to their group, they did not depend on a nest or an egg-mother. Each alone was clever, swift, and dangerous, but in groups they proved even deadlier and more determined.

Contact had led to war. It usually had, no matter what beings were involved. After a series of brief and bloody struggles, worlds that rightfully belonged to the Flock fell under the Others' sway, and worlds that should have belonged to the Flock also dropped into the Others' hands. The creature formed more by its own cultures and environments prevailed over the creature ruled mostly by its germplasm. That usually was the case in conflict between species of this sort.

Defeated, the Iimarae retreated to their own worlds, temporarily abandoning their frontier outposts. For the first time the Flock and all its subordinate pieces had to contemplate failure. The Iimarae considered, thought out, and waited for the right moment to reassert their restless drive. During the wars, the Iimarae had also learned a few things from the nasty hairless mammals. They had placed spies and agents among the humans. True, many were *fah'gid'sla* banished and shunned by the Flock, but they remained Iimarae. Even separated from the whole, they were driven by instinct to serve the species. Through their spies, the Iimarae had learned that strange emotions drove humans, emotions like loyalty and courage and fear and lust and anger and revenge and greed and deceit.

Anger and greed especially intrigued them. Deceit they somehow knew and understood. Then, for the first time, the Iimarae found themselves having ideas, plotting, and intriguing. They knew that humans could be bought, and many of those would betray their own species at the right price. The Iimarae understood that over time squabbles would split humanity. One side would need them. The Flock would take advantage of that. It was simply a matter of finding the right person, because the Iimarae had learned that human beings were for the most part also creatures of habit. In addition, humans — to their misfortune — were also rather predictable.

The Iimarae were patient. The others often fought among themselves and sometimes destroyed each other.

Under the absolute guidance of the queens and elders, the Flock would rest, breed, preen and prepare. The Iimarae would on occasion skirmish, attack and test the human defenses when success seemed guaranteed and would negotiate only where necessary.

Then the Iimarae learned of the existence of the old Gonaymne device at the heart of Delta Pavonis, a star system they coveted and once briefly held. The Great Hens decided that would be where the Flock would strike. It mattered little that the humans had held that world longer than had the Iimarae and were unlikely to relinquish it without a bitter and relentless fight.

In the interim, the Iimarae warriors beat their wings in prayer to the deities of battle and sang their war songs, waiting for the moment of the Swarming.

Then, the Iimarae would strike, a thousand billion strong.

CHAPTER THREE

"Those who stayed behind on Earth dreamed of a new world, but this one forged from the ashes of the old. As the old multinationals collapsed, rebel armies of communitarians seized what they could to keep society alive. They rebuilt much of the great infrastructures, from the power plants to magnetic-levitation rail systems. From this grew a new organization, the Planetary League. Soon it rediscovered the Hyperspace Portals and set out to find new natural resources, establish its own colonies, and locate allies among the Diaspora.

— S. Alexandria Keene, *Among the Enemy Stars: Conflict With Reconstructionist Colonies and Aliens in the Early Great Leap Outward*, New York, 823 New Common Era

Naked, Thom DuBois found himself wandering down a long passageway lit only by a strange red phosphorescent glow. The ground beneath him continually gave way, becoming an oozing, jelly-like mass that sucked at his feet and ankles. Each step became a gargantuan effort to move forward. It sapped his energy, and he soon gasped for breath. He steadied himself against the walls of the cavern, walls that were hard, cold, unyielding. The blood pounded in his temples and echoed in his ears, a persistent drumbeat that drowned out all other sound. Perspiration rolled down his back.

Stumbling blindly for a few moments, he suddenly found a hard surface of some sort. Wresting his feet free of the slime, he clambered onto the rocky outcropping. He soon realized it extended some distance down the corridor. He followed it until it dead-ended against a featureless ebony wall.

"Thom," a voice said. "I'm glad you're here. Now you can stay with me forever."

He turned and saw the ghostly image of Ursula, his mentally ill and unbalanced wife, dead by her own hand seven long years ago. She was dressed in a red Chinese silk gown, her auburn hair flowing behind her in long strands like the hair of a drowning victim moving with the current. Behind her the corridor had vanished, replaced by smooth ebony walls identical to the one behind him.

Her appearance frightened him, for she had the same bloated, livid and bloodless appearance of decomposition she had when a maid found her corpse — three days dead — in a hot, fetid, fly-infested Bangkok hotel room. She had clutched a container of powerful endorphin analog so tightly in her right hand that the nails were imbedded in her palm. The medical examiner had to break her stiff dead fingers to remove the jar.

His heart raced, and he realized that she terrified him. "What do you want?" he asked.

"I want you dead," she replied, dropping the gown to expose her naked, silvery white flesh. She ran a long, thin, bony finger down his chest, then grabbed his genitals. "So you can live with me forever."

He screamed and reactively he slapped her face with the flat of his hand. Stunned, Ursula released her grip, and Thom took advantage and shoved his dead wife aside. Trying to run, he crashed into a wall. He scraped his fingernails along the surface, hoping to find a lever, a button, a crack, or anything to let him escape.

A roaring sound filled the air. He turned to see water burst from a cavity in the wall. It caught him full in the chest and knocked him down. The water boiled and foamed all around him and he struggled to keep his footing, but the torrent kept smashing him against the wall and forcing him underwater. He tried to breathe, but the pressure began crushing his lungs. Blackness swirled around him.

"Come, husband, die for me so I may live," his wife said.

He tried to cry out, but the water filled his mouth and lungs . . .

Thom DuBois woke up screaming. His heart raced and his lungs fought for air. Perspiration rolled down his face, neck and back.

He fell back against the pillow, gasping for breath. "You're awake," Thom told himself. "Just a dream, just like all the others, just like the ones when you were kid. Now, try to relax, try to remember."

He licked his bone-dry lips and tried to remember some of the meditation and relaxation techniques the therapist had taught him. He visualized his beating heart and racing pulse and imagined them slowing down, moving steadily, growing calmer with each second.

Thom decided he needed to walk around the ship. The sleeping pod felt confining. The tube was environmentally controlled, with constantly purified air kept at a perfect temperature. The interior allowed someone to sit comfortably or sleep reasonably well. Like most people, Thom preferred to sleep with his head toward the hatch door. He never understood those individuals who slept in the opposite direction, with their heads toward the closed end and their feet toward the hatch. It was all too claustrophobic for him.

Thom sat up, pulled on his clothes and shoes. He reached up and pulled the hatch lever. The latches released and the hatch irised open like the shutter in an ancient camera. With both hands, he grabbed the exit bar above the hatch and pulled himself out of the pod. Then he climbed to his feet.

The corridor was bathed in soft blue light, simulating the night sky of Earth. It was quiet, except for the low hum of the environmental controls. It made his head hurt.

DuBois walked the length of the corridor to the elevator and waited for the hatch to iris open. He stepped through and said, "Troop level." The elevator did not respond, but the door shut and the elevator dropped the four levels to the barracks portion of the ship.

Thom stepped onto the catwalk that traversed the length of the barracks. He walked about a third of the length of the catwalk before he stopped, leaned leisurely against the guardrail and gazed on the troops. Below him he could see some of the infantry sitting in groups, clearly as unable to sleep as he was. Some of the troopers formed little clusters where they chatted, played cards, drank alcoholic and non-alcoholic beverages from plastic containers, or smoked quietly. Many smoked hemp, but a surprising number used tobacco. It was a habit that had proven hard from which to wean the human race. Despite its health issues, it seemed necessary to calm the nerves of some troopers before they went into battle. A slight blue-gray haze hung above the clusters.

Thom could hear a griot singing a traditional West African song. It seemed strange to hear something so ancient so far from its place of origin. He was reminded of the songs his grandmother sang while working the sugarcane fields in the Caribbean when his family came to Tobago on vacation. That was so long ago, he realized, a lifetime away.

So much had happened since then; he had experienced so much. He had survived too many missions, some of which he now regretted. Now he had just one more mission to complete, one more duty to fulfill. In a few more hours, he would lead his squad in capturing a Tuatha vessel that had attacked a League listening post orbiting Tau Ceti. If he survived, he would receive a transfer to the diplomatic corps. He hoped his life would be less stressful and more organized, but as he looked down at the men and women below, he knew that would never be.

CHAPTER FOUR

"You have this weapon, then?" Ernesto Abu Brion said. He lounged back on a pile of thick, multicolored satin cushions.

"No, we don't possess it...yet," the Iimarae, said, looking away from the human's cold gaze. The little bird-like alien's eyes fell on the three hooded Iimarae elders sitting in a corner of the room. The elders, all females, represented the will of the Flock, the organic entity that was Iimarae society, and whatever the negotiator proposed required their approval.

The small alien stood barely 170 centimeters. It was clearly fearful of the two-meter tall elders and bobbed its thin, orange-colored beak twice, as if apologizing for some offense. The elders did not respond.

Abu Brion watched the three other aliens. Even seated, it was easy to tell the Iimarae were two-and-a-quarter, maybe two-and-a-half, meters tall, taller than all but a handful of humans anywhere in the galaxy. They sat impassively, the hoods covering all their features like the hood of a good hunting falcon. Like most humans, he knew little of Iimarae society, other than that it was possibly matriarchal and that the Flock had a propensity for sudden outbursts of conquest and warfare. These Swarmings resulted from population pressures, the need for strategic resources, and even from a genetic tendency to dominate and control territory. Twice before, humans had had to beat back Iimarae onslaughts, and just two decades earlier Abu Brion himself had taken part in repelling an alien attack on Askander.

Abu Brion found himself curious about the power the three females held over the much smaller male. They reminded Abu Brion of the three ancient Oriental monkeys: See No Evil, Speak No Evil, and See No Evil. That failed, however, to come anywhere near to revealing the aliens' thoughts, which Abu Brion suspected were quite evil indeed. Sitting there unmoving, passive and quiet, the Iimarae females on first observation appeared the male's social inferiors. That observation was clearly wrong. Abu Brion knew Iimarae warriors were female and had fought with a fury that filled many a man with sheer terror.

The male negotiator was obviously terrified of the elders, and the alien's fawning toward the three females disgusted Abu Brion. He preferred to deal directly with

opponents or competitors, but none of the other Iimarae made any moves to take over the negotiations. They
stayed as still and inscrutable as statues.

Abu Brion stroked his beard in thought. "You offer
me a weapon you don't have? Do you take me for a fool?"

"Oh, no, certainly not," the Iimarae said quickly. It
fiddled for a moment with the *voder* at its neck. After
adjusting the translator's tone to create what it obviously thought was a deeper, more assertive voice, the alien
continued. "It is true we don't have this weapon, but we
know where it can be found."

Abu Brion snorted. "You Iimarae must think all
humans are fools, but I'm not interested in purchasing
goods sight unseen."

He rose to leave, straightening his robes as he stood.
He waved a large hand, and his two Tuatha bodyguards
— both eugenically bred members of the elite *Gall
Oglaigh* legion — approached him. "If you can't offer me
anything tangible, then this conversation is over."

"Wait," the creature said, rising and moving toward
the man. It held out its wings to balance itself. The wings
seemed odd: thin, wide membranes, which to Abu Brion
suggested a bat more than a bird. Spindly rudimenta-
ry arms ending in thin, yellow three-fingered talons sat
just below the creature's wings. The arms reminded Abu
Brion of a Tyrannosaurus Rex. The alien waddled awkwardly, struggling against gravity stronger than that of

its home world, which orbited Epsilon Eridani.

The Iimarae reached into its robe, and Abu Brion's bodyguards' hands shot to their holstered weapons, ready to protect their master.

But Abu Brion raised his hands, frowned, and shook his head. The guards stood down. He turned back to the alien. "The negotiations are ended. That is final."

"There is much the Flock can offer you," the alien said, its voice sounding desperate, thin and shrill despite its efforts. It pulled a silvery tube from its robe and held it out between its thin yellow talons.

"*You?* Offer *me* anything?" Abu Brion threw his head back and laughed.

The alien settled slowly on its spindly legs, which it folded under its abdomen. It looked back at the elders and again bobbed its head, but this time the pattern was different. It turned to Abu Brion. "It is true, al Abu Brion, that we cannot provide the weapon, but we can offer you wealth."

"Which I have. This conversation is over." But Abu Brion kept his eyes on the tube. Whatever it was, it held the key to the weapon.

The Iimarae clicked its beak rapidly, a sign of desperation. "There are other things which we know you desire."

"Such as?"

"Control of Jaime ibn Brentholtz's properties, control

of all Askander itself," the alien said. It adjusted its robes and preened itself for a moment, all the while keeping its eyes fixed on the three hooded Iimarae, as if waiting for a sign.

"We can offer you what you wish, what you desire," the Iimarae said after a moment. "Ibn Brentholtz is a great *sèo* and *hausfatah* who possesses much land and rules the largest corporation on Askander. Ciudad Rand is the jewel of your world. But who would not want another man's jewel, if he knew it would look better on his arm?"

Abu Brion frowned. The Iimarae had done their research and knew more about him than he expected. "You Iimarae are in no position to help me there, unless you control stock in ibn Brentholtz's corporation."

"True," the Iimarae said, holding the tube so Abu Brion's eyes could not fail to see it. "We know that ibn Brentholtz is young and has made many mergers with other families. Your family is not so strong. You, the *hausfatah* of your great family, are not nearly so young. Surely he covets those shares belonging to his sister, which are in your keeping. Why let him take your dream of being *sèo* of all Askander from you? He threatens you, and you wish his elimination. Give us what we need, and you may have your desire, *hausfatah* to an entire world."

Abu Brion sneered. "What, a world to rule under the watchful eye of Iimarae suzerainty? That is no deal." He turned for the door. His bodyguards were close by his side, their hands resting on the grips of their flechette pistols.

The Iimarae emissary cried out sharply. Two alien guards, disrupter rifles raised, staggered clumsily to block the doorway.

The Tuatha unholstered their weapons and dropped into battle positions.

Abu Brion laughed. The Iimarae had to know they would be outclassed in a fight with the superior reflexes of the *Gall Oglaigh*. The aliens' own reflexes were slow, and in Askander's gravity they were as clumsy as penguins with clubfeet.

"Your audacity amuses me, little chicken," he said, turning to the emissary. "I could walk out of here unharmed and leave my men to slice you apart piece by piece."

The Iimarae emissary emitted a series of high-pitched whistles and the guards lowered their rifles. "True, we took a chance coming here. The League's ships are fast and its troops well trained. Avoiding them was difficult. We knew that your people hate the League, too."

Abu Brion's men kept their weapons drawn until he raised a hand and nodded slowly. "So, you are desperate."

"We are not desperate, but we are also not fools." The Iimarae gave a short staccato burst of whistles and clicks.

The alien guards returned to their places.

"You are victims of your genes, little chicken, and it is obvious you are gambling," said Abu Brion. He returned to the cushions where he had been sitting, after carefully arranging his long shirt and robe, lowered himself and crossed his legs. His men reformed in a half-circle around their *hausfatah*.

"It is true that the Swarming is near. We cannot control that, as you know," the alien said.

Abu Brion rolled up his right sleeve, exposing a jagged red scar running from wrist to elbow. "Yes, I carry this reminder of your last incursion into our space, when your kind tried to capture Der Merchant twenty or so years ago. I know what one of your talkative jaws can do when it decides to cease talking."

"Nevertheless, it is the Swarming. We cannot resist our instincts."

"Unfortunately for you, we have always resisted your instincts. I have many of your feathered friends in my palace. They make wonderful decorations. You are a very colorful race, after all."

The emissary appeared to take the insult in stride. "You are not the first, Abu Brion. Others have tried to defeat us, but we have survived, even though one of them built the weapon."

"Why is my help so valuable then? Surely you don't need me if the weapon is so powerful," Abu Brion said.

He leaned forward and stared straight into the alien's red eyes. "Or are you just bluffing? Perhaps there is no weapon."

"If you wish a demonstration, I will show you."

The Iimarae inserted the silver tube into a small black cube at its side. In the space between the alien and Abu Brion a small speck of light formed, cartwheeling and expanding at high speed. Then, it grew distinct and a veil of stars appeared.

"Pretty," Abu Brion said, "but it tells me nothing."

"Observe. You will understand," the Iimarae replied.

The stars became a grid map with one star at the center. Abu Brion thought he recognized the sky scene and its constellations, but something was wrong. "It looks like a summer night on Askander, but some of the constellations are wrong."

The Iimarae clicked its beak. "Yes, you are quite observant. Actually, it is a winter sky in the southern hemisphere as it appeared six thousand years ago."

"There is one star I don't recognize."

Suddenly the star exploded. It burned brightly like a gigantic torch flame, twisting and turning. Its light blotted out that of the surrounding stars and the star appeared brighter even than Askander's home star Delta Pavonis.

"The weapon caused this?"

"Yes," the alien said, turning off the machine. "That

star is what you now call the "Crab Nebula." We called it the "Feathery Nest." The Nameless Ones destroyed it with a nova inducer, which collapsed the star's core. All that remains is the neutron star you now know.

"The weapon destroyed many nests and a billion Iimarae. We expected a major attack from the Nameless Ones immediately after that, but they vanished and didn't exploit their victory."

Abu Brion leaned back on the cushions and rubbed his chin. *The hologram could be a fake*, he thought. That was easy enough for anyone to create, but somehow he couldn't imagine the Iimarae going to such lengths to enlist his aid. The aliens genuinely feared the Nameless Ones, which humans had come to call the Gonaymne. The few humans who had dealt with the Iimarae also noted the aliens' reverence for the now vanished race.

In addition, the Iimarae had displayed a literal-mindedness that made them almost too easy to predict in battle. Deception was not the Iimarae's strong suit. That was an all-too-human trait. It had made defeating their early incursions much simpler than expected.

"The hologram?" Abu Brion said.

"Made here on Askander by Iimarae astronomers many years after the attack. The Nameless Ones too later destroyed that colony. Little could the colonists know that we would later face a greater danger from you, human."

The Iimarae said the word "human" with the same sort of venom with which Abu Brion had said *"little chicken."* Abu Brion found himself smiling at that. "But this weapon destroyed itself in the super nova. There must be others, correct?"

The alien nodded. "We know of two, from records the Nameless Ones left behind when they vanished. One is easily obtained; the other, less so."

"And where are they?"

"One is at the core of Delta Pavonis itself," the alien said.

That did not surprise Abu Brion. The Iimarae were justifiably nervous when facing the Nameless Ones. It was also obvious that the weapon had to be obtainable, or the Iimarae would not have bothered to contact him. Getting a weapon out of the heart of a star was, however, literally impossible. So they must be after something else, he decided. "So where is the second?"

"In the heart of the star called Sol, your peoples' birth star."

Abu Brion raised an eyebrow. "If the weapon is only in the star, then it would be useless to you. So, it's not the weapon you want."

"No, not the weapon itself. There is a ship, a vessel belonging to the Nameless Ones. From writings we have discovered, we believe it crashed on Askander. We also believe that the device controlling the nova inducer is on board that ship."

Abu Brion smiled. With the controls, the aliens could threaten the Solar system and the League it sheltered. The League would have either to sit by, helpless, as the Iimarae swarmed or risk having the sun destroyed. It was blackmail. Abu Brion found himself admiring the aliens' audacity. Extortion was something to which he could relate.

This weapon, if it existed, appeared quite formidable indeed. If the Iimarae desired the nova inducer as much as they appeared, then perhaps he did have use for them. After all, the aliens were only a minor hindrance as far as he was concerned. His real enemy was ibn Brentholtz. Despite the veil of cordiality that corporate manners required and despite the fact that his wife was ibn Brentholtz's sister, he found it difficult to hide his venom for the young *sèo*. His grandfather's blood was still on the hands of the Brentholtz clan, and they had not yet paid for it.

Ibn Brentholtz's lands and holding were huge, and he held many subsidiaries. Many minor *sèo* owed uneasy allegiances to his corporation. With luck, and the Iimarae's help, Abu Brion thought, it might prove easy to convince subsidiary *sèo* to accept his overlordship instead. It would be especially easy if he had the weapon. With the weapon no one, neither the Iimarae nor the League, would threaten him.

"Very well, Iimarae. You shall have my assistance, for the price you ask," he said. *And more*, he thought. "Only," he said, pointing to the elders, "if I may deal directly with them."

The Iimarae squeaked agitatedly. Its body shook. "That's impossible. They will not talk to you."

"Why?"

"They are potential egg-mothers and queens. To look on a human face would be a disgusting, impure act," the alien explained. "If they saw your face, they would have to be killed, have their very hearts pecked from their breasts so the impurity would not spread."

That idiocy explains the hoods, and why those fat brood hens don't talk, Abu Brion thought. "So, if we humans are so ugly, why do they let you talk to me?"

The Iimarae avoided Abu Brion's gaze. "I am just a low-caste, not even male enough to be a breeder. I am an unclean, filthy thing, fit only to talk to vermin."

"But smart enough to have important uses, especially when the vermin have something the Iimarae need, correct?" Abu Brion said.

The Iimarae nodded. "All servants have their purpose."

Despite himself, Abu Brion found he sympathized with the Iimarae go-between. He also knew that he would make no headway in talking to the elders. If he cultivated the little bird's friendship, it might be even more to his advantage. "Very well, I drop my request. I will be more than glad to deal with you."

The alien, delighted, bobbed its shiny head repeatedly. It turned to the three hooded elders. The middle elder then did something quite rare. It raised a spindly black hand, extended a highly lacquered red talon — a sign of her rank as head of the elders and her future as a queen. It bobbed its head in agreement. The other two bobbed their heads likewise. It was the first movement from the three that Abu Brion had seen.

"Very well, it is agreed," the emissary said. "Shall our scribes prepare a treaty?"

"May the Hand damn you, Iimarae, a *sèo's* word is his honor," he said with mock anger.

"We know the value of your word, Abu Brion. A treaty is the least we will accept."

Abu Brion smiled. The Iimarae were not complete fools after all. It would be unwise to underestimate them. A treaty disc was just a formality, after all, and it was simple enough to acquiesce to such a thing. It was worthless as far as he was concerned, and he suspected the Iimarae held it in similar regard.

"No honor among thieves, eh, little chicken," Abu Brion said.

"What?" the alien said, puzzled.

"An old human saying, of little importance. Yes, I will agree to a treaty."

"Then it is done. We shall be restored to our glory."

And I shall have ibn Brentholtz's land and yours too, Iimarae, Abu Brion thought. He smiled at the alien, but it was not a friendly smile.

CHAPTER FIVE

"Some of the Reconstructionist colonists of the Great Leap Outward sought not economic utopias but rather perfectionist religious societies or homogenous ethnic ones. They rarely succeeded. Among those who did, however, were the mercenary and callous Tuatha. They had sought to establish an imagined ancient Celto-Aryan warrior world of racial and mystical purity. When faced with the hardships of their chosen world, however, their fantasies collapsed, and they resorted to selling their services as professional soldiers of fortune, ruthlessly killing and destroying for the highest bidder. The result proved quite financially successful."

— S. Alexandria Keene, Among the Enemy Stars: Conflict With Reconstructionist Colonies and Aliens in the Early Great Leap Outward, New York, 823 New Common Era

The Tuatha crew cut the gravity just as the first League trooper from Thom DuBois' company came through the airlock.

A neural flechette struck the trooper in the neck before she could power up her armor. Her lifeless body slowly cartwheeled down a corridor, crashing into a bulkhead just as the second soldier entered the enemy vessel.

The second trooper had enough sense to power up his armor as he entered the Tuatha ship. His fate proved little better than his compatriot's did as an attacking Tuatha *saighdear* breached the armor with a sword. The weapon's slow-moving blade penetrated the gap between the League soldier's helmet and cuirass and embedded itself in the man's throat.

As the mercenary withdrew the sword, he exposed his own chest. Thom DuBois wasted no time and rammed his particle-staff into the man's cuirass and pulled the pistol-grip trigger.

The staff's beam shorted out the armor's defenses, leaving the Tuatha soldier trapped and helpless in a paralyzed exoskeleton. The force of the blow also sent the man tumbling down the corridor. A hail of poisoned flechettes from the weapons of his own comrades stopped his progress.

It was a painless death, or should have been. It was one that Thom wished he could have avoided. He didn't have time to reflect on it as he powered up his armor just in time to deflect a volley of the deadly darts.

Thom reached for a handrail to steady himself and to allow him to vault down a side corridor. Something struck his armor as he jumped. Momentarily out of control, he crashed into a wall, bounced off the bulkhead, and somersaulted out of control down the corridor. The particle staff flew from his grasp.

He knew he'd taken a shot from an alpha-particle projector, not enough to knock out his suit but enough to slow him down. A momentary wave of fear washed over him as he realized his shields had dropped in power and wouldn't stop a flechette from penetrating his armor.

From the corner of his eye, he glimpsed another handrail. Thom thrust out his left hand, straining to catch it. His fingers hooked the railing just as the ship's gravity returned. He landed heavily, twisting his arm slightly. He looked up in time to see a Tuatha with a phase rifle turning toward him.

He sprinted down the corridor, toward the area where he expected his troops to be. His skul-fone crackled as the Tuatha fired at him. The speaker mounted in his mastoid sinus popped, and his helmet screens went blank for a second. He knew another shot might knock out his shields permanently.

Thom turned the corner into the main corridor. His screens blanked briefly and the skul-fone hissed from a near miss. He hurdled the prone form of a Tuatha trooper and spotted a particle staff lying against the far wall. Thom grabbed the two-meter-long, black, javelin-shaped weapon and, like a medieval pikeman, he thrust it out in front of him.

The Tuatha trooper rounded the corner and ran onto the upraised staff. Thom squeezed the trigger. The low-level radiation particles disrupted the suit's electronics, and, drained of its power, the man's armor froze solid as a statue. The trooper, carried forward by momentum, was caught on the end of the staff and catapulted over Thom's head. He landed like a rock and slid along the floor.

Thom laughed nervously. He could feel his heart thumping in his chest, and his breath came in deep, labored gulps. Perspiration rolled down his back. He leaned back against the bulkhead.

Across the corridor a series of red lights went out and a bank of green lights began flashing. The corridor was being repressurized.

He didn't know how the fight was going with his platoon, but he knew League troops had gained control of the ship's bridge and engineering sections. Standard Tuatha battle practice was to create a vacuum in the ship and cut the gravity. That would force the enemy into their pressure suits and armor, not the most graceful way to fight. League soldiers always worked to restore the gravity and repressurize. The Tuatha, when they won, preferred to return to base before repressurizing.

A voice crackled in his skul-fone. "Major DuBois? Where are you?"

Thom tongued on his helmet transmitter. "Sergeant Conrad, I'm in the main corridor. I took a shot that nearly knocked out my screens. It kicked me down a side corridor before the gravity came back, but I'm all right, I think."

"I'm glad to hear you're okay, Major," Keith Conrad replied, his voice weak. "We secured our sector, but we took heavy casualties."

"How many?"

"Six dead, Major," Conrad replied. "And we have two badly wounded."

"Damn," Thom said. Eight casualties were a third of the squad. He checked his helmet chronometer readout and shook his head. The assault had taken five-and-a-half minutes — much too long.

"How many Tuatha casualties?"

"We bagged thirteen. They should all be coming around in about twenty minutes," he said. Thom could detect anger in Conrad's voice. "Six dead, and all those Tuatha bastards will suffer is a goddamn headache. It's not fair, Major."

"Life's not fair, sergeant," Thom said, wishing in his heart that he could make it so and knowing that was all too painfully impossible. "But we all took the oaths when we joined up."

Thom glanced at the Tuatha bodies lying around him. For all their reputation as the fierce descendants of Celtic warriors, the mercenaries all looked fragile and helpless while unconscious. The Dravidian politicos who had hired them to attack the League listening post at Barnard's Star hadn't received their money's worth from their employees this time. "I've got some Tuatha prisoners here with me. I'll need help in securing them before they come around."

"Roger, Major," Conrad said and cut the connection.

Thom reached up to undo his helmet just as his screens flashed red. He ducked his head and rolled, just in time to see a neural flechette glance off the bulkhead where his head had been. Thom looked up and saw a Tuatha *saighdear* fumbling with a jammed flechette pistol.

"Keith, get a fix on me," Thom said. "I've got an armed Tuatha still loose in this quarter." He didn't wait for a response.

The Tuatha looked up as Thom came down the corridor and flung the useless pistol at him. The soldier grabbed a lance from a paralyzed comrade and took off down a side corridor.

Thom easily caught up with the Tuatha. *Too easily*, he thought. The enemy soldier had trouble running, only staying upright by occasionally putting out a hand to catch a bulkhead. After a short chase down the corridor, the mercenary turned down a narrow alcove and tried to open a heavy hatch, but the hatch refused to unseal. The trooper futilely pounded the door.

"It's over," Thom said in Tuatha Gaelic. "We control your ship. It's time to surrender."

The Tuatha turned and thrust the lance at Thom's mid-section. Thom parried the blade with his staff. The trooper lunged unsteadily forward, forcing Thom to step back. The lance point danced crazily, just a few centimeters from Thom's throat. The corridor lights glistened like a rainbow on the blade's edge.

Thom looked beyond the lance. He carefully watched the Tuatha. The soldier's helmet face shield hid the Tuatha's eyes, which made it difficult for Thom to determine the trooper's moves. But the Tuatha moved slowly and heavily, and Thom noticed that the soldier's armor bulged curiously about the waist and abdomen, as if the trooper were overweight.

Thom suspected the extra weight could work to his advantage. He feinted a headshot with the charged end of his staff. The Tuatha moved to parry, but Thom brought the staff up, and then slammed the butt end into the trooper's knee. The Tuatha grabbed the injured knee with one hand and staggered into the wall. He pushed off from the wall and charged, aiming the lance at Thom's stomach. Thom deflected the blade and stepped aside as the Tuatha went past.

With both hands, Thom swung his staff down into the back of the soldier's legs. The trooper tumbled out of control into the wall behind Thom. The trooper's lance came free and slid down the corridor. The Tuatha fell backwards, its hands going to the injured hamstrings. Thom brought his staff about, stood over the wounded Tuatha, and prepared to deactivate the trooper's armor.

"Please, get me a doctor," said a tired, feminine voice in his skul-fone.

He hesitated. The staff's faintly glowing tip hovered over the Tuatha's chest.

"Please," said the voice again. It was the Tuatha's.

Thom opened his face shield, knelt beside the trooper, and undid her helmet. Frightened green eyes stared back at him. The eyes were set in the pale face of a young woman. Thick red hair, reminiscent of her Celtic forebears, was plastered with sweat to her forehead.

Thom began removing her armor.

"League bastard," the woman hissed. "Keep your filthy hands from me." She grabbed for his throat, but he was quicker and caught her wrists in a tight grip. After a moment the strength left her and she fell back, exhausted and perspiring heavily.

Thom resumed removing her armor. As he tossed aside her cuirass, Thom saw that she was very pregnant and that the inside of her thighs were drenched. "When did your water break?" he said.

"Don't remember. An hour, maybe two." The woman groaned, closed her eyes and grimaced.

"Sergeant Conrad, I need a medtek team at my coordinates," he said into his mike. "I've got a woman giving birth here."

"We copy, sir, but it may be a while. We've got a lot of wounded," Conrad said.

"Do what you can," he replied. "Damn the Tuatha," he said under his breath.

Thom knew that while it was generally accepted that women, and especially pregnant women, could more readily withstand the constant atmospheric pressure and gravitational changes on a starship, the pregnant women usually served only on the flight deck.

Yet, drawing on the legends of the Scottish and Irish ancestors they left behind on Earth centuries before, the Tuatha believed unborn children would become great warriors if their pregnant mothers went into battle. Such "great warriors" could earn enormous sums of money from the propertarians who bought their services, just the thing for a poor colony world whose only resource was its people, people driven by ancient hatreds fueled by romantic myth. It was a barbaric throwback to a more brutal time, and it made little sense to Thom.

The woman groaned again and her hands went instinctively to her belly. "The baby," she said through clenched teeth. "It's coming."

He tore apart the woman's trousers to expose the birth canal. He could see she must have fully dilated now as the top of the infant's head had begun crowning.

Thom tried to remember what the doctors told his former wife when their children were born. Only vague images came to mind. "Push," he said finally, not knowing what else to do.

The woman screamed and tried to sit up. Thom gently eased her down. The baby's eyes and nose were visible. He moved between her legs and put his hands under the child's head. "Push, and breathe deeply," he said.

Although he had watched the birth of his own children, Thom didn't remember childbirth being so messy. He was kneeling in a pool of the woman's amniotic fluid, which had spread out across the floor. She shrieked in pain from another contraction, and impulsively she grabbed his right arm, her fingers digging deep into his flesh. Thom gritted his teeth. What pain he felt, he knew, it could never match what she was enduring.

Perspiration rolled down in a torrent from her forehead and she grunted as each contraction of her uterus worked further to expel the baby.

The woman grimaced as she strained to force the

child out. She gasped. The baby slid into Thom's large, dark hands. It unleashed a strong, hearty scream.

As he picked up the infant, he was startled by the waxy, cheese-like membrane, or vernix casèosa, that coated her skin. He hardly had time to think about what to do about the vernix when the child had its first bowel movement composed of the lining of its intestines. He glanced down to see the green, tar-like substance known as meconium spatter his knees and thighs.

Thom's throat and mouth felt dry as he stared down at the child. "It's a girl," he said. "As strong and brave as her mother."

He placed the baby on the woman's chest.

The mother managed an exhausted smile. She undid the front of her uniform shirt and exposed a milk-swollen breast. The baby began to nurse. "I'll call her Grania, after her mother and my mother," the woman said.

"May she grow up to be a great warrior," Thom said in Tuatha, a Gaelic dialect.

The mother looked up at Thom with a puzzled stare, "You know the Old Tongue?"

"I learned it, years ago, on Ramal."

"A bad place and an evil time. Even we regret that." She smiled sadly and stroked her daughter's head. "No, not a great warrior. I think she will grow up to be a great peacemaker, this one. Perhaps it's time."

Thom smiled.

A hand touched his shoulder. "We'll take it from here, Major," the owner of the hand said.

Thom looked up to see two medteks, both carrying full medical kits; they also had a field gurney. He hadn't even noticed them arrive. He mumbled his thanks before getting up and moving out of the way. He found a bulkhead, leaned back against it, and slid down to sit on the deck. He watched the medteks get the woman and her child onto the gurney, check the vital signs, and then take them to the League ship's infirmary. Suddenly Thom realized just how incredibly fatigued he was.

This is the last time, he thought. His tour of duty ended, and he would soon see Earth again. The prospect of rest and counseling pleased him, especially now that he would be mustered out and reassigned to civilian duties.

The Code of the League was difficult, but he had not killed, unlike many others. For him, therapy would simply ease the loss of dead friends. For others, it meant further help in the Zen-like disciplines of *la souffrance*, the suffering. The expunging of the memories of pain and killing could mean facing years of rehabilitation.

He was tired of being a soldier. Even victory tasted bitter. All he wanted was peace. He dreamed of a small beachfront *dacha* on a summer day in New England, the waves rolling across the sand.

He awoke with a start from the daydream when he

felt a hand touch his shoulder.

"Major," Sergeant Conrad said. There was a tone of reluctance in his voice. "Colonel Paget needs to see you. She said it was urgent."

Thom's heart sank. He knew that whatever Paget wanted, it meant he would not see Earth again for some time. His tour of duty wasn't over after all, and he would have to carry his pain just that much longer.

CHAPTER SIX

As a commanding officer, Paget qualified for slightly more spacious quarters than a sleeping pod. Even so, entering a commanding officer's quarters was far from the most comfortable thing to do in the world. Worse, he and the Colonel had a history, making it awkward reporting to a superior officer who was both a friend and a former lover.

Thom, however, could not imagine the colonel to be doing anything but telling him that his request to the League Corps Diplomatique was approved and she would have his new orders ready for him.

When he reached Colonel Paget's cabin, Thom could look through the hatchway into the cabin to see Paget at a small — *very small* — desk, going over messages and reports on the screens of three, maybe four, different *Isaaks*. Using a stylus held in her right hand, she occasionally assaulted the screen of a computer tablet a bit more roughly than was necessary.

He knocked on the cabin door. "Rowena?" he said, "It's DuBois."

Paget looked up from her work. "Why so formal, Thom? Come on in. As you know, I don't bite...often."

He stepped into the cabin.

"It's so good to see you," Colonel Rowena Alexandrovna Paget said. She smiled as she came toward him and took his hand. "Please, take a seat."

"Now who's being formal, Rowena?" Thom said as he sat down. "We've been friends a long time."

Rowena managed a tired smile.

Thom examined Rowena's face. Time and trials had taken a toll on her. Her blue eyes had once almost danced, but now they seemed weary, and there were bags under both of them. Furrows had worried themselves into her brow, and her lips, which usually formed a perpetual grin, now frowned more than he remembered. Even her short blond hair was unkempt and lifeless.

"You'll be pleased to know the Tuatha government on Alba Nuadh and the Dravidian high council have agreed to an armistice," Paget said. "So the Tuatha won't be attacking League outposts for the foreseeable future, or at least not in this star system."

"Good," he said, "but that's not why you asked me here, is it?"

"No, you're right, it isn't," the colonel said. "I know

you've been expecting that transfer to diplomatic. When were you last on Earth?"

"Three years ago," he said, smiling. "And you know it."

"New England was nice then, wasn't it?" she said, managing a smile that briefly brought the dance back to her eyes. "I didn't want those nights on the beaches to end." Rowena sighed. "And it'll be a while before either of us see Earth again."

His heart sank at the realization he wouldn't be going back to Earth for diplomatic training. "So you have new orders for me?"

She nodded. "I know your tour is up, and the Corps Diplomatique requested you, immediately, for a mission."

Thom was puzzled. He had hoped to transfer to the Diplomatic Corps when he returned to Earth, to follow in his father's footsteps. Why had they suddenly requested him now, without his receiving formal training? It didn't sound good at all. "I'm afraid I don't understand," he said.

"What do you know about Askander?"

"Just the usual," he said. "A colony in the Delta Pavonis system formed by radical propertarians during the Great Leap Outward after the Third Zaibatsu War. Supposedly, they were free-market absolutists, but their society collapsed into a sort of patchwork of corporate feudal states within three generations. Hostile to the League. My father and his associate counsel, a fellow named Owen Herriot, I believe, negotiated a brief alliance with them against the Iimarae about twenty or so years ago. That's all I recall offhand."

"And what about Don Jaime ibn Brentholtz?"

The instant Rowena mentioned ibn Brentholtz's name, Thom realized why the Corps Diplomatique wanted him so quickly. It had been a long time, almost twenty years, since he'd seen the *sèo*. Brentholtz had been just a brash and arrogant young student then, as was he.

"I went to school with him briefly on Formalhaut Four, during the thaw in relations years ago. We were fairly good friends, I suppose, but he never talked about his home world. I think it embarrassed him."

"Hmm," the colonel said, nervously chewing her lower lip. "Our intelligence service received a strange, encrypted message from some rebel group on Askander. They claimed to have intercepted it. The message was actually written on paper, of all things, and was apparently from one of the great houses on Askander to its allies. Intelligence said that the message's author, in a rather amateurish attempt to throw off any cryptographers, wrote it with both human and alien symbols, especially those belonging to the Iimarae."

"The Iimarae?" Thom said, a bit incredulous.

Rowena nodded.

The news shocked Thom. Except for scattered skirmishes, the last one twenty-five years ago, the aliens hadn't threatened humanity for a century-and-a-half. He wondered why they would show up now. "Are you sure?"

"Yes. Intelligence told the League embassy that an Iimarae scout ship recently brought emissaries, very important emissaries, supposedly including a Great Hen or two, to Askander. The Iimarae are believed to have contacted someone among the planet's ruling elite, but our main source doesn't know whom. The intelligence service fears some of the Askanderians hate the League so much that they would have no qualms in forming an alliance with the Iimarae.

"If the Iimarae are Swarming again, then the League needs to renew the alliance with Askander," Rowena said. "That's why Diplomatic wanted you now, because you at least know ibn Brentholtz and because he seems well disposed toward the League."

"I see," Thom said softly. He sat up in his chair. "So what am I supposed to do? Tell the negotiating team everything I know about the cagey ibn Brentholtz, so they can counter his every move during delicate treaty talks? Damn it, Rowena, I haven't seen the man in twenty years. I doubt he remembers me."

"It seems ibn Brentholtz asked for you personally," she said. "I think he remembers you very well."

Thom sank back in his chair.

Seeing his disappointment, Rowena frowned. "I'm sorry, Thom, I thought you wanted a transfer to Diplomatic. If everything goes well on this assignment, it's virtually assured."

"If it goes well," he said.

"You're still bothered by that business at Barnard's Star, on Ramal, aren't you?"

"Yes, but that's over and done with. I'll take the assignment."

The colonel's face brightened, but only slightly. "Thanks, Thom," she said. "Now, remember, this is essentially a secret mission. You are to find out what you can about any Iimarae presence and report to intelligence. The diplomats will be handling the exact negotiations."

"So when do I get briefed?"

"You'll learn all you need to know on board ship to Delta Pavonis. In the meantime I'm supposed to give you this." Rowena opened the drawer of her desk and removed a small, hinged plastic box. She pushed the blue and white container across the desk to him.

"What's in that?" he said.

"Databugs," Rowena said. "Two are disposables: briefing software on Askander, its history and its culture. The other is an implant on the Askanderian language."

Thom picked up the box and turned it over in his hand. "When am I supposed to leave?" he said.

"A shuttle's scheduled to pick you up late tomorrow morning." Rowena said. She paused a moment. "Now, you need to get some sleep. I've been getting reports of your nightmares and your late night walks," Paget said. "That's not good for you or any of the troopers."

"Thanks, but I don't think I'll go back to my pod just yet."

Rowena stood up and came around the desk. "You can stay here, if you'd like," the colonel said. She directed his attention with a slight turn of her head and with her eyes. "The couch is comfortable, I'm told."

"Thanks, but..."

"I've also got a real bed, thanks to our naval comrades," she said. She had an oddly tired smile on her face; her blue eyes held an invitation Thom hadn't seen in years.

"It always seems half-empty to me, and makes me feel isolated and alone," Rowena added. "It's yours, to share, if you'd like."

He took her in his arms and kissed her. "I would like that," he said.

Indeed, he did.

CHAPTER SEVEN

"When the first ships of the Planetary League ventured from the rebuilt Earth in the third decade of the second century of the New Common Era [NCE}, they also found the martial relics of a previously unknown, supposedly dead race that the Tuatha had already labeled the Gonaymne, from the Gaelic 'gan aimn,' meaning 'having no name.' It soon proved clear that the Gonaymne, these Nameless Ones, had built the HyperPortals. While the Gonaymne seemed a long dead threat, they were to be an unpleasant portent of the future."

— S. Alexandria Keene, Among the Enemy Stars: Conflict With Reconstructionist Colonies and Aliens in the Early Great Leap Outward, New York, 823 New Common Era

Thom felt himself pushed back in his seat as the shuttle pulled slowly away from the League starship *William D. Haywood* and kicked in its chemical reaction motors. He leaned back and caught a final glimpse of the huge vessel. Thom had three hours to kill until they reached the *L.S.S. Ferdinand Lasalle*, the ship that would take him to Delta Pavonis via a Hyperspace portal. As much as he hated the turbulence of interstellar travel by the Hyperspace portal's Einstein-Rosen bridges, he could at least take solace in the fact that it was quick. By comparison the shuttle he was riding used old fusion engines and plodded on like an old horse.

Better use the time as best I can, he thought. Thom leaned back in his seat, set the databug box on his lap tray, and opened it. He removed the databug with information on Askanderian history, then carefully pushed back the small skin flap behind his right ear and inserted the plug-in. Data roared into his brain like a tidal wave. It was momentarily disorienting.

"Askander is the second planet of six in the Pavonis system," intoned a narrator with a deep, yet annoying voice. "Only Askander lies within the star's 'golden zone' where life can exist. Some argue that Askander just clings to the edge of that zone, far enough out to allow life but too close to make it really pleasant. Askander has two moons, " the narrator added, "a small uninhabited inner moon named Kamar, and a larger outer moon called Der Merchant, where some mining and refueling operations occur." Then the narrator suddenly became pompous and overly melodramatic. "Two Earth decades ago, the avian alien Iimarae attempted to invade Der Merchant and were only repelled with assistance of both League and Tuatha forces." Just as suddenly, the voice became numbingly monotone as it described the Pavonian system's other planets. "The inner planet, which has no agreed upon name, is a barren mass of rock. It lacks an atmosphere and may have originally been a wandering asteroid captured by Pavonis' gravity. The outer four planets — known by mostly obscene sexual names — are all methane gas giants and range in size from twenty to sixty times that of Askander. Several have moons that are mostly like captured space debris, such as asteroids and large rocky comets."

A different voice — a feminine, soft, and unfortunately sing-song monotone, now took over for the geography — or, more correctly, the planetography — portion of the presentations. "Radical members of the Propertarian Party settled it after their defeat by the communitarian forces, following the societal collapse precipitated by the Third Zaibatsu War. Five-sixths of Askander is covered by a massive ocean, the Coase Mare. The remaining one-sixth that is land-mass is composed of one major continent, Stiglera, and two minor ones, Fogelland and Fama. Stiglera is divided into arid and tropic areas, with large

settlements in both regions. Major cities include Friedmanville, Von Misestown and Ciudad Rand, with numerous ones, especially on the more isolated Fogelland and
Fama. The Ciudad Rand, Askander's largest city-state, is
an arcology located on a plateau in the Rothbard Mountains. Sparse woods run down from the plateau to the
Nahr Sakhr, or "Stone River," a major water source and
commercial waterway. The river separates the arcology
from the edge of an arid region. The planet's largest city, it
is named after a now obscure twentieth-century woman
the Askanderians regard as a prophetess and saint. The
culture is neo-feudal, with hereditary titles controlled by
voting stock in the generally single-family ruling coun-
cils, which make all the decisions . . ."

After two minutes of the monotone voice, Thom
popped the databug from the jack. The data-stream of
voices, text and images swamped him and made his mind
spin. He couldn't possibly assimilate the information
quickly enough now to retain it. If he were lucky, some
of the data would sink in on its own. He was tired and
anxious about the Jump. He decided he'd try the plug-in
again later.

He shut his eyes and tried to sleep. He wanted to
dream of New England beaches and the fragrance of salt
water, but the only images he could conjure up were of
desert sand, sirocco winds and bones bleaching beneath
the scorching rays of Delta Pavonis.

"Fifteen minutes till we jump," a stocky noncom named Reynolds told Thom and the negotiating team members. "So I'd suggest you gentlemen and ladies retire to your chambers. It'll take us ten minutes to set everything up so you aren't smashed up too badly by the Portal."

Thom stepped into his personal pressure capsule, a large metal chamber resembling a sarcophagus. He strapped himself in and hit the lever that closed the hatch. He took a deep breath and then swallowed hard as the hatch shut with a dull ringing sound.

He was alone, trapped in a cramped metal womb. Thom wondered if this was how his African ancestors felt, imprisoned below decks in the confined spaces of slave ships making the Middle Passage nearly twelve hundred years ago. He felt a sudden kinship with those who had endured that terrible experience. It did not comfort him.

He glanced at the readout above his head. It indicated his breathing and heart rate were slightly elevated and his blood pressure was rising.

"Would you like a sedative?" the chamber said. "One can be injected subcutaneously."

"No, thank you," he said curtly. As much as he hated Jumps, he preferred to be awake. If he was going to die, he decided to confront it directly rather than slip into the unknown doped into unconsciousness with saliva drooling from the corner of his mouth.

Thom ran a last-minute check of the capsule's readouts. Pressure was normal, the oxygen-nitrogen mix was normal, and the scrubbers had adjusted automatically to handle the extra carbon dioxide his rapid breathing was producing. Everything seemed unexceptional.

He wasn't reassured. Thom remembered reports of sarcophagi failures, of friends pulped beyond recognition or asphyxiated when the life-support systems gave way. He preferred not to gamble, but he had no choice. Einstein-Rosen travel, with its literal bending of space-time, was a risk and always would be.

The green "Go" light came on.

Using the capsule's video screen, Thom could see the *Lasalle* as it neared the Portal. In the center of the Portal, invisible to the naked eye, an artificial black hole with a diameter of forty-six kilometers rotated at incomprehensible speeds. Thom knew the ship had to enter the 600-meter wide area of the Einstein-Rosen Bridge precisely, or it would fall into the black hole's event horizon. Failure meant being instantly crushed by the black hole's immense gravity. Death was said to be instantaneous, but since time was irrelevant in a black hole, Thom wondered if it didn't last for eternity.

The ship's computers carefully calculated the precise mathematics for the Kruskal–Szekeres pathway into the empty space-time surrounding the black hole, the pathway to Delta Pavonis. Thom could hear the hydraulics as the navigational rockets were adjusted. Then the main engines fired to provide enough thrust so the ship would skim past the event horizon of the spinning toroid.

The *Lasalle* entered the Einstein-Rosen Bridge.

High gravity slammed Thom back into the padded couch of the capsule. Seconds felt like hours. The sarcophagus adjusted the air pressure so it maintained a strong oxygen mix at one Earth atmosphere, but still he couldn't breathe. His sinuses pounded, and his eyes hurt. It felt as if a vise were squeezing his chest. He wanted to move, but he couldn't make his muscles respond. The pressure increased each second, yet the capsule clock didn't move.

Just when he wanted to scream, he sensed the pressure of gravity and time lift. The vise unwound. He gulped air and nearly hyperventilated. His muscles ached, and his eyes felt as if they were bulging from their sockets.

When his eyes had cleared, he looked up at the viewscreen and saw the glow of Delta Pavonis, now roughly nine astronomical units away.

The image disappointed Thom. The Jump across

light years was precarious and distressing, but it lasted only a few seconds. The trip across the relatively short interplanetary distance to Askander would take roughly ten days. He would have nearly a week and a half of nothing to do but be briefed by the negotiating team. Thom reluctantly unlatched and opened the capsule and climbed out.

The negotiating team of three men and two women were courteous, but they really had little time to teach him the specifics of the treaty proposal. He began to feel he was a useless appendage to their plans, just some other problem with which they had to contend. After two days, he decided he would attend the briefing meetings but would otherwise leave the negotiators to their own devices. He made no effort to get to know them and instead spent the rest of his time listening to plug-ins and, on an *Isaak*, reading the few other bits of data available on contemporary Askander.

What struck him most was that the name Askander seemed an oddly bland name for a hostile, mostly barren, rocky orb heavily dominated by deserts in the one-sixth of the surface not submerged by the waters of the Coase Mare. The few habitable places were mere oases that could hardly be called "regions." Some people who claimed the name truly befit the planet's ruling class, an elite who cared only for profits and essentially worshiped the free marketplace as a god.

Although it offered little in amenities except for the wealthy, Askander had long tempted some desperate, greedy men with sizeable lodes of precious metals and jewels and rare minerals, supposedly ripe for the picking. The mythic siren song of the propertarians seduced and persuaded the naïve that wealth could be easily had by all and that a lack of governments meant you were free.

The hungry, the desperate, and the greedy therefore indentured themselves to the great family corporations that had inherited the *zaibatsu's* mantles. Only after they were on Askander did the wide-eyed naïfs learn to their regret that the ones who actually profited were the already super-affluent and the cosmically wealthy. For the elite, no government simply meant that no countervailing force existed to control their tyrannical rule, and no institutions were in place to allow other men to challenge their property and power. Askander suited the needs of the rich and the powerful. It provided materials that served to increase their affluence. It was a haven for those who did not wish to share anything with their fellow humans, for those to whom money meant more than any single human life other than their own.

Always there was a seemingly endless supply of those who willingly and foolishly slaved away their lives, hoping one day they too would strike it rich and ascend to the heights of their Masters. Such optimists never led revolutions or dared to believe that injustice might exist. Their faith told them that the god of the market would grant them their rightful reward, and it kept them working themselves, uncomplaining, to their deaths. At their deaths, their remains would be recycled, reclaimed, reused, and sold. Even death was an opportunity for profit on Askander.

By the time the *Lasalle* entered orbit around Askander, Thom had gained some familiarity with Askanderian, a language blend of mostly Arabic origin with German and Spanish influences. He had also gleaned a more than serviceable understanding of the planet's culture, which was an amalgam of pseudo-medievalist and utopian free market fantasies, blended with odd bits of old Middle Eastern, American nativist conspiratorial and Twentieth Century counter-culturist traditions. It was far from even being a remotely democratic and egalitarian sort of place, he decided. Still, he suspected little of the plug-in's data could help him fully dissect the reality of the planet's social and political intricacies. Experiencing a world first-hand would provide a fuller portrait. Thom hoped that the rest of the negotiating team, who were trained to play such mind games, would handle the political intrigue aspects.

He told himself that he was just along for the ride and tried to recall what he could about Don Jaime ibn Brentholtz. Despite his past familiarity with the man, he found he could remember little that might be helpful. He had known Don Jaime well twenty years ago, but now the man seemed just another stranger.

When it came time to debark, he walked down the deck to the waiting shuttle with a growing sense of apprehension and worry. The other diplomats acted as if he didn't exist. He had, inexplicably, the same strange feeling about them.

Each passenger had a separate pod in the passenger shuttle. The separate pods were a precaution unique to League diplomatic and military shuttles entering hostile territory. The principle behind them was simple: in the event of a disaster at least some of the passengers and crew could escape and a command group would not be thoroughly disrupted.

"Can't say I wish I was going with you," Reynolds said as she helped strap Thom into his pod.

"You don't like adventure?" Thom said with a forced smile, trying to put any doubts out of his mind.

"Nope. I have a family back on Earth," she replied. "My wife and I are expecting a kid soon. She's supposed to deliver when I get back next month."

"Your first?" Thom said.

"Second. I carried the first, a really sweet little girl. She's three now. But we had real trouble with egg fusions this time," Reynolds said. She brushed a sweat-soaked clump of brown hair from her face. "Okay, you're all set. Now, do you see that D-ring on the right side of your seat?"

Thom looked down. The yellow D-ring was recessed into the side panel. "Yes. What about it?"

"That'll activate your escape pod manually," Reynolds said. "When you pull the ring, the latching bolts detach from the main fuselage and a pair of chemical rockets eject you. If you're lucky, your parasail will deploy once you've hit dense enough air. Otherwise, it's one hell of a roller coaster ride."

Before Thom could say anything, she had locked the pod hatch and left the dock. He felt the shuttle shake as its engines roared into life. Watching through the pod's porthole, he could see air condense into thin, wispy clouds as the shuttle bay was purged of atmosphere.

The shuttle rose slowly from the flight deck. It hovered, and then rotated on its axis until its nose pointed straight at the slowly opening bay doors. After the doors were fully open, the shuttle's engines throttled up, and it moved forward into space. The whole operation reminded Thom of a whale giving birth as seen from the baby whale's perspective.

Once outside the *Lasalle*, the shuttle fired its retro-rockets and began the reentry sequence. The starship itself would break orbit and move out toward Kamar, the inner moon, before rendezvousing with the outer moon Der Merchant. From there, it would watch for any Iimarae vessels entering the system.

Thom glanced out the porthole. Below him, he could see that night covered the half of Askander in which Ciudad Rand lay. Only the glow from the lights of the huge arcologies indicated that anything dwelled on the planet's surface. He realized that landing at night was meant to hide their presence on Askander, and to protect ibn Brentholtz from possible accusations from other *sèo*. The darkness, however, left him with a sense of foreboding.

He felt the tug and pull of air as the shuttle entered the upper levels of Askander's atmosphere. The shuttle bucked heavily from the turbulence. Thom's fingers dug deeply into the seat's armrests. Remembering a Zen-style discipline from *la souffrance*, he began counting his breaths to ease the tension.

Through the porthole he glimpsed bits of the shuttle's protective outer heat shield flying past. The particles burned with a reddish gold brilliance. Thom found the fireworks somehow soothing. He let himself relax, let his mind drift. His fingers released their grip on the armrests.

The shuttle soon hit the thicker lower levels of the atmosphere, and its air-breathing jet engines kicked in. The ride smoothed out, and the descent slowed.

"Sorry about that turbulence," Thom heard the pilot say over his skul-fone. "Seems we hit a little upper level disturbance. Should be smoother from now on. We're estimating ten minutes to the Ciudad Rand spaceport."

Thom looked out the port. The shuttle appeared to be flying over some woodlands, possibly the small stunted timber forests in the foothills outside Ciudad Rand. He guessed they should soon be coming to a large plateau overlooking the narrow, yet elongated, *Nahr Sakhr*, the Stone River: Askander's longest waterway. The arcology of Ciudad Rand was built into that plateau, which translated as "Treason's Tooth."

The shuttle dipped a wing and began a slow turn into its final approach.

Thom watched the starlit landscape roll past. Then he saw something explode from the woodlands. He watched it flare briefly, and then vanish. After a moment, he could see something coming toward the shuttle, something with a glowing tail.

He touched the mike at his throat. "Captain, this is Major DuBois. Somebody just fired a surface-to-air missile at us."

"A SAM? Are you kidding, DuBois? They've been obsolete for centuries," the pilot said.

"Captain, I've seen a lot of SAMs on colony worlds, where they're not so obsolete."

"Sir, he's right," the copilot said. "I've got something on my screens, and it's heading for our exhausts."

The force of the pilot's hard right turn flung Thom

hard to one side. Instinctively Thom grabbed the arm-rests as the shuttle banked and dropped heavily to the left to evade the heat-seeking missile.

"No use," the copilot shouted. "The damn thing's sticking right to us."

The shuttle turned right again, but this time in a steep climb.

Thom managed to twist his head around to look out the porthole. He could see the missile complete a turn of its own, which would bring the projectile right behind the shuttle. He knew it would soon catch them.

"It's gaining on us, captain. In five seconds it'll be up our tailpipe," the copilot said.

"*Merde*," the pilot said. "Okay, folks, I think we may have to abandon ship."

Thom reached for the D-ring before the shuttle's computers could automatically eject the pods. As he yanked the ejector release, the shuttle exploded.

CHAPTER EIGHT

The escape pod tumbled uncontrollably. Then the drogue chute deployed, stabilizing the capsule until the main parasail fully inflated. The pod, swaying wildly, descended quickly through the thin mountain air toward a thick stand of trees.

Inside the pod, Thom was heaved from side to side. The joystick that controlled the parasail leaped from his hand as he attempted to steady the capsule. He tried desperately to contact the others with his transmitter, flicking his tongue against the micro-switch in his right lower incisor to get a signal. Only static crackled in his skul-fone.

Clamping the joystick between his knees, Thom managed to stabilize the pod and the buffeting slowed. Through the porthole, he could see the trees outlined in moonlight as the pod drifted toward them. The forest went on for kilometers without even the hint of a clearing. Thom knew that if he hit the trees, he would be just as dead as if hc had never ejected.

Up ahead he spotted what he thought was a clearing. He kicked the joystick to his left. The parasail responded swiftly, bringing the capsule about in a long, wide turn. His descent was still too fast. He pulled back on the controls, but the pod failed to respond. If anything, the capsule now seemed to plummet more rapidly.

The trees loomed beneath him. Thom jammed the joystick against the seat. The clearing was just scant meters away, if he could just keep from losing any more altitude. Already he could hear the treetops scraping the capsule bottom.

A large tree sprang up in front of him. Thom braced himself and held tight to the joystick. The pod hit the tree, and then twisted about. The parasail lines tangled, and the capsule fell suddenly. The pod struck the earth. Bouncing twice, it slammed into the ground a third time and rolled, coming to rest upside down against a large tree trunk.

Thom slapped a large button next to the hatch, and then covered his face. Explosive bolts blew the hatch into the air. Undoing his harness, Thom eased himself from the seat and through the exposed hatchway.

The ground was muddy and wet from a recent rainfall. Thom's feet sank into the moist earth. With legs already weak from the journey, he almost lost his balance, and he had to hold onto the capsule to keep from falling.

Thom saw that he had landed on a steep portion of a hillside. Farther down the slope he could see the glow from a large fire caused by the shuttle's impact. The tall flames produced enough light for him to see two other escape pods slowly descending from the night sky.

Something was wrong. In horror, Thom watched as first one pod, then the other landed right in the heart of the fire. He turned away and shut his eyes.

The clearing suddenly filled with brilliant light and a strange stiff wind whipped the treetops. Thom looked up and a bright flood lamp nearly blinded him.

"Are you all right?" a voice in his skul-fone said. The voice spoke Askanderian.

Thom shaded his eyes and made out the shape of a *veetol* — an obsolete vertical takeoff and landing aircraft — floating over the clearing. The long, silvery, cigar-shaped craft hovered on four ducted propeller units mounted at the ends of two sets of stubby wings. Red, green, white and amber lights blinked along its fuselage.

"Are you all right?" the voice repeated.

"Yes, I think so," Thom said. He felt dizzy and leaned back against the escape pod. "Who are you?"

"We are with Brentholtz-Madden Gesellschaft, a search team from the Ciudad Rand spaceport," the pilot said. "Please wait. We are lowering a rescue harness for you."

The harness, which resembled a heavy fishing net, descended on a thin polymer cable. Thom climbed into the webbing and was pulled up into the vee-tol's belly. The craft, its insides painted a dull gray, was empty except for cargo ropes, the rescue crane, and the pilot's seats and controls. The only light came from the control panels and the only occupants were the two crewmen. It gave Thom a feeling of desolation. They had rescued no one else.

"How did you find me?" he said once they had him on board.

"We spotted your parasail," a thin, dark crewman said. He helped Thom into a small seat behind the pilot. "It was just after your shuttle exploded."

"Then we picked up a signal from your pod transponder," the pilot said. A toothy smile spread across his pale, round face. "It wasn't difficult to find you after that."

"Are there any others?" he said. "Did you find any others?"

The pilot and the crewman both frowned and shook their heads.

"We saw other parasails. Perhaps another vee-tol has found them," the pilot said.

"I don't know," Thom said. A chill rolled down his spine as he realized it was possible no one else had survived the missile attack. "Did any other pod send out a rescue signal?"

The pilot opened his mouth to respond, then stopped. He placed his right hand against his helmet and appeared to be listening to something. He smiled. "I have a transponder signal similar to yours," he said.

"Where?" Thom demanded, reaching forward to grab the pilot's shoulder and turn him around.

The crewman pulled Thom's hand from the pilot and pushed him back in his seat. "Please, *sidi*, stay in your seat."

Thom realized he had overreacted. "Sorry," he said.

The pilot smiled. "I take no offense, *sidi*. May the Invisible Hand which rules all things guide you in this terrible time."

They flew on for several minutes, and then the vee-tol slowed and hovered over a bare patch of hillside.

"Here. The signal is here," the pilot said.

The crewman turned on the ship's searchlight and began scanning the area.

Thom could see something protruding from the ground farther up the slope. In the moonlight it appeared to be a large, round boulder. "Up the slope, about seventy-five meters," he told the crewman. "Can you see it?"

The crewman aimed the beam at the shape, and Thom could see an escape pod, one side mashed so it resembled a broken eggshell. The searchlight revealed an unopened parasail still tucked into its storage compartment. The brightly colored parasail against the white of the pod resembled the iris of a huge eye, which now stared unblinkingly at Thom.

"I am sorry, *sidi*," the crewman said, snapping off the light. "But no one could have survived that crash."

Thom, shaken, eased himself back into his chair.

"The other vee-tols, they report no more signals," the pilot said. "The remaining pods are all with the main wreckage."

"I see," Thom said. He swallowed hard. It was obvious someone knew the negotiating team was arriving in Ciudad Rand, and that someone wanted them all dead and had almost succeeded. Now Thom was the negotiating team, and he hadn't the slightest idea of what to do.

The vee-tol pilot made a quick sweep of the area at Thom's request. They found nothing. Thom reluctantly agreed to let the vee-tol return to Ciudad Rand. He sat back in his seat.

The crewman offered Thom a squeezeflask of brandy, which the crewman said was called "*araki*".

Thom accepted the squeezeflask, and let the liquor scald his throat as it went down. Soon he felt nothing but a dull warmth, and that was just fine.

Dawn was breaking over Ciudad Rand as the vee-tol approached the spaceport. Pavonis' first rays bathed the arcology in golden light. The light sparkled off the glass and metal girders of the city's outer skin. The city was an urban monad: a single huge architectural construct built directly into the side of the plateau called Treason's Tooth. Nearly one hundred twenty stories tall, the arcology showed only a single side to the world, a side that caught the sunlight to power the long black solar panels that gave much of the city life. It reminded Thom of the cliff dwellings and pueblos he had seen in the Republics of New Mexico and Arizona, only on a grander scale.

Treason's Tooth itself was an eroded volcanic plug thrusting up from the more gently sloping, forested hill country around it. Coming directly toward the geological feature, Thom could see that it did indeed resemble the blackened tooth of some long-dead giant.

The vee-tol rose above the plateau's rim, and he saw that the summit of Treason's Tooth stretched on for several kilometers in every direction, forming a huge, craggy rectangle. The spaceport and its long, flat runways occupied only a small corner of that rectangle.

The vee-tol circled a small complex of long hangars. Then the aircraft, its engines whining, descended slowly to a well-lit square of tarmac. A cloud of reddish dust rose from the back-blast of the vee-tol's engines. The dust hung in the air even after the pilot cut the power and only slowly began to settle.

Thom spotted three figures standing at the edge of the landing pad. The trio all wore long, loose robes, billowing pantaloons and heavy boots. Hoods and breathing masks hid their faces. As the dust settled, they approached the aircraft.

The vee-tol hatch opened. One of the three stuck his head into the aircraft. He removed his breathing mask and a broad grin crossed his thin pale white face.

"So good to see you, Thom," said Don Jaime ibn Brentholtz. "It's been far too long, old friend."

CHAPTER NINE

The two men sat at a heavy table made of dark wood. The room, though well lit, was decorated with ornate, heavy furniture of deeply stained wood. The walls were covered with the somber, brooding portraits of the ibn Brentholtz family and their cadet clans. All of it gave the room a depressing, serious mood, but a mood not shared by its two occupants.

"Ambassador Stephens inquired as to your safety," Don Jaime said. "I told him you were quite all right, and I added it was probably better that you stay here in my quarters, rather than have to journey from the embassy each day."

"I see. When do I get to meet the ambassador?" Thom asked.

"I'm having a private function tonight: a few guests, the ambassador among them."

A servant brought in two luncheon platters of steaming food on a carved ivory tray. The foods' delicate spicy aromas filled the room. Thom selected a flat, orangish cutlet and a yellow vegetable covered with an odd-looking green sauce. Despite the spices, it all tasted fish-like and oily. He reached for his water glass to cut the flavor.

"Forget that. Here, you must try this *araki*." Don Jaime pushed a wine bottle across the table to Thom. "It comes from my own vineyards. I believe you had some last night, under less than optimal conditions." The young *sèo* leaned back in his large, opulently decorated chair and sipped his brandy.

Thom watched Don Jaime carefully. Overall, he seemed to have changed little from the headstrong youth at the university. He sat with the relaxed ease of a rich and powerful man who cared little for others' opinions. Yet despite the man's outward mask of calm and joviality, his narrow, high cheek-boned face showed fine lines of worry, especially around his mouth and eyes. He drank too much, and when he grinned his lips smiled, but his dark blue eyes remained serious, even fearful.

"We think the Mukhalafi tried to kill you," Don Jaime said.

"The Mukhalafi? Who are they?" Thom said, pouring the dark wine into a glass by his plate. "They weren't mentioned in my databugs."

"Your League's intelligence about my people is old, no doubt," Don Jaime said. He dismissed the servant with a stiff wave of a hand. "The Mukhalafi are a band of bandits, cutthroats, criminals who call themselves revolutionaries. They blaspheme the power of the Hand, blessings upon Its invisible ways. They profess to support the *mostazafin*, the laboring people and the disinherited, and they want to destroy the power of the great *sèo*."

"But how could they have known we were coming?" Thom said. "I thought the meeting was secret, arranged personally by you and our ambassador."

"True, Ambassador Stephens and I kept this private," Jaime said. He knocked back his wineglass, refilled it, and then continued. "But a few of my closest advisors and some of the embassy staff knew. Remember, walls have mice, and mice have ears. The Mukhalafi are very clever mice."

"Well, whoever shot down the shuttle did a good job. I'm not prepared to negotiate with you, because I simply don't have all the details the other diplomats did."

Jaime dismissed Thom's concerns with a broad sweep of his right hand. "Don't worry, friend. Negotiations with the League are a small matter. You and I both know the threat the Iimarae pose. My problem is convincing the other nobles, and agreeing with allies is far more difficult than making treaties with one's enemies." He picked up his wineglass, downed the contents, and slammed the glass back on the table.

"But enough of business," Jaime said. He smiled and leaned forward. "Damn, Thom, it's good to see you. You've done well. And what about Ursula?"

Thom placed his fork down by his plate. "We're divorced." He stood up and walked over to a bank of smoked glass windows. He stared out across the Nahr Sahkr, past lightly forested mountains, to the *Shaul Khala* — the Great Desert — beyond. "It's been five years. She went crazy, you see, some sort of untreatable form of manic depression comorbid with schizophrenia. She began having these grandiose delusions, that she was God or Buddha or Lao Tzu. Then one day she took our two children, a boy and a girl, and disappeared." Thom paused a moment. "I don't know where she went, and I frankly don't care anymore," he lied.

Jaime rose, picked up the wine flask, and came to Thom's side. He placed his right arm across his friend's shoulder. "I am sorry. I didn't mean to offend you, my friend. She must have hurt you very much."

Thom smiled. "*'The wedding is a fog, but the marriage is a cyclone,'* according to one of your Askanderian proverbs. Ursula proved worse than that."

"Be thankful you only had one bad marriage. I've had four, at least," Jaime said with a loud laugh. "I only married them because of the stock it gave me in their families' corporations. One of my few bad business decisions."

"We all make mistakes," Thom said.

"Like the time I convinced you to go out to the Bintelkhatiye District in Formalhaut City the night before you took your general exams?" Jaime said. "I have never seen anyone drink as much as you did that night."

Thom smiled at the memory; or rather what his friends had told him afterwards had happened. "You should talk, the way you tried to pick up every woman you saw, saying you would whisk them away to Askander and fulfill their every dream."

"It was the truth, I swear." Jaime knocked back his glass of *araki*. "Anyway, they thought I was charming."

"They thought you were crazy," Thom said. "Then you fixed us with those two sisters. Those amazons damn near killed us."

"How was I to know they'd been stevedores before they had sex changes?"

"They had arms as strong as tree trunks," Thom said with a laugh. The laughter and the wine began to make him feel better. He no longer felt sorry for himself.

A servant entered the room.

"Yes, what is it, Rustam?" Jaime said, his voice suddenly serious.

"Colonel ni Mhaonaigh is here to see you, Don Jaime," Rustam said.

"Well, show her in, man," he said.

"Very well, *sidi*," Rustam said, and he left the room.

A moment later, a tall, striking woman entered the room. She wore the drab black uniform of a Tuatha infantry officer. The dark uniform with its silver markings contrasted with her hair, which was golden blond. A flechette pistol hung in a holster from a belt at her waist and a short dagger, a *skean dubh*, was in a scabbard at her knee.

The colonel was something Thom had not expected. While he knew that the Askanderians hired Tuatha security units, he wondered if League officials were aware that Tuatha ground troops were on Askander.

"Thom, I'd like you to meet Colonel Siobhan ni Mhaonaigh," Jaime said. "She and her associates are training my personal army and police forces to fight the Mukhalafi."

"My pleasure," Thom said extending his hand.

The colonel did not respond. Her dark blue eyes gave Thom a quick examination, but her lips neither smiled nor frowned.

He withdrew his hand.

The woman had the look of a mercenary, but she was one of the regular Tuatha forces and not the *Gall Oglaigh*, the elite genetically engineered and utterly ruthless soldiers-for-hire. Her face was tanned, almost amber from years of exposure to the suns of many worlds. Standing just a bit under Thom's own height of one hundred ninety centimeters, she was the perfect model of Tuatha eugenics, a pure Celtic warrior bred from generations of humans who claimed ancestry from the ancient stock of Briton, Scotia, Eire, and Helvetica.

Such purity was doubtful, Thom knew, as true Celts had not existed much beyond the fall of ancient Rome. Thom wondered how those old Gaels who valued their independence would view their descendants, now reduced either to selling their military prowess to the highest bidder, or to raiding League outposts to support marginally viable colonies on the edge of human habitation.

Thom glanced at Jaime. He was surprised to see an odd expression on his face. Thom knew instantly that Jaime would gladly forsake all his wives for the woman who stood before them. But he also suspected it was unrequited love at best.

"And Siobhan, this is — " Jaime began.

"I know Major DuBois, by reputation at least," she said. "Many of my comrades have tasted defeat at his hands."

She stared at him with cold, sharp eyes. "I would have thought you'd be with the League forces opposing the Dravidians at Tau Ceti."

Thom smiled. "There was an armistice and a peace treaty, which I'm surprised you didn't know. I just came from there. A change of assignment."

"No doubt a reward for your victory," Siobhan said.

"No reward, just a new challenge," he replied. "I

didn't know the Tuatha were selling their services so widely these days."

"You know Alba Nuadh is a poor world, Major Du-Bois," she replied. "We earn what we can, where we can. We've served on Askander for some time, more than fifty years."

"I meant working for the Dravidians," Thom said.

The colonel smiled. "Not all of us support every contract the Dail makes. Our government can be a trifle dazzled by large amounts of money dangled before it, even money dangled by thugs like the Dravidians."

Don Jaime moved to stop what was a potential dispute between Thom and the colonel. "Well, I am pleased to have two such important guests," he interjected. "Would you like some brandy, Colonel?"

"Thank you, yes, a very small one" she said, a faint smile crossing her lips.

The three sat down at the table, and Don Jaime poured out the last of the araki. He drank his quickly, and Thom could see Jaime was growing more than a little intoxicated, both with drink and with Siobhan. Thom elected to drink no more.

The colonel barely sipped her liquor. "Our informants can tell us little about who shot down the major's shuttle. They either deny any knowledge of it, or they say it might have been the Mukhalafi, or might not. Most lean toward 'Not.'"

"Have you tried all your informants?" Jaime said.

"All but two or three," she replied. "Two of them are merchants who arrived in Ciudad Rand this morning for the market. They had to pass through rebel territory, so they might know something."

"Are they in the bazaar?" the *sèo* said.

She nodded. "I plan to send men to interrogate them this afternoon."

"No," Jaime said. "I want you to personally question them."

Siobhan looked at Jaime and raised an eyebrow, but otherwise she did not react. "Very well, as you wish."

"I'd like to come with you," Thom said.

"But what about your safety?" Jaime protested.

"I think I would feel quite safe in Colonel ni Mhaonaigh's company," he said. "If she doesn't object."

The colonel's cold eyes shot him a piercing glance. Thom could almost feel anger emanating from her. She opened her mouth to speak, paused, then said, "I have no objections."

Jaime clapped his hands with delight. "Very good." He rose from the table. "Now, you must excuse me. I have a business meeting I must attend to."

Thom saw that the harsh expression on Siobhan's face did not soften when Jaime left the room.

"Shall we go?" she said.

"By all means," Thom replied.

Thom began feeling uneasy as he and the colonel rode the turbo-lift down the twenty-six levels from Don Jaime's quarters to the *souk*.

He knew part of his discomfort was the *araki* and the food, which made his stomach a bit queasy, and part of it was also Colonel ni Mhaonaigh. Her cold stares made him restive, and he sensed she merely tolerated him and wished he were not here. Thom was unsure if she disliked him personally or detested him because he was a League citizen. Tuatha often held grudges simply because it was expected of them to despise someone.

Neither of them spoke in the turbo-lift. The colonel calmly stared out the glass windows of the lift, across the mountains to the desert, the bleak *Shaul Khala*. She hardly moved through the entire descent.

Thom fumbled with the Askanderian robes she had convinced him to wear instead of his uniform. He granted her that point. Certainly someone in a League uniform would be an object of suspicion, if not hatred. While the burnoose and long shirt were snug, the pantaloons Rustam had provided were large and proved a little difficult to deal with.

He managed to tie a knot in the drawstring at the waist and hoped the pants would not come loose. As the lift came to a halt, he adjusted his *kaffiya* so the kerchief covered all of his face, except his eyes. Then he reached back behind his ear to make sure his Askanderian language plug-in remained in place. Even if he did not speak, he could at least understand what was being said.

"Colonel ni Mhaonaigh," Thom started to say.

"Forget the formalities, Major," she replied, as her lips curled into an ever so slight smile. "You can call me Siobhan. We're working together, at least informally, and rank and origin have little meaning here for folks like you and me."

The remark took Thom aback. It seemed odd, especially if she could not stand him, but before Thom could respond, the door of the turbo-lift opened, and they stepped out. The bright light momentarily blinded him. Thom's nostrils were assaulted by a wild array of pungent, fetid odors mingled with the aroma of spices, herbs and cooking food.

"Quite a sight, isn't it?" the colonel said. She explained the souk was the massive open-air bazaar held daily on a terraced area built above the poorer, more squalid lower parts of the arcology. Those underground portions, buried directly beneath the main structure, were called the Jura, or the underbelly. "As you can imagine, those areas never receive any sunlight from Delta Pavonis, so the inhabitants are often quite pale, like those colorless animals found in caves on Earth."

Before Thom could respond, he found himself surrounded by children dressed in rags. All of them begged for money or food. He looked into their small faces and was horrified to see how scarred and disfigured they were. Some thrust fingerless hands toward him. Others bounced up and down on a single leg. Still others had only one arm, or one eye, or had faces disfigured by hideous silvery scars or festering red sores. A few sores appeared to move, as if something were alive under the skin.

Thom felt paralyzed. He tried to say, "I have no money," but his plug-in seemed unable to provide the phrase. He reached into the folds of his robes, hoping that perhaps Rustam had forgotten a coin in a pocket.

Siobhan spared him the trouble. She took a handful of coins from her jacket and flung them on the ground. Scattering like a swarm of insects, the children raced after the coins. As the children fought among themselves, Siobhan grabbed Thom's arm and dragged him away.

After they were some distance from the lift, they slowed their pace to a walk.

"Those children," Thom said. "It was horrible. Their faces!"

"They're from the lowest class of *mostazafin*, and they're always here in the bazaar," she said. "It's a fact you must get used to."

"But why are they so disfigured?"

Siobhan stopped and looked at him. "Their mothers do it. It increases the child's value as a beggar."

"Value?"

"The Beggars' Guild maintains a strict control over begging, with the corporation's blessing. Only cripples, mutants or the mentally defective can legally beg. So mothers maim their offspring. Some mothers even try to maim their fetuses, just to be sure."

"And it's condoned?" Thom said.

"Don't be such a fool. Certainly it's condoned," Siobhan said. "It allows the wealthy to be charitable. They say the Hand rewards the generous."

Thom detected more than a hint of sarcasm in her voice, which surprised him. "But you don't believe that," he said.

"I believe what I have to believe," she said. "Now, we have business to attend to."

He let his senses absorb all he could as he walked through the bazaar. The marketplace was a chaotic assemblage of the sublime and mundane, the truthful and the deceitful. The bazaar itself seemed to stretch out for several square kilometers. Although there were some permanent structures, most of the stalls were temporary, haphazard huts. Canvas tents and awnings, ranging in color from white to dazzling rainbow hues of blues, golds and reds filled the area.

Above the tents, holographic billboards blared out

their continuous advertisements. The bazaar displayed all the magic and contradictions of the Askanderians' faith in "free" trade. Anyone could sell anything, including what was left of his or her dignity. The images and sounds produced a meaningless cacophony that a majority of the people in the bazaar — mostly lower-class *suma*, including some of the laboring *mostazafin* — seemed to ignore.

Thom watched women, hidden from head to foot under long shapeless black dresses called *chadors*, as they haggled with merchants over the price of overripe fruits and vegetables. Less modest women in colorful long-sleeve dustcoats purchased toys for their children, whose state of dress contrasted sharply with that of the beggars.

Hawkers shouted the qualities of their wares, from produce and meats, to pots and pans, ceramics and even electronics. One merchant tried to sell genetically altered mice, their fur colored in several shades of pastel. The mice scrambled frantically around their rusty wire cage. Thom shook his head, not surprised at the shoppers' lack of interest. No matter where humanity had gone among the stars, mice and rats had followed. He felt sorry for the merchant. Most people still regarded mice, even colorful ones, as vermin.

Another merchant offered only the finest cybernetic merchandise: ROM chips, plug-ins, databugs, circuit boards, even prostheses and personality modules. All of it was either obsolete or illegally obtained, but the trade in it was brisk. Thom had heard rumors that the Askanderians smuggled, stole and pirated software and all manner of technology, all under the auspices of various *sèo*. Most *sèo* also claimed that paying the developers amounted to restraint of trade.

Thom spotted another merchant measuring powders and pills out for two young men. The men were well dressed and appeared wealthy. They laughed and joked as they inhaled samples of the powders. Thom suspected they were lower-ranking Ciudad Rand officials out on a spree. With a simple thought, he accessed the databug. Through the interface wired into his brain, it told Thom they were probably *jhereks*, the junior executive sons of nobles who would one day rise to the rank of *manaj* or *dhirek*, if they had enough stock and possessed the proper friends and wives to help them become those managers and directors.

Thom and Siobhan continued walking through the bazaar. Whoever her informant was, his stall was well on the outskirts of the market. Siobhan maintained a steady pace. After so much time in artificial gravity, Thom had trouble staying up with her.

He was grateful when she stopped a moment to chat with another Tuatha, a large bearded and well-muscled *saighdear* — a foot soldier — who was part of her training contingent.

Thom wandered over to a stall that sold silver trinkets and jewelry. As his eyes carelessly strayed over the merchandise, he felt a tug at his left elbow. He turned to see the heavily decorated face of a young woman with long, oiled black hair.

"Is *sidi* seeking pleasure?" she said, her full red lips forming a seductive smile. She ran a long wine-colored fingernail down his forearm. "I have implants. Modules. Whatever you desire."

He gently removed her hand and shook his head. "Some other time, perhaps."

She frowned and walked over to the two young *jhereks* Thom had seen earlier. They seemed more willing to take up her offer. As he watched the three, Thom spotted a man in a black *jallaba*, a unisexual robe-like garment. A breathing mask covered the lower half of the man's face, but his eyes were fixed on Thom. Thom had the impression that the man had been observing him for some time.

Thom stepped away from the stall and looked for the colonel. He was relieved to see her still talking to the other Tuatha. He walked quickly over to Siobhan and grabbed her by the forearm. "We're being followed," he whispered.

"Are you sure?" she said, still looking at the other Tuatha.

"No, but I saw a man in dark robes and a breathing mask watching me."

"Liam," she said, "look past us — carefully now — and see if someone is spying on us."

Liam smiled and nodded. He scratched his beard and pretended to look directly at Thom. "I did see a man in a black *jallaba* of some sort, but he ducked behind a stall. He could be anything though: a *suma* out buying goods, a Mukhalafi agent, or just a desert nomad."

"Find him and follow him," Siobhan said. She glanced at Thom and smiled. "You have sharp eyes."

The first merchant that the colonel sought had a stall near the far edge of the marketplace. Thom noticed the area appeared grimmer and filthier than the part of the bazaar that abutted the arcology itself. The tents were faded and patched. The more permanent-looking structures looked run-down and were covered with graffiti. From the numbers of men and women entering and leaving some of the canvas-covered stalls, it was obvious that many of the businesses were whorehouses. The women stood on the porches and advertised their skills, which included nerve-stimulating implants, personality cartridges and cybernetic enhancements.

Beyond the men and women and graffiti, Thom also noticed posters and stickers in red ink. Most had been covered over with splashes of white paint, but a few new ones had been added. They all showed a fist thrusting up from the ground. He read the delicately curving letters printed above the pictures. Each poster or sticker read the same thing: "There is no Hand but the Human Hand. Resist the Hand which crushes you."

"This is the tent," Siobhan said.

She ushered him into a stall completely covered by bright yellow and burgundy tarpaulins. The inside was filled with heavy rugs and carpets of various abstract designs. There was no other merchandise. Thom wondered if the rugs and carpets actually were the merchant's wares or if they served another purpose, perhaps hiding the merchant's real wares, whatever those might be.

A smallish, gray-bearded man in white robes and a pale blue headscarf sat in the middle of the enclosure. He was tending to several boiling pots on a small alcohol-fired cookstove.

"Maarat, may the Hand uplift your fortunes," Siobhan said.

Maarat looked up and a broad grin appeared on his weather-beaten face. His chestnut-hued eyes almost glowed as he rose to greet them. "Siobhan, my dearest one, the Hand may do to me what It may," he said in a voice deep and somewhat raspy, "if I may have such guests as thou. I am humbled that you grace me with your presence." He spotted Thom. "And you brought a friend."

Siobhan introduced Thom using the Askanderian form for male names: the person's first name, then the designation "son of" and the man's father's name. "Maarat ibn Steiner, this is Thomas ibn Andre. His family, the DuBois, is from Earth. He is a friend of Don Jaime."

Maarat's grin softened to a smile. "You are welcome, Thomas. Please, make yourself welcome. Share some *kawhi* with me."

Thom leaned over to Siobhan and whispered. "What kind of merchant is Maarat? I don't see any merchandise in his tent."

"Maarat has the best kind of merchandise for sale," she replied. "He sells information."

They all sat around the small stove. Maarat produced three small, old, and very worn blue ceramic cups —Thom recognized them as demitasse cups — from a compartment under the burners and proceeded to pour dark, steaming spiced coffee into the cups. He proffered a steaming cup to both Siobhan and Thom.

"Not as fine as Earth *kawhi*, but who besides a *sèo* can afford that?" he said, "One as poor as I must make do with what local *kawhi* or ersatz — no matter how mediocre — that one can obtain."

"Nonsense, Maarat," Siobhan said. She smiled and all the hardness left her face. "Your hospitality makes it the finest *kawhi* in the universe."

Thom sipped the coffee. He could taste cardamom,

which grew well on Askander and was even a rare agricultural export for the planet. There was also something else, a native spice probably. It had a mild earthy taste, but it was also very sweet. He finished the cup, and before he could set it down, Maarat had refilled it. It occurred to him that the coffee drinking was part of a ritual required before a serious conversation could begin.

They each drank three full cups. Maarat then removed a small, tooled leather pouch and a slim, highly decorated ebony and red lacquered pipe about a half-meter long. The databug plug-in told Thom the pouch was called a *mutui* and the pipe was a *sebsi*.

Siobhan leaned and whispered, "He's offering us *fredaris*. It's made from plant resin, just like hashish on Earth. The drug heightens the senses and makes one less susceptible to being swindled. Merchants like Maarat can't be too careful."

Maarat filled the pipe with a sticky maroon-colored ball from the pouch and lit it from the jet on his stove. He sucked on the pipe, and then exhaled a cloud of pungently sweet smelling smoke. Maarat handed the sebsi to Siobhan.

"*Baraka l'aufic,*" she said. She inhaled deeply, exhaled a plume of smoke, and then handed the pipe to Thom.

"*Baraka l'aufic,*" he said. He sucked on the pipe. The smoke was hot and acrid. Thom managed to suppress an urge to cough. He exhaled and then handed the pipe back to Maarat. Maarat nodded and smiled. He laid the pipe aside. The ritual was completed.

"Maarat, I have a favor to ask of you," Siobhan said. "A shuttle carrying friends of Don Jaime's was to arrive yesterday. Someone shot it down. You have passed through the Mukhalafi's lands. Have you heard anything about this cowardly act?"

Maarat threw up his hands and shook his head. "Alas, beloved Siobhan, no one on the road has mentioned it." Then he paused, picked up the *sebsi* and took a puff. "Now, on the other hand, I have heard talk in the *souk* about such a thing."

He looked directly at Thom. "They say one man survived, a good friend of Don Jaime's."

Thom avoided Maarat's eyes. He began to feel decidedly uneasy. The tent was warm. His mouth was dry and his head pounded, both probably aspects of whatever drug was in the pipe. *The drug might indeed heighten the senses*, he thought, *but if it makes one less susceptible to being swindled, it does so by making one a little paranoid.*

"What else do they say?" Siobhan asked.

"All they do is talk, talk, talk. They don't know anything," Maarat said. He poured himself a cup of *kawhi*. "Some say the Mukhalafi destroyed the aircraft on Al-Saba's orders."

Thom looked at Siobhan. "Al-Saba?" he whispered.

She ignored him. "Yes, the Lion is a clever man, but

he is also no fool."

"True," said Maarat. "They also say it might be a war among the great houses." He paused to sip his coffee. Again his eyes focused on Thom. "They do agree the shuttle was from the Planetary League. The other *sèo* fear that Don Jaime meant to betray Askander. After all, only he has a League ambassador in his house."

Thom wet his lips nervously. Jaime was right. The walls had mice and the mice had ears.

Maarat smiled and put his cup down. "But it is only rumor, friend Thomas. I would not worry."

"Your merchandise is excellent, Maarat," Siobhan said. "Let me know when you have more." She rose to leave. From her jacket, she removed a cloth purse. The coins inside jingled dully.

Siobhan tossed the purse to Maarat. The merchant caught it and placed it within the folds of his robe. "I replenish my stocks often. I may have the goods you seek soon enough."

"*Yadd la yuhish minnak,*" Siobhan said.

Thom's databug plug-in told him she had rendered the common Askanderian farewell of "May the Hidden Hand bless you," perfectly. It was much better than his own cyber-assisted version of the language.

"Perhaps the Hand may bless me, but the Hand is capricious, too," Maarat replied.

A sirocco wind was blowing in from the desert as

they left the tent. Thom pulled his *kaffiya* over his mouth and walked on. He had not gone far when he noticed Siobhan was not with him. He looked over his shoulder and saw her standing still, staring at something.

Thom went over to her. "Something wrong?"

"Over there," she said. She pointed at something near the edge of the bazaar. "Can you see him? I've never seen one come this close to an arcology."

Thom looked out. He saw a tall, painfully thin, almost cadaverous figure standing very still, just outside the rather primitive chain-link fence that marked the outer perimeter of the marketplace. The figure wore a loose-fitting shirt and pants of some silvery fabric. A hood of a similar material covered the figure's head, while a large breathing mask hid the face. There was something odd about the figure, Thom noticed. Its arms and legs seemed exceptionally long, and its head appeared larger and more elliptical than normal.

The figure raised a hand and gestured, beckoning them to come.

Thom saw that the being had seven spindly fingers on its hand. He felt a shiver go through his body. "Who is that?" he said.

"An *Ajnabi*," she said as she turned to him with a look of almost child-like awe on her face. The expression startled Thom, contrasting as it did with her usual harsh demeanor.

"They're humanoid desert dwellers," she continued. "They live in caves along the *wadi.* Those are dried river beds."

She started toward the alien. "Amazing," she said. "They rarely contact humans."

Thom followed her. He noted that no one else seemed to have seen the Ajnabi. They all went about their business as usual.

Siobhan stopped about a meter from the fence and raised her hand in a gesture of friendship. "You are welcome, honored visitor."

Thom watched the Ajnabi nod. It stood roughly a head and a half taller than a human, and its body appeared gangly and emaciated. The alien removed its breathing mask and goggles. The face behind the mask startled Thom. The alien's head was a flattened oval, like a thin, narrow egg. Two large black eyes, seemingly with neither iris nor pupils, stared out from under the hood. The alien had no nose, just two small nostrils above a thin slash of a mouth. Its skin was the silvery color of a dead mackerel.

"Are you servants of the *sèo*?" it said in heavily accented Askanderian.

"I serve Don Jaime, if that's what you mean," Siobhan replied.

"Good," the alien said. "Then you must give him this message: There is great danger in his mines beneath the city. He must stop working the mines before something terrible happens."

"Something terrible?" Thom said. "What do you mean?"

"My people have long known the evil that lies within the mountain," the Ajnabi said. "You must believe me."

The alien looked up. "Someone is coming. I must go." It quickly donned its breathing mask and started down the steep hillside toward the river. In a moment, the Ajnabi was gone. It was as though it had never been there at all.

The alien's warning disturbed Thom. If the Ajnabi rarely dealt with humans, then the alien had made an extraordinary effort to make contact.

"Strange," Siobhan said. She stood transfixed, her eyes watching where the alien had gone. After a moment, she shook her head, as if waking up from a dream. She turned to Thom, an anxious look in her eyes. "There was an Ajnabi here, wasn't there? You saw him too?"

Thom nodded. "Yes, I saw him, but I don't know if anyone else did."

"Probably not," Siobhan said. "The few humans who have met them claim the Ajnabi can cloud people's minds and make themselves seem invisible."

"I think we should tell Don Jaime about the mine," Thom said.

"Yes," she said. "Yes, by all means."

"Colonel," someone shouted.

Siobhan and Thom turned to see Liam running toward them.

"Colonel," Liam said, nearly out of breath, "I lost him. He disappeared somewhere nearby."

"Don't worry," she replied, "it probably wasn't import —"

A scream filled the air. *"Meded! Meded!"* someone cried. It was a desperate call for help.

"That came from Maraat's stall," Siobhan said. She sprinted toward the merchant's stall with Thom and Liam in close pursuit.

CHAPTER TEN

Siobhan flung back the tent flaps, looked inside and froze in her steps. When Thom caught up with her, he saw why she had halted.

Maraat, his robes slashed and bloodstained, lay across his unlit stove. Blood poured from his slashed throat. Mixing with spilled coffee, it flowed down the stove, staining the carpeted floor. The merchant's assailant stood over the body. His right hand clutched a long, crimson-stained dagger. He looked up, and his eyes met Thom's.

There was no mistaking the assassin. It was the black-robed man from the market.

The assassin flung his dagger at them and ran. Thom knocked Siobhan to the ground. He felt the knife catch the folds of his robes, the blade grazing his right shoulder.

Liam fired his flechette pistol at the fleeing man, but

the assassin threw himself to the ground and rolled under the bottom of the tent. The neural darts embedded themselves in a wooden tent pole, and Liam ran after the man.

Thom scrambled to his feet and dashed out the back of Maarat's stall into a narrow alley. Once outside, he looked about, hoping to spot either Liam or the hooded man. Both had vanished into the swirling crowd of people who now filled the bazaar.

"What the hell do you think you're doing?" Siobhan yelled at him as she came out of the tent.

"Trying to catch a killer," Thom said. His eyes darted about.

"Don't be a damned fool. It's not your business. I've already alerted the security forces. They've sealed off the turbo-lifts, and the outside gates to the bazaar are well guarded. Either they, or Liam, will find him. He can't get out of here without being spotted."

"It is my business," he said. "Someone has already tried to kill me."

Then he saw the concern in her eyes, and it surprised him. He felt ashamed and swallowed his anger. He muttered an apology and started walking briskly down the alleyway in the direction he thought the killer had taken.

Siobhan came jogging up at his side. "If you're going to be a fool, especially an unarmed fool, then you'll need a bodyguard."

Thom started to argue with her but stopped himself. She was right. Being unarmed was one thing, but being unarmed and alone was foolish. "All right," he said.

Thom and Siobhan strode through the crowded alleys, scanning back and forth, hoping for a glimpse of Liam or the assassin. Siobhan tried to contact Liam on her skul-fone, but the trooper did not respond.

The alleys were now congested with customers. It seemed more *suma* had come to the *souk*, many to buy food for dinner. All of them appeared intent on arguing loudly over prices with vendors who were equally, and vocally, unwilling to lower those prices. Those not haggling were flitting from stall to stall or insulting recalcitrant sellers and buyers.

He waded through what had become an ocean of people, all moving, all talking and cursing, all somehow sensing exactly where he wanted to go and moving to the precise spot that blocked his progress.

After a moment, he realized he had now lost Siobhan. Apparently the crowd had swept her along down another alleyway. Thom swore and pushed past several heavily burdened women wearing *chadors*. The women dropped their mesh bags of groceries, spat in his direction, and hurled epithets regarding his lineage from assorted animals. At that point, he wasn't about to argue with them. He would feel guilty about it later.

As Thom pushed through more people, noise rose

up over the sound of the crowd from a nearby booth. A merchant began shouting angrily. A figure dressed in black burst into an intersection just ahead. Thom could see that the hooded man was limping badly on his right leg. The man stumbled and turned down the alley, heading straight for Thom.

Another intersection stood between them. Thom shouldered his way past a crowd of old men, hoping to block the assassin's escape route.

The man stopped next to a stall, supporting himself against a heavy wooden post. He seemed out of breath.

Thom edged toward the man.

The assassin, still breathing heavily, looked up and saw Thom. He grabbed a pot from the stall, threw it, and ran. Thom knocked the pot away and began chasing him. "Stop that man," he shouted. "He has murdered Maarat the merchant."

Two men moved to tackle the man, but he slashed at them with a short knife. One man grabbed his injured left shoulder, blood pouring between his fingers. The other, hands clutching his chest, fell backward into a stall. Fruit and vegetables tumbled over him.

Even with an injured leg, the assassin was able to run a few meters ahead of Thom. Thom could feel his heart beating rapidly. His lungs burned at each breath. The muscles in his legs ached. Thom ignored his brain's protests and his body's pains, which were caused by the change in atmosphere and the gravitational pull.

Thom saw the assassin head down one alley and quickly turn into another. Thom was closing the gap. The limp had slowed the man considerably. He turned down another alley and Thom followed.

As Thom turned the corner, a wine cask hit him in the chest and knocked him off his feet. He crashed heavily into a stack of baskets. He rolled onto his stomach, gasping for air. The world spun, and his eyes wouldn't focus.

Thom thought he saw a figure in black ahead, ducking into a covered stall. He struggled to his feet, his lungs still trying to pull in oxygen. Each breath produced sharp pain. He staggered toward the stall he thought the assassin had entered.

Thom tossed open the heavy brown canvas flap and stepped inside. The stall was empty, except for a carpeted floor like that in Maarat's tent. One rug was thrown aside, exposing an open manhole. Thom glanced down the hole. The odor wafting up from the depths was overpowering. Thom covered his face with his scarf to avoid smelling it.

He could see metal rungs running down one side to the bottom, which was several meters below. From the odor, he realized that the shaft descended into the arcology's sewers, which ran untreated to the river. A dull glow, which Thom assumed was from artificial lighting, emanated from the depths. Thom took off his outer robe, tied his scarf over his face, and started down the manhole.

He estimated the shaft dropped about five meters. It finally opened out onto a large drainpipe about ten meters in diameter. He lowered himself carefully down the last rung to the drainpipe floor.

The air almost made him gag. The atmosphere was a stew of odors that included human waste, assorted chemicals, garbage, and runoff from various industries within the arcology. A stream of scummy brown water, with occasional patches of bluish suds, ran down the middle.

Besides the artificial lights, he saw the entire length of the pipe glowing with an eerie emerald luminescence. The walls were covered with a phosphorescent substance. It was hard to tell whether it was animal or plant, but it was abundant in the moist, nutrient-rich atmosphere, and the light it gave off made it possible for Thom to see where he was. That made him feel a little better, knowing he would not have to stumble around in the dark. Injured or not, the hooded man could easily be waiting for him.

Thom heard something ahead of him, some distance down the pipe. He moved ahead cautiously, not wanting to expose himself. He heard a scream and quickened his pace, but the footing on the slime-covered plasticrete made it difficult to keep his balance. The screaming grew louder. Then it abruptly stopped. He slipped and stumbled, landing on his knees in the sewage. Cursing, he got to his feet and continued toward the place from which the screams originated.

Thom had not gone much farther when he came across the intersection of two pipes where about a dozen rats were devouring the freshly killed body of a large brown, scaly creature with six legs. The creature, about the size of a small dog, had clearly made the screams.

Thom knew that the six-legged things were just the latest creatures unable to compete with the rats, which were taking over this environmental niche just as they had conquered similar ones on other worlds. The rats made ugly, moist noises as they enjoyed their meal.

The taste of bile came to Thom's mouth. Slowly, he edged past the rodents and was just past the creatures when the assassin leaped from an intersecting drainpipe. The two of them tumbled into the fetid water. The rats, frightened, shrieked and scattered in all directions. Thom came to his feet, gasping for air. He ripped the now-drenched scarf from his mouth and stood face-to-face with his attacker.

The assassin was favoring his injured leg, but breathing clean air through his mask. He carried a short, double-pointed dagger attached to a long cord. A heavy iron ring was at the other end of the cord, which he swung in a slow arc.

Thom recognized the weapon. It was a *kyoketsu-sho-gi*, an ancient weapon used by the Japanese ninja. Thom slowly backed his way down the drain, not wanting to give the assassin room to hurl the iron ring. The man managed to keep pace, and Thom found his movement slowed by the thick, gelatinous sewage swirling about his ankles.

He took one more step back, and pain shot up his leg. He looked down and saw a sharp dart projecting from the back of his left thigh. Just when he realized he had triggered a booby trap, he felt the cord of the *kyoketsu-shogi* wrap around his ankles, and he was yanked onto his back.

The assassin, screaming, threw himself at Thom. Thom caught the full weight of the man. Seeing the terrible blade as it came toward his chest, he grabbed the assassin's wrist with his left hand and reached for the man's throat with his right.

The assassin pushed Thom's head underwater. The foul, clotted water poured down his nose and throat. He slammed his right knee up into his attacker's crotch. The man howled in pain, his hands going instinctively to protect the injured area.

Thom came up sputtering, feeling sick to his stomach. He pushed the man to one side and scrambled out of the water. The cord from the *kyoketsu-shogi* was still wrapped around his ankles, so Thom grabbed the cord and yanked, trying to get the knife.

The blade clattered against the plasticrete sewer pipe. Thom grabbed for it, but the assassin was just as quick. Thom had the handle firmly in his grasp, but both of the assassin's hands clutched his wrist. The assassin placed his full weight on Thom's chest and slowly forced Thom's left arm back toward his throat. Thom thrust his right fist into the assassin's face, but his punch glanced off the man's breathing mask.

The assassin increased the pressure on Thom's arm. The tip of the knife blade wavered, just centimeters from Thom's throat. He grabbed the assassin's throat, probing for the man's carotid artery. Thom's fingers brushed against something hard on the assassin's neck. Recognizing the object, he grabbed it and pulled it free.

Instantly, tremors jolted the assassin's body. His fingers released the knife as he convulsed and toppled over. Gasping, Thom pushed the man away and rolled onto his side. He found the knife, cut the cord, then sat up and rubbed his ankles.

"That was a damn fool thing to do, Major. You're lucky I found out where you went."

Thom looked up to see Siobhan walking toward him. She had her flechette pistol drawn. "Well, I managed all right on my own," he said, trying to stand up.

"Oh, really?" she said, helping him up. She gestured

with the pistol toward the attacker. "Take another look."

He glanced at the body and could just make out the circle of tiny neural darts embedded in the assassin's lower back.

"You're a good shot," he said angrily. "Another few centimeters, and you might have hit me."

"If I hadn't fired, you'd be dead, Major," she said as she holstered her pistol.

"I think not," he said. He tossed her the object he had pulled from the assassin's neck. "Recognize it?"

Siobhan caught the hard black plastic cube and rolled it between her fingers. "It's a personality cassette."

"I'd lay odds it's for a Japanese *ninja*, probably seventeenth-century by old Earth Common Era dating," Thom said. "That's a thousand standard years ago."

She stared at him for a moment, and then looked down at the body. "I see," she said, nodding slowly. "So our assassin was a brain-wipe, just like from the Zaibatsu Wars, plugged-in with a software personality and programmed to perform a specific mission, to kill Maarat?"

Thom shook his head. "No. He wasn't programmed to kill Maraat specifically. That was a diversion so he could kill me."

"What?" Siobhan said, her face a puzzled mask. "You? You were the target?"

"Think about it for a moment," Thom said. "If Maraat was the target, the assassin could have killed him quietly and slipped away. Instead, he created a commotion and stayed in the tent apparently admiring his handiwork."

"Yes, I think understand," she said. "He *wanted* our attention; he wanted to be found."

"He wanted to lure me down here to kill me," Thom said. Things were growing clearer. "I *am* the target, and I haven't the foggiest idea why I am so important that I must be killed."

Siobhan looked down at the module in her hand. "Perhaps it's all programmed right in here."

"The particulars of the form of attack, at least," Thom said. "The information about Maarat or me could be added later, but you won't find the motive in there. There's no reason for the assassin to know that or even to care."

The colonel scowled. "Damn. This means Don Jaime has a spy in his house, or they couldn't have known about you so quickly." She nudged the assassin's body with her boot. "I think we'd better have Don Jaime's security forces find out who this fellow is, or was."

"I doubt it'll do any good," Thom said. "Whoever programmed this thug has probably erased all records of him."

"That may be," Siobhan said. "I suspect whoever planned this attack was also behind the one on your shuttle. I can't help wondering if the Ajnabi's warning isn't also tied into all of this."

Thom looked at her, then at the assassin. He felt

a chill roll down his spine and frowned. "Colonel, I'm afraid you're quite right, but we may just have to wait to see how it all unfolds."

CHAPTER ELEVEN

"The elders wish to know how your plans are progressing," the Iimarae said, waddling up to Abu Brion's side. "Time is very important."

Abu Brion glanced down at the alien and felt nothing but disgust. "Events must take their own time, little chicken, but the plans are progressing as I hoped. Now, I have business to attend to."

"Have you located the Nameless Ones' vessel?" the emissary said, tugging at the sleeve of Abu Brion's robes.

Abu Brion jerked the sleeve away. Anger burned in his dark eyes. "Don't ever touch me again, little chicken."

The Iimarae, frightened, backed away from the human. "A thousand pardons," it croaked, "but the elders wish to know. I must tell them, please."

Abu Brion's anger softened. He knew it wasn't the little alien's fault, and withholding information might make the Iimarae elders suspicious. He stroked his chin and thought a moment. His lips curled into a cruel smile. "You may tell them that I believe I know where the weapon is located. It may take me a few days to complete my plans, but I will start tonight at ibn Brentholtz's reception. Can you tell them that, little chicken?"

The alien looked at the floor. "Please stop calling me 'little chicken,'" he said softly. "My name is Ryf'Tael. It means 'lowly messenger' in your tongue."

Abu Brion snorted with amusement. The little bird had an ego after all, and a bruised one at that. He also knew that to know someone's name also gave him some control over that individual. "All right, Ryf'Tael," he said, deliberately overemphasizing the alien's name. "You may tell them I will soon have the weapon, but they must be patient. This is my world, and they must obey my rules. I will let them know when I am ready to act. Is that understood?"

The alien remained silent for a moment, then slowly rolled its head from side to side, a sign of consent. "It is understood, but they will not like it."

Abu Brion smiled. "That's their problem, friend Ryf'Tael." He adjusted his robes. "Now, you must excuse me. There is much business requiring my attention. *Yadd yin'im alek.* May the Hand favor you." But may It favor me most of all, he thought to himself.

Hree'Rchee, chief among the three Iimarae elders, dismissed her sisters with a wave of a red-lacquered talon. "We will discuss our plans later," she chirped. "Now we must meditate and consider the greater designs."

The two lower-ranking elders dropped their heads to the floor, prostrating themselves in a sign of respect. Then both raised themselves, keeping their eyes fixed on the ground, and slowly retreated from the room. Neither spoke as they exited.

Hree'Rchee folded her legs under her and sat on the floor. With disgust, she pushed aside the table of food the humans had provided. Though she had been hungry, she had eaten little. She could still taste it, thick and oily on her tongue, and the odor of the cooked meat and grains assaulted her nostrils.

But now was the time for the *ki'ind'rou*, to shut off all sensory input and merge with the Flock. It had been far too long since she had indulged herself in this way, to savor the emotions and thoughts of the Flock, and perhaps she had even neglected this part of her duties as a *se'bes'vos*. Yet there were other things to do, even more important duties such as attempting to comprehend the alien minds of the humans.

The effort of dealing with minds so vastly different, so disgustingly mammalian, had drained her. Only the *ki'ind'rou*, the merging with the Flock, could restore her strength. Even though she would only merge with the crew of the scout ship, it was still *ki'ind'rou*.

Hree'Rchee brought her wings over her head and placed the control band around her head with her spindly hands. She closed her eyes and began consciously slowing her heart rate and her breathing. Gradually, she sensed her mind leaving her body, an act of delight in itself. Her soul sang an ancient melody of exaltation and joy.

She found herself inhabiting the body of a worker-drone, and enjoying the warmth and communality in sharing the mind of such an inferior creature. Hree'Rchee savored the sensations and reactions of the worker as it monitored the vast propulsion units that allowed the ship to pass safely through the Hyperspace portal's gravity fields. The simplicity of the worker's actions and its devotion to the Flock shamed her. She had sadly shirked her duties to her own nest, and if she let it continue, there would be disorder. As a *se'bes'vos*, she had to insure order and harmony, eschew and destroy dissonance. Otherwise, she would never become an egg-mother to her race, become one of the few chosen to reproduce, to create a genetically superior line destined to rule the galaxy.

Drifting among the minds of the crew, Hree'Rchee sorted and analyzed their thoughts; forcibly extirpating anything she knew would destroy the harmony of the Flock. The large number of rebellious thoughts she found both disturbed and appalled her. It had been too long since she had merged with the Flock. Fortunately, although the strength and intensity of those rebellious ideas had grown since her last merging, they were easily suppressed and removed from the workers' minds. But the realization still disturbed her.

Hree'Rchee found one worker in the weapons section whose mind harbored fully formed plans of mutiny. The anarchy of the creature's mind terrified her, for the worker possessed knowledge that could easily destroy the ship. She knew what she must do. To let a *fah'gid'sla*, one who had drifted from the Flock and even held seditious ideas against the Great Hens, survive was itself a threat to the Flock. The integrity of the Flock had to be maintained.

She entered the worker's mind. The worker put up a valiant, but brief, struggle, for Hree'Rchee was much stronger. The control band allowed her to control the worker's brain stem, and she told the worker's heart to stop beating and its lungs to stop breathing. The creature was dead within minutes. With equal ease, she summoned other workers to dispose of the corpse and to see the result of attempting to think for one's self against the harmony of the Flock. They would make use of the remains, for nothing would be wasted.

She rejoiced that her Nest was secure. If the Nest was secure, then the Eggs that were the source of life were safe, and if the Eggs were safe, then the Flock would survive, the Iimarae would prosper and more worlds, more booty, more slaves, would fall into the Flock's claws, and more power would come her way.

Hree'Rchee sang a song of victory, but a sound at the door cut her rejoicing short. The control band, sensing the presence of someone in the room, instantly returned her mind to her own body. Hree'Rchee grew angry at having her *ki'ind'rou* — her meditations and prayers — so rudely interrupted. Her eyes focused on the cowering shape of Ryf'Tael before her.

Such a scrawny thing, and he stinks of humans, too! she thought, her nostrils wrinkling at the odor. *Still, even if he is unfit for breeding, I may find other uses for him when I need him.*

At just 150 centimeters tall, the little male was even shorter than human females. He kept his face toward the floor so his appearance would not offend her. Hree'Rchee stood and stretched to her full height of more than two and a quarter meters, but kept her own gaze fixed on the far wall of the room. Her shadow alone standing over his body would put him in his place. "Yes?"

"The human Abu Brion says he has located the weapon, my *se'bes'vos,*" Ryf'Tael said.

Hree'Rchee repressed an urge to crow with joy at the news. "Has he said where it is?"

"The human said he must attend to further business before he can obtain it," Ryf'Tael said. With his beak, he tugged nervously on the cuff of his robe. "He did not say what that business was."

Hree'Rchee cursed to herself, but she did not display any emotion. To expose her feelings to an unclean *shin'kmiqt* like Ryf'Tael would be a shameful and humiliating act for an elder, especially for a *se'bes'vos* and future egg-mother whose children would be of the noble line. "Then we must find out what he has discovered."

"Yes, my *se'bes'vos*," Ryf'Tael said. He raised his head and looked at Hree'Rchee, a gross violation of propriety. "Forgive my forwardness, my *se'bes'vos*, but I do not trust Abu Brion. I fear he has plans of his own and will betray us."

Hree'Rchee clenched her beak tightly, suppressing her anger at the behavior of the *shin'kmiqt*. Her black eyes burned with her fury. "How dare you offend me, thing," she said coldly.

Ryf'Tael flung himself prostrate and hid his head under his right wing. "It was not meant as an insult, my *se'bes'vos*, but I believed it was important for you to understand my fears."

She glared at him, almost enjoying the intensity of her emotions and her ability to turn Ryf'Tael into a quivering mass. Part of her realized the words of the unclean male carried truth. Humans had proven their deviousness, and Abu Brion showed particularly well-developed skills in that trait. Hree'Rchee released a low clicking sound from the back of her throat.

"You press my goodwill, *shin'kmiqt*," she said, taking care to add the proper amount of contempt to her phrase. "But I will let this insult pass. Your candor is noted. You know the humans well." She paused for effect. "Perhaps too well."

Ryf'Tael did not respond but remained on the floor, shaking.

"You may rise," she finally said to him.

Slowly, Ryf'Tael picked himself up, taking care to keep his eyes firmly fixed on the floor. When he was on his knees, he started a series of gestures and clucks that signified his apologies.

"Your apologies are accepted," Hree'Rchee said. "You have done good work. Now, you may leave."

"Thank you, my se'bes'vos," he said, his voice a series of nervous clicks and chirps. Carefully, he got to his feet and backed out of the room.

When she was sure he had gone, Hree'Rchee unleashed a joyful cry. If she used the ansible to call her home world this moment, it would take just a short time for two Iimarae star cruisers, with crews loyal to her, to arrive at the hyperspace portal hidden among the comets and debris of the Pavonian system's Oort cloud. And Abu Brion, if he did plan some treachery, would have no chance to use the weapon for his own purposes.

Ryf'Tael paused outside the door to the elders' quarters. Though muffled, the pleasure calls of the se'bes'vos were easily heard as they enjoyed each other and invaded the minds of those humans whose depravity and criminality the hens found…amusing. Their power left him crestfallen. Both Abu Brion and Hree'Rchee sought to use him for their own ends. He did not trust the human. A fear that Abu Brion would betray them gnawed at his vitals, but the elders would not listen to him if he expressed those fears. After all, he was unclean, untrustworthy, a thing that conversed with aliens, especially the humans, foulest of the foul. Yet while he feared the human, he was terrified of Hree'Rchee and wished her dead.

The urge to resist grew within him, but he quickly repressed it, for the moment. He had no choice, for the *se'bes'vos*, once she knew of his true feelings, could squeeze the life from him. *If only I had a band of obedience*, he thought, *then I would show them! If only that Hand Abu Brion spoke of would favor me!*

That, he knew, was an impossibility. Ryf'Tael clicked his beak together three times, a sign of resignation. There was nothing he could do. He hurried down the corridor to his quarters, hoping for the welcome numbness of sleep.

Ernesto Abu Brion poured himself a glass of *nebid*. As he brought the glass to his lips, he first savored the bouquet of the wine, then took a sip. He let the liquid roll across his tongue, enjoying the flavor. The wine was dry, with a hint of astringency: a fine vintage. It seemed comparable to the finest French cabernèt and the best California merlots, were they still available and not cost an arm and *two* legs. Even League traders knew the value of their products. Abu Brion decided the wine certainly equaled, if not bested the grandest that ibn Brentholtz's vineyards could produce, and soon those vineyards would be his. He leaned back in his chair, content with himself.

Abu Brion looked up at the tall, gaunt Tuatha officer of the *Gall Oglaigh* who sat across from him.

"General Kreus, you must try my *nebid*," Abu Brion said. "I'll wager you'll find none better on Askander."

"Wine is not a warrior's drink," General Haakon Kreus said, pouring himself a glass of *Tuatha uisge beatha* from a decanter on the table. His right hand made a faint whirring sound as he picked up the glass. The general knocked the whiskey back in one swallow, then wiped his lips and thick, drooping moustache with the back of his sleeve.

"I'd imagine the ancient Romans would disagree with your opinion of wine," Abu Brion said. "As would medieval knights."

"And look what happened to them," Kreus said testily.

"I can see what endeared you to King Daffyd," Abu Brion said, a slight smile on his lips. *Perhaps*, he thought, *it's best not to press such silly issues with the General. The man's short fuse, even with friends, is well known on many worlds.*

Kreus sneered, something that Abu Brion thought seemed a regular occurrence with the general. The mercenary's mouth was set in a perpetual scowl, an expression made worse by the man's cold and dark eyes, eyes of hate. Thick black oily hair framed his tanned, drawn face, a face crisscrossed with thin, pink scars. It was said Kreus could name each battle where he had received those scars, but few dared ask him.

He poured another glass of the dark amber whiskey. This time he merely sipped it. "King Daffyd was a fool. But he paid well, so I tried to save his stinking little realm for him. And little thanks I got," he said bitterly, staring at his hands. Then Kreus smiled, a cruel and crooked grin. "But you pay better than Daffyd, and you appreciate my skills."

"I buy only the best," Abu Brion said. He topped off his wine glass. "But to business. How long do you think it will take your men to eliminate the Mukhalafi in my lands?"

"The resistance is weak here, hardly worth dealing with," Kreus said. "Your own security forces have done an excellent job in keeping the populace in line."

"Terror is an excellent business tool, general," Abu Brion said. "I'm sure you in the *Gall Oglaigh* know that well."

"I know what brings obedience from the *suma*, Don Ernesto." Kreus curled his fingers around his whiskey glass and leaned forward. "The Mukhalafi, however, will not be so easy to eliminate in the other realms. The other *sèo* are weak, and the resistance is clever and resourceful. But with a big enough fist, I can crush them all." To emphasize the point, he clenched and unclenched his left hand. The fingers hummed as he moved them.

Abu Brion smiled. "You will have that fist soon enough."

Kreus swallowed the remainder of his whiskey. "When do you plan to move against ibn Brentholtz?"

"Tonight."

"Then you have the shares? The other *sèo* will remain loyal to you?"

"Some will prove loyal. The rest will stay conveniently bought until they can find a better deal down the road. That is long enough for my purposes."

"But the others don't know the road is short and will soon dead end," Kreus said with a laugh. "No better deals, eh, Don Ernesto?"

"I don't weep over my competitors' poor business decisions," Abu Brion replied.

Kreus stopped laughing. "But what of your own? I'm not sure I would trust the Iimarae."

Abu Brion dismissed the problem with the wave of his hand. "The Iimarae are no problem. Once I have the nova weapon, then they will have to do as I tell them."

"But if there is no weapon?"

"Rest assured, general, the weapon exists. I know where it is, and I will soon have it."

Kreus shook his head slowly. "I don't know, Don Ernesto. The Iimarae are bad allies. I would rather wring their scrawny necks and serve them for dinner, cooked in their own juices."

Don Ernesto smiled. "Perhaps that time will come, and I will enjoy the meal with you." The *sèo* finished his wine and set the glass on the table.

Outside, the wailing of an *adamsumit* announced the afternoon prayers.

"Ah, how unfortunate," Abu Brion said. He rose from the table. "You must excuse me while I attend to my prayers."

Kreus sneered. "I didn't know you were a religious man, Don Ernesto."

"I pray to whatever gods will help me. But the Hand, blessings on Its invisible ways, helps those best who force Its fingers." He left the table and began to leave the room, but he paused in the doorway. "General, do you have a dress uniform?"

"Yes," General Kreus said, somewhat puzzled. "Why do you ask?"

"Ibn Brentholtz is holding a party tonight. Something to do with honoring an old friend, a Planetary League official."

"What, one survived?"

"Yes, unfortunately, but that is no matter now. We are invited to attend, and I wish you to come along, to witness how we Askanderians handle things."

"Very well. I will be delighted to accompany you."

Abu Brion smiled. "Good. So, until tonight, then?"

Kreus nodded. "Yes, until tonight."

CHAPTER TWELVE

"Betrayal!" Don Jaime cried. He slammed his fist into the table. "Those *sèo* had promised they would sell their minority shares to Brentholtz-Madden Gesellschaft and accept my protection as *hausfatah* in return for seats on our board."

The twelve *dhireks* seated at the table said nothing. A few looked down at the screens of the Isaaks set before them. Others fiddled nervously with a writing stylus or poured a glass of wine.

"They received a better offer, Don Jaime," an elderly white-haired *dhirek* said finally.

"But all five of them, Uncle Rafael?" Jaime said. "That smells suspicious to me, may the Hand damn them."

"Business is not done as it was in your father's and my time," Rafael said with a sigh.

"Yes, in your time a *sèo* who sold his shares stayed bought," Jaime said bitterly. He poured himself a glass of *araki*.

Rafael stroked his chin and smiled sadly. "Nephew, in my time there were many daughters and sons to wed off for alliances."

Jaime looked up angrily at his uncle. "What are you saying, uncle, that I don't have enough children? I have six children and another on the way. They should be worth many shares and mergers."

"Yes, Don Jaime," another *dhirek* said softly, his eyes still fixed on the tabletop. He looked up. "But they are still too young to marry."

Rafael leaned forward in his large brown leather chair. "You misunderstand me, Jaime. The problem was your father's and mine. We didn't have enough children to form the correct alliances. You and your sister were your father's joy, and mine, but we had to rely on our own strengths to make our mergers. Our allies *shared* our vision and loyalties."

The old *dhirek* leaned back and sighed. "Although their sons have their fathers' avarice, they don't share their fathers' morals and restraints. Nor do they consider family bonds formed through marriage to be binding."

"So they find quick, personal gain more important than long term profit and loyalty, then?" Jaime said.

Rafael nodded slowly. "Sadly, my dear nephew, that's the reality of things."

Don Jaime leaned back in his chair. He sensed his

anger starting to grow out of control. His heart beat loudly in his chest and his head pounded. He pressed his fingertips together, took a deep breath, exhaled.

"All right," he said, trying to seem calm. "Do we know who is behind this maneuver, and how he is leveraging it?"

No one spoke.

Jaime looked at the *dhirek* who had spoken earlier. "Reynardo? Any ideas?"

Reynardo bit his lip. His face flushed. "Don Jaime, we suspect many people, all of them heads of the great families of the arcologies: Abdul Al-Murdock, Ibn Branson, Abu Adelson, even . . ." he paused and licked his lips nervously.

"Out with it, man," Jaime said.

Reynardo opened his mouth to speak, then looked at Rafael, his eyes filled with anxiety. Rafael smiled and nodded slowly.

"We suspect Ernesto Abu Brion," Reynardo said.

Jaime sighed heavily. He picked up his glass and finished off the rest of the *araki*. The news disturbed him. Although the shares from the traitorous *sèo* did not threaten his power in Ciudad Rand, his sister could prove another matter. He glared at Rafael. "Does my sister know what her husband is doing?"

Rafael shrugged. "Who can tell? Isabella defers everything to Ernesto, except her shares in this house."

"She only has twenty-five percent of the shares, and I still control her voting rights," Jaime said.

"But if she gives her voting rights to Ernesto, instead of you — " Rafael interjected.

"How many shares are outstanding or are in questionable hands?" Jaime asked.

"We can't be sure," Reynardo said. "All of our shares, and those of the high-ranking *manaj* account for perhaps forty-five percent. Another two or three percent for the smallholders and the *jhereks*. It's not much."

"Ernesto has ten percent shares, mostly through his subsidiary *séo*, and the other thirty-odd percent is scattered among the other great houses," Rafael said. "Only your sister's shares prevent us from being majority shareholders."

Jaime sank back into his chair. He should have expected that Abu Brion would eventually try a power play. The peace had lasted far too long, and Ernesto's ambition could not remain in check forever.

Jaime's father, Don Hernando, had once told him that the ibn Brentholtz and Abu Brion families had been rivals, actually bitter enemies, since they had colonized Askander, and even longer, back to the days of the Zaibatsu Wars on Earth. It had gone on for generations, until the murder of Ernesto's beloved grandfather by an assassin allegedly in the pay of Ciudad Rand.

After that, his father and his uncle Rafael had wearied of the pointless competition, as had Ernesto's dying father, Don Ignacio. Therefore they had agreed to an alliance and married Isabella to Ernesto. The peace was sound, at first, but the marriage was not.

Then Jaime's father had died from a heart attack, and Don Ignacio soon followed Don Hernando to the grave. Some whispered that Ernesto had poisoned his father, but none proved it, and Jaime doubted his rival was that cruel.

Jaime knew Ernesto hated the ibn Brentholtz clan and blamed them for his grandfather's death — and for the fact his own Abu Brion family was not the most powerful on Askander. Isabella had kept Ernesto in check, keeping her stock under Jaime's control. That fact should have made him feel comfortable, but something nagged at him. Although his sister's loyalty was never in question, Isabella's mental health was another matter. He often wondered how the biochips implanted in her brain to control her epilepsy affected her. It could not be good.

"Have you spoken to my sister lately?" he asked.

Rafael shook his head. "Neither I nor your Aunt Imelda has spoken to her in months. I'll ask about her tonight, at your function."

Jaime smiled. "Thank you, uncle."

The cries of an *adamsumit* calling the faithful to prayer came into the room.

"Well, gentlemen, let us adjourn," Jaime said. "I'll see

you tonight. May the Hand protect us."

"Especially now," Rafael said.

"Yes, uncle, especially now." Jaime looked at his uncle and for the first time, he felt a tinge of fear. He rose from the table and went into his own office, closing the door behind him.

The office was cool and dark, the perfect place for Jaime to gather his thoughts. He felt a little intoxicated, and he knew he should reduce his drinking. The alcohol seemed to soothe him, calm his heart, and ease his fears.

The chants of the *adamsumit* sounded particularly beautiful now, lilting across the sky from the prayer tower atop the arcology. What he heard was the digitized reproduction on the sound system, an almost perfect recreation of the cleric's songs, but somehow it wasn't the same as being down in the marketplace, among the small merchants.

He envied them for their faith in the Hand, a faith he knew was sincere, though misguided. They truly believed the Hand rewarded those who did not resist Its will, that the god-like Hand blessed the faithful, yet those who reaped the greatest success manipulated the Hand at every chance. The market was never free.

The Hand would never help the small merchants, nor the peasants, nor the workers or any of the *mostazafin*. It only helped those who already controlled It. He knew the thought would be judged heresy by the *adamsumit*, but perhaps the Mukhalafi were right when they said the only Hand was the human hand.

But Jaime could not be sure. From a cabinet, he removed a small green prayer rug decorated with ancient signs for profit and gain. Spreading it on the floor, he knelt on the rug and began the prayer he had learned in childhood.

"I submit with all my heart and mind to the will of the Hand," he chanted. "The Hand uplifts, the Hand casts down."

Yet those properly cast down always threatened to rise up, like the fists the Mukhalafi claimed they were, he thought. *And those uplifted were in a precarious situation, afraid of both enemies and supposed friends, like those sèo who had betrayed him for their own gain.*

"The Hand molds, the Hand crushes."

Surely if the Hand were not malicious, it would not mold Ernesto Abu Brion, and certainly not the Iimarae, into weapons to crush the clan of ibn Brentholtz and Ciudad Rand, the city that lovingly followed Its ways. But perhaps he had not followed Its ways, perhaps it had been a mistake to try to deal with the League. Yet the Iimarae were a threat to all humanity.

"The ways of the Hand are hidden and unknowable."

Jaime fell face forward on the rug and found himself weeping. If the ways of the Hand were unknowable, then there was no use in doing anything. He could not accept that, and he knew his long-held faith had crumbled.

"I'm sorry, colonel," the guard said, "but Don Jaime is in an important meeting with the other nobles. He cannot be disturbed."

Siobhan tried to protest, but then thought the better of it. "Very well, we'll wait. But I don't like it."

Angrily, she turned from the guard and walked back to the foyer where Thom stood looking out the huge tinted windows.

Thom watched an *adamsumit* calling from a prayer tower. He thought the tower, one of several, seemed a strange eruption, a pimple on the otherwise smooth, flat face of the arcology. The *adamsumit*, dressed in robes of gray flannel, appeared almost comical as he called the followers of Yadd-Khabba, the Invisible Hand, to pray. Thom could make out a few of the words of the cleric's songs:

"Submit to the will of the Hand, and It will guide you to success," sang the cleric, his voice pure, high and clear. *"The Hand rewards those who do not resist. Blessed is Don Jaime, for the Hand has chosen the sèo in Its hidden ways."*

As a student, Thom had wondered how what had once been a completely secular theory of economics could have evolved into a religion. Belief systems that held that there existed some mysterious force beyond human control had often become the basis for religion. There had been signs in the late twentieth century of the ease with which mysticism and superstition merged with politics and overwhelmed it. Peasant saviors became millionaires who ran great corporations rather than healing the sick, feeding the hungry, or clothing the naked. Pastors reaped large fortunes from the poor and desperate who wanted hope and riches of their own. The almighty male deity was said to have endorsed the system of self-aggrandizement and was portrayed as chairman of some sort of cosmic board of directors. Freedom — defined as riches — was parceled out to the faithful, to be bought and sold only to those who fit the new consumer profiles, who fit the traditional roles of husband, wife, and child, and who condemned sin, except when it was profitable. All who opposed the cosmic plan, the preachers declared, were devil worshippers.

"Do not touch the Market," the faithful had said, "the Market is in balance. The Market decides everything. Man must free himself of any ideas that he can rationally control the Market, for the Market is perfect, everlasting, forever and ever." It was not too much longer until the more extreme propertarians had sanctified their beliefs and expelled heretics. Then they had created a priesthood, the *adamsumits*, that tried to interpret the ways of the Hand, the very Hand they had declared was unknowable.

The new messiahs proved as false as the old. The leadership cared far less for souls than they did profit margins. When the people grew tired of their bread and circuses, the leaders gave them war, especially war between the multinationals. The leaders claimed war justified the spirit of competition in the marketplace. The rulers offered "Liberty," which became corporate rule. What humanity received was destruction, death, disease, and devaluation.

Corporations, which the Japanese had called *zaibatsu*, replaced nations states and made war a more personal, privatized, and profitable affair, at least for the winners. Like the East India Company of old, they could afford to have military forces beholden to no one but the boards of the great multinationals. Corporate logos replaced flags, but nothing changed. The wealthy still ruled, and the only rights were property rights, and every employee was property of their employer until their value as an asset declined.

Still, Thom understood the true believers. Even among the League's precursors there had been the fanatics who took everything as gospel. They wanted certainty, order, and reward. He almost envied them their faith, those fanatics on both sides.

They had moved mountains, but at great price. What

had he done? He had fought for the ideals of the League, which he knew he believed in, but he did not know how he could integrate them into his own self.

Gandhi, Ulyanov, Badshah Khan, Debs, Bevan, all of the philosophers who inspired the League had integrated their ideas of the world into their personalities and had actualized them. Their descendants, the humanist communitarians, had seized the centers of power and the means of production after the devastation of the Zaibatsu Wars as the various economic, ethnic, and religious fanatics had fled to the stars in the Great Leap Outward. The communitarians had rebuilt the world into a world without war, without racial strife, or ethnic hatred, but with a spirit of cooperation and responsibility, with enough for everyone's need, a rational, thoughtful world. But that world was sometimes overly demanding of self-sacrifice. Thom believed in the strength and power of the League's ideals, difficult as they were to live by. Intellectually, he knew that an injury to one was an injury to all, and that violence was no solution. Riches should be awarded to all the community, not the greedy and crafty select few. Republic, *res publica*, did not mean the wealth of the rulers, and *commonwealth* meant the riches held common by all, and not just greedy individuals. The Zaibatsu Wars betrayed all those values, those ideals. There were times, though when Thom still found himself hard pressed to feel it emotionally, to make it a part of who he was.

Then again, since Ursula had left him, he had found that he felt few emotions other than anger and fear. All he felt were personal emotions, sometimes even selfish and self-pitying ones. Not even the meditations of *la souffrance* helped him get past the egocentric aspects of his pain.

The *adamsumit* finished his chants with a flourish, a high-pitched, wobbling vibrato.

"Very beautiful," Thom said, admiring the art if not the content of the song.

"They pick only the best young singers and mathematicians to be *adamsumit*," Siobhan said.

Thom looked and smiled when he saw the colonel. "Well?"

"He's in a board meeting," she said. "The guard won't let us in."

"I thought you were in charge of security," Thom said.

"I am, but Don Jaime hired me, and his orders supersede anything I say," she replied. "Still, I'm concerned about this meeting. Don Jaime has faced a lot of business setbacks recently, and the Mukhalafi attacks seem centered more on his territory than the other *sèo*."

Thom raised an eyebrow. "Setbacks? What kind?"

"Nothing spectacular, other *sèo* refusing to honor contracts or failing to deliver goods on time, ambushes of merchant trains coming to Ciudad Rand. Each in itself not serious, but collectively dangerous."

"But there have been too many of these occurring all at once, as if someone is planning it?"

Siobhan nodded. "Exactly."

"How do you know these things?"

She smiled and gave a slight laugh. "I underestimate you, Major. Well, Don Jaime tells me many things, at night, when he feels safe."

Thom found himself envious of Don Jaime. It wasn't simply envy, it was jealousy. He realized that he desired the colonel and wanted it to be him who shared her rooms and her bed. He found himself embarrassed at the feeling, an emotion he hadn't felt in a long time, not since Ursula left him. To hide his feelings, he turned away from Siobhan and stared out the window.

"Are you all right?" Siobhan said, putting a hand on his shoulder.

"I'm fine," he lied. Her fingers rubbed his shoulders and he enjoyed their strength. His throat was dry. He swallowed, but it didn't help. "I'm just tired."

His eyes fell on two small, winged creatures attacking a sinuous, six-legged animal trying to steal eggs from a nest on the window ledge. He recognized the six-legged animal as the same sort the rats had killed in the sewer.

The bird-like animals each came at the creature with four ebony-tipped claws. The animal lashed at one bird-like being, but missed. The attack left it off-balance, and a blow from the other flying animal sent the creature tumbling from the ledge into the open air.

Thom's mind focused less on the battle than on the creatures' appendages. Six legs, or four legs and two wings. He wondered if all the native Askanderian species were sextopeds. It certainly seemed that way. But then, the Ajnabi were humanoid. They had only two legs and two arms. Somehow that appeared out of place in the scheme of things.

"What do you know about the Ajnabi?" he asked.

Before she could answer, a guard appeared in the foyer. "Don Jaime will see you now."

Jaime had his back to them when they entered. Thom thought his friend was watching the same *adamsumit* he had seen earlier. He looked past Jaime to the prayer tower and saw that it was empty, the cleric long gone. Jaime was staring at something farther on in the distance, but Thom had no idea what it could be.

"Don Jaime, so glad you could see us," Siobhan said. "We have some important information for you."

"I see," Jaime said, turning toward them.

Thom was shocked by how drawn and pale Jaime appeared. The *sèo's* eyes were red-rimmed and moist.

Jaime wiped his face with the back of his hand, then

sat down behind his large, ancient oak desk. He sat up straight, his hands before him. "I'm sorry the meeting took so long, but we had important business." He took a deep breath, then gestured for them to sit, which they did. "Now, what do you have to tell me?"

Thom looked at Siobhan. She glanced at him and he nodded.

"There are two things, excellency," the colonel began. Her tone was firm and business-like, probably not the one she used when alone with Jaime. "The first is that Maarat ibn Steiner has been murdered."

A shocked expression crossed Jaime's features. "How did this happen?"

"An assassin. He came in the tent after we had spoken to Maarat," she said. "We have captured the man."

"Has he been interrogated?"

Siobhan shook her head. "No. And it won't do any good, excellency."

"And why not?"

"This is why," Thom said. He tossed the black plasteel cartridge onto the desktop. "Do you recognize that?"

Jaime picked it up and looked at it a moment before tossing it back to Thom. "A personality matrix cartridge," he said. "They're common enough, especially among the souk whores. It lets them be any woman a man desires. What does it have to do with the assassin?"

"He was a brain-wipe," Siobhan said. "I have security trying to trace his real identity, but that may prove difficult. His owners may simply have erased any record of him."

"That matrix cartridge is for a Japanese ninja, probably late sixteenth or early seventeenth century, old Earth reckoning," Thom said. "Very popular among assassins centuries ago, especially during the Zaibatsu Wars."

He held up the cartridge. "But this is a new matrix, not some antique. I'll wager it has a lot of sensory enhancements."

Jaime said nothing for a moment. He looked down at his hands, then sighed. "Do you suspect the Mukhalafi, Colonel?"

"They seem likely candidates, but one can't be sure. Ibn Steiner had many enemies of his own."

Jaime turned to Thom. "But you don't think it's the Mukhalafi, do you?"

Thom smiled. He'd always prided himself on having something of a poker face. Still, even though Jaime had clearly read his mind on that point the *sèo* could not know that Thom was the assassin's real target. And Thom was not about to tell him just yet. "No, I don't think the Mukhalafi are behind this. From what I've been told, they're just a dissident rebel movement living hand-to-mouth in the hills and desert. But this assassination seems very sophisticated, and the hardware is state of the art. I doubt the Mukhalafi could afford it, let alone bother to use it to kill someone as relatively unimportant as ibn Steiner."

"I should have suspected something like this," Jaime said. He leaned back his chair. "It seems I have many more enemies than I knew." The *sèo* paused a moment and glanced at Siobhan. "Well, Colonel, you said you had another message for me?"

Siobhan nodded. "Yes, sir. After we met with ibn Steiner, Major DuBois and I encountered an Ajnabi."

"What?" Jaime said, sitting bolt upright. "Where did you meet him?"

"Outside the fence of the bazaar, excellency," Siobhan said. "He didn't speak long, but he asked us to deliver a message to you."

"Yes? What was the message?" Jaime leaned forward and sat on the edge of his chair.

Siobhan paused a moment and licked her lips nervously. She glanced at Thom, who gave a nod of support. "The Ajnabi said you should stop production in your mines under the city. He said there is something dangerous there."

"The Ajnabi threatened me and the city?"

"The Ajnabi seemed concerned for our safety," she said. "It wasn't a threat; it was a warning."

"Well, it's impossible to close the mines, no matter what the alien said," Jaime snapped.

Jaime's sudden anger made Thom feel uneasy. He

sensed something was disturbing Jaime, and it was something besides ibn Steiner's death and the Ajnabi's warning.

"Perhaps it would be prudent, excellency, to stop work until the mines are inspected," the colonel continued.

"It's out of the question," Jaime said sharply. His face was flushed. He stared directly at Siobhan. "Ciudad Rand receives nearly sixty percent of its income from those mines. The rare earths alone probably pay for half. Without the mines, Ciudad Rand would be ruined."

"But, Don Jaime — " Siobhan protested.

"But nothing, colonel," Jaime said, slamming his hand down on the desktop. "I have recently learned of an attempt to gain controlling interest in Ciudad Rand. I need all the liquid capital I can get to stave off this attack. The matter is closed."

With that, Jaime pushed back his chair, rose, and left the room. He slammed the door behind him.

Siobhan turned to Thom. "I've never seen him act like that before. This takeover attempt must be very serious to have upset him so much."

Thom didn't say anything for a moment. He considered the events that had happened in the short time he had been on Askander, and he found himself seeing a disturbing pattern. Someone had tried to shoot down his shuttle, and he suspected the same someone had

Steiner murdered. Undoubtedly the same someone was behind the hostile takeover.

Siobhan grabbed his left wrist. "Are you all right? You looked like you were in a daze."

"Sorry, just thinking," Thom said. He stood up from his chair. "I'll tell you about it tonight, at the reception. Maybe Jaime will be calmed down a bit by then."

"I doubt it," she said. She smiled. "But we can hope."

"Yes, we can always hope."

CHAPTER THIRTEEN

As he left Jaime's offices, Thom had the odd sensation he was being watched. He glanced over his shoulder down the long corridor. The hallway was empty and still save for the rumble of the air conditioning. That failed to reassure him. While logic told Thom that he was alone, his survival skills, honed over years of military service, warned him to trust nothing here.

As a precaution, he reached into his pocket, pulled out his sense enhancers, and jacked in. His faculties responded with heightened awareness. The air conditioning had grown to a dull roar, and his nostrils detected a faint odor of dust and decay in the air masked only by equally noxious disinfectants. His eyes scanned the corridor, looking for any clues, especially telltale shadows cast on an intersecting hallway. He found nothing.

He turned down an adjoining hallway, went down a short set of steps, crossed a foyer where a bank of turbo-lifts were located, then turned again. His room was the fourth from the end. Thom reached the door, but before he keyed open the door, he looked back in time to see a shape at the end of the hall.

"Hey, you," he shouted, sprinting after the figure.

As Thom reached the end of the hall, he heard the electronic bell of a turbo-lift and the soft *whoosh* of its doors. He rounded the end of the hall in time to see the doors close. A read-out over the door said the turbo-lift was ten floors below, but it also showed the lift rising to his floor. It didn't take him long to realize that whoever had followed him had opened the lift doors manually and probably used an access panel inside the lift-tube to escape.

Thom felt a knot of fear in his stomach. He sprinted back to his rooms and examined the doorjamb. His enhanced senses did their job well as he spied a slender metal tube on the doorframe.

Roughly ten centimeters long, it was as thick as a large sewing needle. The shaped charge of the kneecapper would have done more than just prick the skin like a needle. It would have blown both his legs off at the knee, and he would have bled to death before help arrived. The Tuatha were particularly fond of the weapon, as it carried on a tradition of revenge dating back to the Earth's twentieth century.

Scarcely breathing, Thom painstakingly extracted

the kneecapper. Two hair-thin wires protruded from the top of the weapon. He broke each one separately. With its detonator disconnected, the kneecapper was harmless. He followed the thin wires up the doorjamb to the door latch on the wall. The wires ran under the metal guard plate and were probably connected to the lock. Had he placed his hand against the latch plate to have the sensors read his fingerprints, the bomb would have exploded.

He swallowed nervously at the thought. He placed his index and forefingers against the plate, the door opened, and he went inside. He headed straight for the bathroom. His hands trembling, he ran cold water into the sink, and then scooped the water onto his flushed face. After a moment, he sat down on the toilet, took a towel from its niche in the wall, and dried himself.

When he felt better, he sat on the edge of the bed, popped the enhancement cartridge from his skull jack, and tossed it onto the nightstand. He spotted a bottle of *araki*, no doubt a gift from Jaime, and some glasses on the nightstand. He poured himself a stiff drink. The liquor burned his throat as he swallowed, but soon it relaxed him, calming him.

Thom realized now that he'd been terribly wrong in believing that the attack on the shuttle was aimed at the entire League delegation. It had been aimed at him alone, as was the murder of Maarat. The others had died simply because they were in the way. This time there were no other potential victims. The intruder clearly knew when Thom would come out of Jaime's quarters and had followed him accordingly. In fact, in each prior case, the potential killer or killers knew exactly where Thom was at any given time. He knew now that he was the main target and had been all along. But why? He had no real negotiating skills. What good was he dead?

A knock on the door interrupted his thoughts.

Thom tensed for a moment. "Yes?" he said cautiously.

"Major DuBois?" a young boy's voice responded. "I have a package for you, from your embassy. Don Jaime told me to bring it to you."

Thom rose from the bed and went to the door. He had left it unlatched, so he carefully locked it. "What is your name?" he asked.

"I am Ishmael abdul Jaime, the *sèo's* servant, Major," the boy said.

"Place your fingers on the latch plate, please," he said. He glanced at the small read-out screen on the door. After a moment, red letters formed against the silver background.

"Abdul Jaime, Ishmael," they read. "Personal servant to house of Brentholtz. Identity confirmed."

Relieved, Thom opened the door. A young man, wearing the plain white jacket and blue turban of an indentured servant, stood outside the door. Poor parents often sold their children as servants until they were twenty-one in order to pay off family debts. Thom estimated Ishmael was about thirteen years old and probably had eight more years to serve on the contract his parents had negotiated.

Ishmael held up a limp, plastic wrapped package for Thom. "Your embassy sent this, Major. It is for Don Jaime's party."

Thom took the package. "My thanks to you, Ishmael and to your master. May the Hand find ample reasons to bless you."

The boy bowed slightly, then left. Thom closed the door and locked it. He glanced at the room clock and saw he had two hours before the reception began. He decided to take a nice long, hot bath.

After bathing, he checked the package containing his dress uniform the embassy had sent. To his relief, there were no explosive devices of any kind. He removed the uniform and dressed carefully. The uniform fit perfectly, as if it had been tailored for him. The trousers had a sharp crease, and the red-and-white lacquered stars and dove glistened on the epaulets of the dark blue jacket. The embassy had even found replicas of all of Thom's military ribbons, including his Hero of the People's Peace medal. Whoever provided the uniform had done his research. Thom felt uncomfortable in dress uniforms, pre-

ferring the anonymity of his fatigues, but he knew now
he could never be anonymous again.

The reception hall was relatively empty when Thom
entered. A few white-jacketed waiters, mostly young indentured servants, carried tureens of soup and trays of
sandwiches and vegetables to the long tables on either
side of the hall. Older men carried bottles of liquor and
large coffee urns. They ordered the younger servants
about with gruff shouts and curses.

Across the hall, a band of musicians practiced on a
strange mixture of instruments. Thom could make out
a rebab, a cittern, several varieties of drums, a large santour, some shawms and flutes of various kinds. There
was also a pair of synthesizers. The music they played
was equally eclectic, blending the sounds of ancient and
medieval Earth cultures with divergent forms found
among the assorted planetary societies. "Universe music," critics called it.

"You're early," Siobhan said stepping up to him.

"I've never learned to be fashionably late," he said,
finding himself pleased to see her. "So why are you early?"

"I'm chief of security, remember?" she said.

The colonel wore a traditional Tuatha woman's dress

uniform of a white silk blouse, black bolero jacket with silver trim, and a long red and green tartan kilt. An orange, green and white sash ran down from her right shoulder to her left hip. The sash was fastened at the shoulder with a large silver brooch. Her face was tastefully made up, and her short hair was pulled back and smoothed to her head.

"You're looking quite lovely this evening," Thom said.

"How kind of you to notice," she said. He detected she was wearing a perfume scented of jasmine and clove. Quite a contrast to her military kit, he thought.

Thom grabbed two wineglasses from a passing waiter and handed her one.

Siobhan thanked him and sipped her wine. "You're really quite dashing for someone who comes from such an egalitarian society as the League."

"My dear Colonel, we learn very young to stress courtesy and civility as a means to show respect to everyone," he said, "and not to draw distinctions between social classes, as some cultures do." He paused. "Or like whoever tried to kill me today."

Siobhan looked puzzled. "You mean the assassin who killed Maarat?"

He shook his head. "No, I was followed when I left Jaime's offices. I spotted the intruder, but he got away. When I went back to my room, I found someone had planted a kneecapper in the door."

"What?" she said, genuinely shocked. "But that's impossible. I've had your room monitored since you arrived." Then she stopped, realizing she had said too much.

The news that she had monitored his room didn't surprise Thom. "Well, it wouldn't take much to get around that. Maybe one of your guards works for the other side, waits till a friend plants the kneecapper, then carefully erases the record."

The colonel frowned and furrowed her brow in thought. "Yes, that's a possibility, Major. Definitely a possibility."

By then, more guests had entered the room. The majority were nobles from the other corporate families, but there were a few minor off-planet officials, including two male Tuatha in full regalia and two women and one man wearing the robin's egg blue uniforms of the League *Corps Diplomatique*. Ambassador Stephens was not among the League officials, so Thom suspected the three were security officers scouting the area.

"Well, I'm afraid I must attend to my work, Tho — Major," Siobhan said. "If you'll excuse me."

"Certainly, if you'll allow me the chance to dance with you later," he said.

"I think that can be arranged," she said with a grin. Without another word, she sauntered toward a group of minor nobles who were talking with one of the Tuatha officers.

Thom watched her for a moment as she easily slipped into the group's conversation, smiling and laughing. He envied her ease with social skills, and he found his attraction to her growing.

The musicians began playing. Thom recognized the tune as an *estampie*, an ancient dance form, although the harmonies were decidedly modern. He scanned the room, watching the guests as they talked and drank and toyed with the food at the tables. He spotted a middle-aged bearded and balding man in a League diplomatic uniform holding a small plate of food and a glass of wine. Thom crossed the room toward the man.

"Ambassador Stephens?" he said.

The man looked up. "Yes?" Then a smile crossed the man's face. "Ah, Major DuBois, I presume," he said, speaking League Standard Volapük, a nineteenth century artificial language first used by the Austro-Hungarians. League diplomats had revived it, knowing few Askanderians or other human exile groups would understand them. Stephens put his plate down and extended his right hand to Thom. "So good to meet you."

Thom took the ambassador's hand. Stephens's grip was firm, and his handshake was friendly. "I'm sorry I didn't have the chance to speak to you earlier," Thom replied, also in Volapük.

Stephens dismissed the apology with a brief shake of

his head. "Think nothing of it, Major. The embassy staff is busy enough as it is, even if we are only an unofficial delegation."

"Thank you, sir," Thom said.

"I must say I'm glad you're well. We were concerned when we heard the shuttle had been shot down. Nasty business." He sipped his wine as he strolled away from the table.

"Have we learned who did it?" Thom said, following the ambassador.

Stephens shook his head. "Not yet. Our contacts tell me the Mukhalafi have denied any involvement. Hard to say with them, though. They deny everything, and with good reason."

"Good reason?"

Stephens chuckled. "You haven't been here long, have you? It's become standard practice to blame the Mukhalafi for everything from bad business deals, to inflation, to domestic disputes among the *suma*, and the cattle that run amok in the *souk*. They routinely deny everything, even when they are guilty, which I'm inclined to believe is not that often."

The ambassador stopped, placed his empty glass on a waiter's tray, and took two fresh glasses. He handed one to Thom. "The wine is tasty, but not especially strong. Don Jaime seems to prefer his parties not degenerate into drunken bacchanals." He pointed toward another waiter. "The round sandwiches are made from a bean paste, something like hummus. I think you'll like them."

Thom picked one up from the table and took a bite. To his surprise, he actually enjoyed the smooth, nut-like taste, heightened by several spices. *Ginger and mace?* he wondered. Quite expensive, if so, as they were imported from off-planet and only the wealthy could afford such an extravagance. He finished the sandwich and washed it down with a swallow of some unexceptional wine. "Tell me, Mr. Ambassador, has the League assembled another negotiating team?"

"We've contacted the *Lasalle*, and they tell us it will take another month or so to find a new team as qualified in negotiation," Stephens replied. He hesitated a moment. "I hate to tell you, but they've been recalled to Tau Ceti — some unfinished business with the Tuatha I gather. I'm afraid you're on your own until the next ship comes."

The news surprised Thom, but he could have anticipated it. To have the *Lasalle* tied up, waiting around Der Merchant for an earth standard month was expecting too much. The starship was far too valuable for that.

"Well, it'll give me more time to get to know this place and to renew my old friendship with Don Jaime," Thom said, trying to sound upbeat. He noticed that the ambassador was actually looking past him toward the main entrance.

"Well, if it isn't the wicked brother-in-law," Stephens said.

Thom turned about to see a tall, well-muscled man in a dark gray formal suit. He wore a red and white *kaffiya* that covered all of his head except his olive-skinned face. The main features of that face were high cheekbones, a long and thin razor-like nose, and a dark black goatee trimmed to a sharp V-shape.

"Who is that?"

The ambassador glanced at Thom. "That's Ernesto Abu Brion, *sèo* of Friedmanville. He's married to Don Jaime's sister."

"He's Isabella's husband?" Thom clarified.

"Yes, I believe that's her name. An arranged marriage, I understand. I can't say she would have wanted to marry Abu Brion out of love. He's quite an unpleasant person, and Friedmanville is an equally unpleasant arcology. Steer clear of him if you can."

Thom barely heard the ambassador's words. His eyes focused on a figure in a black and silver uniform of the *Gall Oglaigh* who now moved from the doorway to stand at Abu Brion's side. The man had a face the color of parchment, crisscrossed with thin pink scars, and thick black hair. The ends of a long moustache hung down from his upper lip. It was a face Thom remembered well. "Haakon Kreus. What's that bastard doing here?"

"He's Abu Brion's military chief," the ambassador replied. "What about him?"

Thom looked at the ambassador. "You mean you don't know?"

"Know what?"

"He's the Butcher of Ramal."

A shocked expression crossed Stephens's face. "He crowded all of King Daffyd's political opponents into that sports stadium and had them all killed?"

Thom nodded.

Pinocheted was the proper expression for the crime, Thom recalled, named for a twentieth-century Chilean general who had brutally overthrown a democratically elected government and then massacred its supporters. Kreus had, however, lifted the act to new levels of cruelty and brutality. He paid a price, though. The Ramalese rebels preferred forms of revenge that left their victim alive, but minus certain body parts. To his regret, Thom had allowed the rebels to extract that revenge.

"This does put new light on things. You'll have to excuse me," Stephens said. "I need to let intelligence know about this. They can relay it to the *Lasalle* before they leave. It might just keep them here a while longer."

The ambassador crossed the room to talk to one of the three League officers, who were now busying themselves about a large, ornate glass punchbowl.

Thom considered joining them until he saw a tall, willowy woman enter the room and join Abu Brion. As she came to Abu Brion's side, she slid her arm around his crooked elbow. Thom thought the motion appeared mechanical, emotionless, and somehow mindless. Abu Brion's patting of his wife's hand seemed equally emotionless, but there was no mindlessness to the *sèo's* action. They strolled toward the center of the hall.

The woman wore a loose dress of white and gold that hung to the floor. Her upper arms were bare except for a golden armlet on her left arm, a sign that she was married. Golden mesh gloves covered her forearms from fingertip to elbow, while her face, except for her dark eyes, hid behind a thin gauze veil. Her skin and hair were almost as white as the dress and made her appear preternatural and ghostly. The woman's resemblance to Jaime was striking, and Thom recalled that they were fraternal twins. She had always been the physically weaker of the two. One reason Jaime had come to Formalhaut Four was to keep an eye on Isabella as she underwent biochip implant surgery to treat her epilepsy.

Yet Thom thought Isabella now seemed surprisingly docile. She was almost servile and not at all the vivacious young woman he remembered for being as strong-willed as her brother. Thom watched Kreus leave the side of Abu Brion and Isabella and walk toward the two Tuatha officers at the reception. He took that as his chance to speak to Isabella.

"Isabella, how are you?" he said, stepping toward the

couple.

She stared at him without recognition, her eyes black and empty dots. "Should I know you?" she asked, her voice thin and reedy.

"I'm Thomas DuBois, a friend of your brother's," he said, shocked at how pale and sickly she seemed. "We went to school on Formalhaut together."

"So long ago," she said. Her eyes drifted from him and seemed to stare off into the distance.

Abu Brion smiled, but his eyes belied any kind nature. "I must apologize for my wife, Major. She has not been well lately," he said, gently patting her hand. "Come along, my dear, we have much to do."

The *sèo* led his wife away from Thom, and they drifted toward a knot of nobles and their wives conversing at a large oak dining table at the far end of the hall.

"I'm free to dance now," Siobhan said, touching his arm. She stared at him when he didn't respond. "Are you all right?"

"Oh," he replied. "Yes, I'm fine but I'm worried about Jaime's sister. She seemed like she was sleepwalking. She didn't remember me."

Siobhan nodded. "Yes, I know. We suspect Abu Brion keeps her drugged. She reportedly has a great appetite for 'Midnight Lace.'"

"I never would have expected that of her," Thom said, taken aback. The psychotropic was known for its deadly properties, as well as for the vivid hallucinations it created.

"Some people prefer it to reality, I'm afraid."

"But where would she get it?"

"Anything is available on Askander, especially for the wealthy," the colonel said.

The musicians struck up a lively minuet.

"Come on, let's enjoy ourselves. She's beyond your help," she said. Siobhan pulled him toward the dance floor and into a clutch of other dancing couples.

Thom tried to put Isabella out of his mind as he and Siobhan danced. He was surprised at the grace and ease with which the colonel made each step, while he was hard pressed to remember the dance and keep his feet untangled. He felt so clumsy around this fascinating woman, who attracted him in ways he was pressed to explain. Soon the flow and rhythm of the music caught him and made the minuet almost seem second nature.

"I haven't seen Jaime," he said suddenly. "Don't you think it's unusual for him not to be at his own reception?"

Siobhan executed a turn, pirouetting perfectly. "He'll be here. He seems to prefer waiting until everyone has arrived before making an appearance. Watch your step."

Suddenly, the music changed to a *pavane*, a contemporary composition from a recent neo-Elizabethan revival. The couples formed into two lines, men on one side and women on the other. The movements were stately and precise, with the couples gradually exchanging partners until the dancers at last returned to their original partner.

Then the band broke into a fast and furious *tourdion*. The energetic medieval Burgundian dance, driven by an incessant drumbeat, contrasted starkly with the stately pavane. The couples whirled about madly until a flourish of drumbeats signaled the end of the dance. The dancers, exhausted, applauded the musicians, and then staggered happily from the dance floor toward the punchbowls and carafes of wine. A new set of dancers replaced them, and the band began a *czardas*, an old Hungarian folk dance derived, curiously, from a dance for military recruiters.

Thom, his arm around Siobhan's waist, walked breathlessly to a table. "Goodness, I haven't danced like that in years." He felt his heart pounding in his chest. "I think my heart hasn't stopped dancing yet."

Siobhan laughed. "Yes, it was fun."

She smiled, and Thom felt happy to be with this woman, who somehow melted the barriers he'd put up against all his pain — and his joy.

Although his hands shook from the exertion of the dancing, he still managed to fill a cut-glass goblet with the ruby red punch and hand it to Siobhan without spilling a drop. Then he filled one for himself.

She drank all of her punch, then held out the cup for

a refill. A waiter readily obliged her.

Thom wanted to kiss her then, but felt awkward. Instead, he held her hand tightly in his. "Thank you. You've given me back something I haven't had since — "

"I understand. Your wife hurt you very much," she replied.

Thom was shocked. "How..." he started to ask, but caught himself.

"Oh yes, I know all about that. My intelligence officers are good."

"Yes, she did hurt me, deeply," he said. "But I try not to think about it."

"You don't do a very good job of showing it, Major," Siobhan said.

A slight smile crossed her lips.

"Perhaps I don't disguise it well," he replied, returning her smile.

"I see you have decided to fraternize with our enemies, Colonel ni Mhaonaigh," a dark, heavy voice said.

Thom turned to face Haakon Kreus. A scowl filled the Tuatha's scarred face, and his eyes had the slightly glazed look of someone who had had too much to drink. Kreus held a half-empty glass of whiskey in his right hand.

"He is my employer's guest, General Kreus," Siobhan said curtly. "And you should show him some courtesy."

"That's all right," Thom said. "Let him be rude."

Kreus snorted. "You can afford to be kind then, Du-Bois? After Ramal?"

Siobhan looked at Thom. "You know each other?"

Thom nodded. He was a little surprised that she did not know that fact. *A failure of her intelligence officers perhaps?* he wondered. *Or is my involvement still a well-kept secret?* "I'm afraid so. I was an advisor to the Ramalese guerrillas who overthrew King Daffyd."

"How could he forget?" Kreus spat. He seemed unsteady on his feet and his speech was slightly slurred. "The major led a Ramalese commando force which kidnapped me from my bed. Quite brave."

The general extended a finger of his left hand. There was a slight whirring noise. Kreus pushed the finger into the middle of Thom's chest. "Then he did nothing when those bastards turned me over to their women, who proved to be excellent amateur neurosurgeons."

"I tried to stop them," Thom asserted. "But you had their husbands killed in the stadium."

"Oh, certainly you tried to stop them," Kreus said mockingly. *"A League soldier never kills,* and all that bullshit."

"I'm sorry for what they did," Thom said. He felt his throat tighten and his mouth grow dry. His cheeks were flushed and warm. He tried to suppress the anger rising in him, anger aimed as much at himself for failing to stop the Ramalese as it was at the Kreus's provocations.

Kreus stared at Thom. "I'll bet you're sorry." He gulped down the last of the whiskey in the glass. "Actually, I should thank you, DuBois. My new hands are so much better than my old ones." His right hand whirred softly, the fingers clenched, and the glass shattered noisily. Kreus dropped the moist fragments on the table. "Perhaps next time it will be your neck, eh, Major?"

"There won't be a next time, General. I'm transferring to the diplomatic corps, so I suspect our paths won't cross again."

Kreus opened his mouth to speak, but before he could talk, he was cut off by a sharp voice.

"General Kreus, I will not have you arguing with my guests," Jaime Brentholtz said. He stepped between Thom and the mercenary officer. "Now, General, your employer and I have business to attend to regarding you. He has requested your presence."

Kreus stared at Jaime and scowled. "We'll see, Major DuBois. I am not finished with you." The general turned and stalked off. The drunken stumble seemed to have disappeared.

"Bastard," Jaime said under his breath as he watched the mercenary leave. "Perhaps they should have cut his tongue out and left him with his damn hands."

Thom sighed with relief. "Thank you, Jaime."

Jaime didn't respond. His eyes remained fixed on Kreus until the man left the hall.

"Thom, your hand," Siobhan said.

Thom looked down and saw he had clenched his right fist so tightly that his fingernails had left bloody indentations in his palm. "I didn't realize I was that angry."

"It's very easy to become angry with Kreus," Siobhan said. She found a napkin on the table, moistened it from a water glass, and dabbed at the wound. "The Dail of Alba Nuadh became disenchanted with him early on, after he recklessly wasted warriors' lives. He can, however, also command great respect from his men."

So he rose through the ranks, Thom thought, *and when he could rise no further, Kreus sold himself to the highest bidder, from King Daffyd to Ernesto Abu Brion.* Thom turned to ask Jaime a question, but the *sèo* was no longer at his side.

"Did you see where Jaime went?" Thom asked.

"No," she replied, "I thought he was standing next to you."

Thom glanced around the hall, hoping for a glimpse of Jaime, but the *sèo* was nowhere to be seen. "He said he had business with Abu Brion. Could that mean the takeover bid he feared — a takeover by his own brother-in-law?"

Siobhan thought a moment. "I don't know, but I think you're right."

"Something's wrong," he said. "And we'd better find out what."

CHAPTER FOURTEEN

Thom spotted the *Gall Oglaigh* guards as he and Siobhan approached Jaime's offices.

The *saighdearan* posted outside the doors of the office appeared more heavily armed than Don Jaime's personal guards. In addition to their flechette pistols and ceremonial knives, the troopers also carried weapons that were clearly not ceremonial.

Thom recognized the large caliber weapons as siege rifles intended for infantry combat. He'd seen the damage that the guns' rocket-propelled, tumbling bullets could do to the human body.

"Damn it, now we've got to find some way out of here," he whispered.

Siobhan laughed loudly, grabbed Thom's right elbow, and led him down a side corridor. "Your rooms? What a wicked idea, Major," she said, making her flirtations loud enough for the guards to hear. She gave a little giggle to add to the effect. Once they were out of earshot, her tone changed. "Something is definitely wrong. Those guards are Abu Brion's men, not Jaime's."

"I know. It's the takeover Jaime feared."

She nodded. "I'm afraid so."

"We've got to find out what's going on in there," Thom said. A smile crossed his lips as he remembered the turbo-lift. "And I think I've got a way to do it. Come with me."

"Where are we going?"

"To my rooms," he said, starting down the corridor.

Siobhan smiled. "My, you are wicked, aren't you?"

In his room he located a small set of tools and an enhancement cartridge from a survival kit all League troopers were issued. He usually carried it strapped to his leg, but hadn't thought he'd need it until now. He also changed from the dress uniform into a set of fatigue pants and an undershirt. He was relieved Siobhan didn't make any comments about his physique, which he knew, that while healthy, couldn't match hers for strength.

"Now, Let's go find a lift tube and see what we can learn," he said.

It didn't take long to find a lift tube. They stood outside, waiting for the car to arrive and its doors to open.

The wait was short. The turbo-lift arrival bell chimed and the lift doors opened.

"You're certain there is an access hatch in the tube?" Siobhan said as they entered the lift.

"I'm almost positive," he replied. "It was the only way the intruder could have escaped."

"I suppose I'll have to believe you."

The lift doors closed. Thom undid the access panel to the lift controls. He found the circuit for the emergency alarm bell and disconnected it. "We'll take it down one floor," he said.

The lift capsule descended one floor. Thom hit the emergency stop button, and the capsule shuddered to a halt. "Now, there should be another access panel in the ceiling," Thom said, looking up. The ceiling itself was hidden behind a gold-colored metal grill, above which was a sheet of frosted plastic covering the fluorescent lights. Thom ran his fingers along the edge. "There should be a latch along here," he said.

"Here it is," Siobhan said. She reached up, located the snap, and pulled.

The hinged grid dropped away.

Thom caught it and lowered it slowly to the floor. "And there's the hatch," he said, staring up at the ceiling. He reached up and pushed. The hatch popped open.

He reached into his pocket, pulled out the enhancement cartridge, and jacked it in. Immediately, his senses grew heightened. He could smell the ozone generated by the lift motors, taste the hot lubricating oil, hear the throb of the huge motors, and see the two columns of small lights running up the sides of the lift-tube.

"You're sure you'll be all right?"

"It's safer than star travel," he said, "and I hate star travel."

"All right," she said. "I'll give you fifteen minutes, then I'll have to go back to the reception."

"I hope this won't take more than ten."

"Good luck," Siobhan said.

Thom looked at her, and their eyes met like mutual tracking systems locking on a target. He felt an almost electric thrill come over him. He leaned forward, compelled to kiss, but to his surprise Siobhan acted first. She grabbed his head between her strong hands, pulled him down while she stood on tiptoe, and planted a passionate kiss on his lips firmly.

She released him reluctantly, then said, "If it all works out, we'll go back to your room."

Her actions startled him. Thom had no idea she was attracted to him, although he found her extremely attractive. He had believed she merely tolerated him. He realized that some of her flirting with him during the dance was not an act at all.

"I'll be back shortly," he managed to say.

He jumped up, caught the edge of the hatchway,

and pulled himself through. Once on top of the lift, he crouched down and scanned the side of the tube, looking for the access panel. He ran his hand along the edge of the cylinder, but all he found was smooth, highly polished metal and the recessed handholds on one side. Those, he realized, were what the intruder held onto while in the tube.

Then his eyes spotted a dull red marker blended smoothly into the curved wall. It looked like it had once been illuminated, but the bulb had long since burned out. He pushed the button. The panel in the tube slid silently, smoothly open. A soft yellow light spilled from the opening.

"I found the panel, and I'm going in," he said.

The shaft ran a short distance to a small maintenance room. The room was bathed in a dim red glow. The multi-colored lights of a monitoring panel glowed dully under years of dust. Thom saw that the panel controlled both the turbo-lifts and the local air conditioning and ventilation.

He heard a voice coming from one of the shafts. It was a shouting voice, and Thom suspected he could have heard it even without the cybernetic enhancements plugged into his brain. It took him just a few seconds to find the shaft from which the voice originated.

The ventilation panel was loose, so he simply pulled it away and crawled into the shaft. The shaft itself was not tall enough to crawl through, so he slid along on his stomach. He tried to remember how far it was to Jaime's offices. The voice grew louder and his eyes, with their vision enhanced, made out some light just ahead.

"I will not stand for your trickery," Thom heard Jaime say. "You've drugged my sister. She's not in her right mind."

"Your sister's fondness for illicit drugs began long before she was married to me," Abu Brion replied. "And with all the hardware in her brain, I doubt any of us can say what is her right mind."

Thom eased himself up against a vent. Through the gaps in the grid, he could see Jaime, Abu Brion, Kreus and several of Ciudad Rand's nobles and minor outside *sèo*. There were also at least a dozen armed troopers, and Thom suspected they were not Jaime's men.

On the opposite side of the room sat Isabella. She seemed to be staring off vacantly into space. She was smoking a cigarette, probably containing Midnight Lace. A long grey ash hung from its tip, then tumbled to the floor. Isabella played with a strand of her hair and began giggling softly.

"But just look at her," Jaime said. "She's clearly mad. This document you have, transferring control of her shares of stock to you, is worthless. No adamsumit would approve of it."

"I beg to differ," Abu Brion said. "Every *adamsumit*

in Friedmanville has found it without fault, as have many of your own leading clerics." He crossed to the table and poured himself a glass of *araki*.

"But, if she is as mad as you say, then I as her husband, would be her guardian in any case, and have control of her shares. All the *adamsumit* in Askander would agree to that. You would still be the loser."

He raised his glass. "A toast then, to the new *sèo* of Ciudad Rand."

Jaime flung himself at Don Ernesto. He knocked the wineglass from Abu Brion's hand, and then tried to place his fingers around his brother-in-law's throat. They tumbled to the carpet. The nobles rushed to their leader's aid, but Abu Brion's troopers leveled their rifles at the unarmed *dhireks*.

Kreus walked over to the brawling pair of *sèo*, grasped Jaime's left shoulder, and began to squeeze. Jaime howled in pain and released his grip on Abu Brion. He struggled in the mercenary's grasp, but the general's plasteel fingers were too strong. Kreus tossed Jaime to the floor and placed his right hand on the young *sèo's* throat.

"Move, and I'll break your scrawny neck," Kreus hissed.

Jaime did not move.

The general's voice was sharp and clear, not at all the drunken slur Thom had heard earlier in the evening.

Thom suspected that Kreus was either a good actor or had an enhancement cartridge that suppressed the effects of alcohol.

Abu Brion slowly rose from the floor and steadied himself against a chair. The fingers of his right hand gently rubbed the area on his neck where Jaime had tried to throttle him. Isabella's eyes focused on him, and she laughed uncontrollably. The long ash from her cigarette tumbled to the floor.

"A foolish move, Jaime, and a futile one, too," Abu Brion said. "Let him up, general. He has business to attend to."

Kreus's fingers snapped away from Jaime's throat. The mercenary stood up, towering over the young noble. "Get up."

Jaime stood up. Thom could see his friend's chest rise and fall rapidly at each breath. Jaime's face was flushed and perspiration rolled down his forehead. Thom wished he could help, but stuck in the ventilation shaft, he knew that he was as impotent as Jaime.

"Call the meeting to order," Abu Brion said.

Jaime paused a moment, then licked his lips. "This emergency meeting of the board of Brentholtz-Madden Gesellschaft is called to order."

"Good," Abu Brion said. He lowered himself into a chair next to that one reserved for the *sèo*. He gestured to the other nobles. "Gentlemen, be seated."

The other nobles sat around the table. They said nothing. Most looked at their hands or stared at the ceiling, perhaps hoping for the direct intervention of Yadd Khabba. But the Unseen Hand remained invisible, as always.

Jaime pulled back his chair and sat. "The business before us is the removal of the present *sèo* and his replacement. There will be a vote."

An older *dhirek* Thom didn't recognize rose to his feet. He held an Isaak, a small computer in his trembling hands. Thom's databug informed him that the Askanderian elite did not use databugs or plug-ins, which they saw only as tools to control the servile poor. "I, Rafael ibn Brentholtz, representing five thousand proxies and forty-eight percent of all shares, vote to continue Don Jaime Ibn Brentholtz as *sèo* of Ciudad Rand." He tapped the device's screen to send his votes. The older noble sat, his eyes fixed on Abu Brion.

Abu Brion stood up. The *séo* had a larger tablet-sized Isaak on the table before him.

Thom couldn't quite tell, but the screen seemed to display thousands of proxies and perhaps more votes that Don Rafael controlled. "I, Don Ernesto Abu Brion of Friedmanville, representing myself and five thousand proxies and fifty-two percent of all outstanding shares, vote for the removal of *sèo* Don Jaime ibn Brentholtz and his replacement by myself, in the name of the majority of shareholders."

There was silence in the room. Abu Brion signaled two of the guards. Rifles at the ready, they came over and stood at either side of Jaime.

"Don Jaime, please vacate your chair," Abu Brion said.

Jaime looked up at the guards. Thom could see the noble's face had changed from being flushed with anger to being almost bone-white in its paleness. He pushed the chair back and stood. Then one of the guards took him by the elbow and led him from the table.

Abu Brion, a cold smile on his face, walked around the end of the table and seated himself in the *sèo's* chair. He turned to face Kreus. "General, as the new *sèo* of Ciudad Rand, it has come to my attention that a conspiracy may exist against the body of this corporation and against me personally."

He reached into his jacket and withdrew a data crystal, which he handed to Kreus. "These are the names of the alleged conspirators. You will find them seated at this table."

The other nobles rose to protest, but the remainder of Abu Brion's guards, their flechette pistols drawn, placed themselves behind the various *dhirek*. Seeing they had no choice, the nobles settled uneasily back into their seats.

"Take them into custody and question them to find the roots of this conspiracy," Abu Brion said. "Treason must be weeded out at all cost."

"It shall be done, Don Ernesto," Kreus said. He nodded toward his men. Each guard pressed the barrel of a flechette pistol into the neck of a *dhirek*. With their free hands, the soldiers grabbed the back of the nobles' robes and pulled them up. Each *dhirek* came slowly to his feet, not showing any resistance. The troopers quickly ushered the nobles from the room.

After a moment, Abu Brion got up from his chair. He walked across the room and came face to face with Jaime. The guards now held Jaime's arms tightly so he could not move.

"You bastard. You're no better than a common thief." Jaime yelled. He spat in Abu Brion's face.

The soldiers jerked Jaime backwards, and one of them slammed the butt of a flechette pistol into the side of his face, snapping his head back.

Thom winced, feeling Jaime's pain.

Abu Brion calmly reached up and wiped the saliva from his cheek. "Quite the contrary, all of our wealth, even yours, has been built on theft. The very foundations of our society require us to steal land, labor, and dignity from others. Your ancestors and mine both knew that, only you seem determined to ignore it. A pity."

Jaime raised his head. A trickle of blood ran from the corner of his mouth. "So what do you intend to do to me? Kill me?"

Abu Brion frowned. "How little you think of me. If I were to kill you, that would create a martyr for those who oppose me. I have better plans than that. I intend to destroy your reputation, after I render you harmless, of course." He stepped aside and gestured to Kreus. "General?"

The mercenary pulled a small laser pistol from a holster and walked toward Jaime. The two guards forced Jaime to his knees, then one of then grabbed the noble's hair and yanked his head backwards. Jaime grimaced in pain.

Thom watched in horror as Kreus reached down, and the mercenary's fingers separated Jaime's left eyelid. The general raised the laser pistol and aimed it into Jaime's eye.

"A simple operation," Abu Brion said. "A squeeze of the trigger, and the laser will scar the optic nerve at the point where it leaves the retina, rendering you permanently blind. You may begin, General."

"No," Thom shouted, unable to control himself.

All the eyes in the room turned toward the ventilation grid.

"It's DuBois," Kreus shouted. He swung the pistol about and fired. The laser spat a thin red beam that hit the metal grid. The metal melted and sagged where the beam struck.

Like a blind crab, Thom scuttled backward from the

grid. His heart pounded, and he was drenched in sweat. His knees scraped along the bottom of the shaft, and he could feel little sharp ends of metal tearing through the cloth of his trousers and ripping his skin. He kept going as fast as he could. He ducked his head down and tried to look between his scurrying legs to find the dim red light from the control room that meant safety. He could hear Abu Brion's shouts and Kreus's cries, and he could hear alarm buzzers and sirens screaming down each side shaft into his.

Not much farther now, Thom thought. He thought he could see a crimson glow ahead. He came to a side shaft. Carefully, he backed himself into it, turning himself around so he could continue his journey headfirst. Now he could clearly see the light. If he was lucky, he could take the turbo-lift down to the lowest levels of the arcology. *Once I'm in the lower levels, I can probably find the sewer system and get out into the mountains*, he thought.

The maintenance room lay just a short distance ahead. He quickened his pace. "Not much farther, just a little ways," he panted. He reached the opening and began to pull himself through when something struck him in the left leg. Pain surged through his body. He rolled from the opening into the room, clutching his leg.

He gritted his teeth and looked down at the injury. A neural flechette was embedded in his calf. The dart's golden stabilizer fins glistened around the growing circle of blood on his trousers. He reached down and yanked the projectile free. Someone had been hiding in the ventilator shafts, he realized, someone who had been waiting patiently for him. He had no idea how much longer he had before whatever toxin the dart contained took effect, but he knew if he reached Siobhan, they might find an antidote.

Thom crawled toward the access panel. Through the opening he could see the lights of the lift tube and the top of the turbo-lift. Then he heard a roar and a gust of wind lashed his face as the turbo-lift dropped away.

"No," he screamed. "It can't be fifteen minutes."

He stretched his fingers, hoping to touch the access panel so he could climb down the handholds.

The access panel slammed shut. Thom's vision began to spin. Darkness crept over him, and he tumbled down a long, nightmarish corridor into unconsciousness.

CHAPTER FIFTEEN

Jaime took a step. The rock under his foot gave way. He nearly tumbled to the ground, but managed to steady himself with the twisted old branch he was using as a walking stick.

"A blind man needs a cane," the soldiers had said, laughing, as they had thrust the stick into his hands.

"And a begging bowl," another had shouted, throwing some crockery at his feet. He heard the bowl, if it was a bowl, shatter on the jagged rocks.

"Oh, too bad," a third soldier said. "It should have been a wooden bowl. Well, we can't be wasting time. Get you gone, Don Jaime ibn Brentholtz, never darken our *hausfatah's* domains again."

Someone had pushed him heavily in the back. He staggered, then fell headlong into the rocks and sand at the end of the vast *Shaul Khala*. Jaime tasted grit and the saltiness of blood on his tongue. Hands grabbed him, lifted him to his feet, and pushed him forward into the cold desert. Despite an eternal darkness that enveloped his now sightless eyes, he could tell by the temperature that it was night.

It seemed as if he had walked for days, yet he knew it had only been a few hours since they had taken him from his cell and transported him by flyer to the desert's edge.

He wondered how many more hours remained until dawn. When the warming rays of Delta Pavonis crossed the horizon, he would have an idea of what direction he was heading. He would find shade, drink the last of the water the guards had given him, and if the Hand willed it, some nomads would find him. Then he would plot his revenge against Abu Brion.

With his stick, he tapped the ground ahead of him. The wind brought the tang of the desert to his nostrils. He could detect the honey-like aroma of *mirjan'zhur*, the coral flower whose blossoms only opened at night to avoid the killing heat of day. While they usually grew singly, he recalled, they often grew into numerous large bushes near a water source. His nostrils were then assaulted by the sickly stench of the *keriha wardi*. He remembered that the stink-flower's odor belied the beauty of its rose-like blooms.

Then the sirocco wind brought a stronger scent of scent of *mirjan'zhur*. This was not a single plant. It had to be many, and large numbers of blossoms could only mean water was nearby. He poked ahead excitedly until his walking stick fell on empty air. His momentum carried him forward and, before he could steady himself, he felt the ground under his feet giving way. Screaming, he tumbled over the edge of a *wadi*.

"Still no sign of DuBois?" Ernesto Abu Brion said to the young Tuatha officer who stood before him. The *sèo* himself sat behind the desk that had once been Jaime's. Before him were unsigned warrants for the arrest and execution of several former corporate officials.

The soldier shook his head. "No, we've searched everywhere. He's not in his quarters, nor in the League delegation offices. We also scanned the ventilation system, but there is no sign of him."

Abu Brion frowned and laid his stylus on the desktop. "General Kreus will not be pleased. He so wanted to deal with the major." He sighed. "Well, what about the woman, the Tuatha colonel?"

"She, too, remains missing."

Abu Brion had already taken a great risk with the League delegation. Should either one get to the League starship he knew was lying in wait somewhere, then all of his plans would be ruined. His only hope was that Kreus could extract the necessary information from

Ambassador Stephens.

"If I may be allowed to speculate, Don Ernesto," the officer said, "he may have escaped the arcology with the aid of Mukhalafi agents, or he might be down in the *Jura.*"

Abu Brion considered the man's speculations. Unfortunately, he had to admit that both possibilities had a high likelihood of being true. The rebels would undoubtedly have a use for someone with DuBois' experience. "And if he were down in the sordid underbelly of the arcology?"

"We might never find DuBois among those low-lives in the *Jura*, but it is highly unlikely he would survive long. Certainly he will be unable to contact his League comrades as long as he's there," the officer said.

"Yes, lieutenant, I think your suggestions are worthy, but keep checking out all the possibilities," Abu Brion said. "I want the major and that woman found."

Someone screamed in the next room.

The officer looked up. "Sir?"

"Dismissed, lieutenant."

The officer began to speak, but then he turned and left the room.

Abu Brion waited until the door had shut before he closed his eyes and rubbed his brow. Kreus had promised he would have results without difficulty. It seemed the ambassador had more strength and courage than the general expected an effete League diplomat to possess.

He rose from his desk and went into the adjoining room. Kreus had converted the room, which had served as the boardroom, into an impromptu interrogation chamber. Ambassador Stephens was strapped into a large, heavy wooden chair. His head lolled on his chest, and a thin trickle of saliva dribbled from the corner of his lips. His hands were bloodied and mangled. Kreus's own powerful hands had bent back the ambassador's fingers and snapped them like twigs.

The sight of the injuries nauseated Abu Brion. Only with great effort did he control his stomach. Lined up against the opposite wall were the corpses of the rest of the League delegation. Their arms and legs askew, their necks broken, they resembled marionettes whose strings had been cut. Kreus clearly intended them as a warning to Stephens of his own fate if he didn't provide the information the general wanted. But the ambassador had refused to cooperate and had suffered all the torture Kreus could provide.

"I will ask you one more time, Ambassador," Kreus said. "Where is the League starship? Or will I have to break an arm this time?"

Stephens stared blankly at the opposite wall. He failed to respond.

"Your crude methods are getting us nowhere," Abu Brion said. "We still don't know where DuBois is, nor do we know where the League ship is."

Kreus glared at his employer. "My methods have already proven effective with his subordinates, who were less courageous. We know the starship is the *Ferdinand Lasalle*, and she is a *Kautsky*-class vessel, quite large."

"But you don't know where she is."

"I have my suspicions," the general replied. "Give me time, and I will have that information too."

Abu Brion walked in front of the chair where Stephens was strapped. He raised the ambassador's head and looked carefully into the man's vacant eyes. "I'm afraid you won't be getting it from him."

Kreus scowled. "What do you mean?"

"This man is in catatonic shock, probably induced from all that unnecessary pain you caused him." He looked up at one of Kreus's soldiers. "You there, unstrap this man. Take him to the hospital. Have the doctors tend to his injuries and save his fingers, if they can."

The soldier seemed disoriented for a moment, then nervously looked up at Kreus.

Kreus did not speak, but the anger clearly showed on his face. "Do as Don Ernesto says."

The soldier and a companion moved to unstrap Stephens. Abu Brion smiled, then he turned and left the room. Kreus followed on the noble's heels. The general slammed the office door behind them.

"I could have extracted the information," Kreus said.

"No doubt," Abu Brion said. "And what you have obtained is useful." He sat down behind his desk, leaned back in his chair, and carefully folded his hands across his stomach. "But I could have used other, less wasteful ways of getting that information."

There was a knock on the door.

"Come in," Abu Brion said.

A young *dhirek* entered. He carried a large Isaak in his right hand.

Abu Brion smiled broadly. "Reynardo, good to see you." He glanced at Kreus. "Here, General, is a good example of my less wasteful ways of persuasion. Reynardo is a cousin of Don Jaime's, but he is wise enough to know his fortune lies with me."

Kreus arched an eyebrow. "So you were the spy?"

Reynardo nodded.

"Reynardo learned of the League negotiating team and of Captain DuBois. He procured the assassins, and he also made all the arrangements for last night's reception, so we would have no trouble. Don Jaime trusted him implicitly, the fool," Abu Brion said. "Now, what do you have for me?"

"First, we cracked the League legation's computer codes and dumped all the data into our mainframe. You should be able to access it whenever you want. Second, we found these among their files."

He laid the tablet on the desk and opened a series of files. "It's all the communiqués between the legation and the starship *Lasalle* and a rough itinerary for what appears to be a negotiating team. There are also orders dispatching the ship to Tau Ceti."

"Excellent," Abu Brion said. "You see, general, you shouldn't criticize bureaucrats so much. All of your finger-breaking would never have produced this."

Abu Brion used a stylus to go through the messages. Each message bore a time-stamp and date of when it was sent and when it was acknowledged. Abu Brion noticed that there seemed to be a slight time delay between a transmission and acknowledgement of its reception. "This time lag?" he asked. "What have you learned from it?"

"We suspect the message was bounced from a satellite to the ship," Reynardo said. "I ordered a computer check on the transmissions, and we discovered something very interesting."

He removed a small, hand-held *Isaak* notepad from his robes and handed it to Abu Brion.

Abu Brion examined the *Isaac's* display for a moment. "The satellite appears to be orbiting Der Merchant. That means the *Lasalle* is not on its way to Tau Ceti. The orders must have been a ruse so the ship remains here, hiding on the dark side of the outer moon."

"Perhaps we should alert the Iimarae, Don Ernesto, and let them attack the vessel," Reynardo said.

"Yes, a good idea," Kreus said. "Eliminate one threat

now."

"I think not," Abu Brion replied. "I have a better idea. They don't know of our little coup, so let's keep them in the dark. Reynardo, I want you to send them regular messages, properly encoded, letting them know everything is all right."

"Very well."

Kreus opened his mouth to speak, but Abu Brion cut him off.

"I know what you're thinking, general, but we must wait," Abu Brion said. "We don't yet have the nova weapon. When we do, then we shall dispose of the *Lasalle*, and our worrisome little allies as well."

CHAPTER SIXTEEN

Hree'Rchee and her sisters clicked their beaks in delight. *Such exquisite pain*, she thought as she watched the tortures through the eyes of the soldier the elders had commandeered with their control bands. She admired the human Kreus's great skill in producing agony in his victims.

It was unclean to inhabit the human soldier's minds, but the deliciousness of the experience and the taste of the pain-waves coming from the other humans pleased her. It gave her a giddiness she rarely experienced when she excised rebels from the Flock. Each shattered finger, each broken neck carried her to new heights of ecstasy. When Stephens screamed, Hree'Rchee and the sisters swooned, their minds flooded with ecstasy.

The sight of the prostrate elders writhing in pleasure at the humans' pain repelled Ryf'Tael. Hree'Rchee's perversions and those of her sisters sent shivers of cold terror up his bent spine.

Ryf'Tael knew that Hree'Rchee delighted in extirpating *fah'gid'sla* and enjoyed the pain she caused them. She told him as much when she took him to the mating nest in her quarters, forced him to perform for her, then humiliated him. The insults had hurt him more than the injuries to his reproductive organs. He had endured her taunts because he knew that if he responded to her, she would have him killed the next time she performed *ki'ind'rou*. She would have enjoyed it and felt no remorse afterward.

Ryf'Tael had had enough of her and of the other elders this time. He knew that when the elders were in this state of ecstasy, they were vulnerable. He could escape. He went through their belongings and took what he would need. He stuffed it in a bag that he tied around his abdomen. He still didn't know why he had taken the extra bands of obedience stored in the elders' belongings. It was a foolish act because he had no idea how to operate them, but he did not want the elders to have them once their current bands ran out of power. He also knew that if he stayed, his crime would be discovered, and Hree'Rchee would create exquisite tortures for him to suffer and for the sisters to enjoy.

Now was the time to leave, in the night, while the *se'bes'vos* and the two other elders lay asleep. Taking care to avoid being seen, he took a turbo-lift to the roof of the arcology. The spaceport was deserted; not even its landing lights were on. That was a relief to Ryf'Tael. He waddled to the edge of the building.

The warm updrafts carried terrifying odors, of the desert and of the Friedmanville arcology's power plants, up one hundred stories to Ryf'Tael's nostrils. Flight would be difficult but not impossible, even with the bag containing the control bands and a few of his belongings. If he fell to his death, that would be preferable to facing Hree'Rchee again.

He had no idea where he would go, but that was to his advantage. If the *se'bes'vos* did not know where he was, then she would have tremendous difficulty finding him while in *ki'ind'rou*. With luck, he would soon know the secret of the control bands, and when she did find him, he would meet her blow for blow and gain his revenge.

He leaped into the starry night.

Dull aches coursed through much of Jaime's body, especially his legs. It hurt to breathe. The palms of his hands throbbed, probably from when he had thrust them out to catch himself as he fell. Something sharp was jabbing him in the lower back. He rolled over and discovered he had landed on a patch of broken rocks, their pointed edges now digging into his knees and chest.

He got to his knees, and his fingers fumbled for the walking stick he had lost. The gnarled branch was nowhere to be found. Jaime felt the sun's heat on his face and the sting of sand carried by the gusting desert wind. It was now well past dawn, he realized, and Delta Pavonis would soon turn the *Shaul Khala* into a blazing cauldron. He knew he needed shade. Unsteadily, he got to his feet and staggered a short distance. Fortunately, he had not lost his shoes — a small blessing. It would mean he could still walk and not have the rocks tear his feet. He thought he smelled the scent of aromatic plants, a scent he recalled from the previous night, and he realized he had stumbled into a *wadi*. The plants only grew near pools of water, so water had to be nearby.

Caves, he thought, *there might also be caves or bushes, someplace where I can rest until night.* He imagined he could hear the water gurgling nearby. The plant scent seemed stronger. His mouth grew dry. The mere thought of water made him thirsty. Suddenly, the air seemed a bit cooler, as it would if the air was just a little more humid. He dropped to his hands and knees and groped ahead of him. He crawled about madly, his need for water now an obsession.

His hands slipped into the cool, flowing spring. Jaime shouted for joy and plunged his hot burning face into the stream. His pain forgotten, he lifted his head from the spring, cupped his hands, and brought the water to his lips. The water stank and tasted of filth and stagnation, but he could not recall a better, finer drink in all his life.

"You are hurt," a voice said.

Jaime sat up, nearly falling over. "Who is there? Where are you?"

"You cannot see me?" the voice said. It had a strange accent, one Jaime could not place.

"I am blind," he said. The realization that he was sightless now hit him, and he started to weep.

"I will help you. Our dwellings are not far from here."

Jaime felt a hand gently clasp his right wrist. He placed his own hand over it. The fingers of the helping hand were long and thin. He carefully counted the fingers. A chill went through his body. There were seven.

"You're an Ajnabi," he said.

The alien did not reply. He grasped Jaime under his left arm and lifted him to his feet. "Come, we will tend to your wounds, Don Jaime ibn Brentholtz."

"How do you know my name?"

"We know many things," the alien replied. "Let us leave it at that, for now." The Ajnabi lifted Jaime onto his back and carried the injured man across the desert.

CHAPTER SEVENTEEN

A harsh white light flooded Thom's eyes. He covered his face with his hands and blinked until his vision adjusted. The light came from huge flood lamps mounted on a ceiling that was ten meters or more above where he lay. The lamps cut through an atmosphere swirling with steam, smoke and a greasy haze that left oily black deposits on everything.

His head pounded, a side effect of the neural dart. Thom had no idea what neurotoxin the flechette contained, but clearly whoever shot him had not intended to kill him.

Thom sat up and discovered that he was wearing dingy ochre-colored coveralls. Scuffed black rubber boots covered his feet. He sat on a yellowed, thin mattress speckled with small brown stains. The mattress itself lay on a bare metal frame bolted to a thick plasticrete wall. Other bunks like his, stacked in threes, ran the length of the wall and the one opposite. Overhead was a heavy iron grid. Moisture dripped from the grid and pooled on the floor below, where an oily, green scum had formed.

A guard, his heavy boots resounding on the metal, walked along the grid. A helmet and visor covered the guard's face, but it was clear he was looking down into the huge cellblock. Thom recognized the uniform as Tuatha, but with the black and silver skull insignia of Kreus's *Gall Oglaigh* divisions. He could see a strange silver box on the man's belt.

The guard fingered the strap of his seizure rifle with black-gloved fingers. "Time to wake up, you dogs. Second shift is about to start. Don't want any slackers today." The guard turned and started down toward the opposite end of the cell.

All around Thom, the other prisoners began to wake. There was a mixture of groans and yawns as a few men climbed out of their bunks. All the men wore the same soiled ochre coveralls and scuffed, dull black boots as Thom had. Their backs were bent, and they moved slowly, shuffling their feet as they walked. Their eyes remained fixed on the floor. They reminded Thom of some of the concentration camp prisoners he'd seen on Ramal.

His neck hurt. Reaching up to massage it, his fingers touched a leather collar. He tugged on the collar, but it was bound fast. He ran his hands around and felt a small box on one side. A thin cable ran from the box and ended in a cartridge jacked into his mastoid socket. He grabbed the cartridge and tried to pull it out. A searing pain shot through him. He fell back onto the bunk, his arms and legs shaking uncontrollably. The spasm passed after a moment, but it left him gasping for air.

Although his brain was wired to stop pain when interfaced with a matrix, it was clear that the cartridge's software could subvert the wiring and directly stimulate the pain centers.

"Get moving," the guard yelled from above.

Thom looked up and saw that there were now five guards, all with seizure guns slung across their shoulders and with silver boxes on their belts. He slid from his bunk and joined the ranks of the other men.

As they passed through the iron doors at the far end of the cellblock, the men were handed plates of food. Thom's plate contained a slab of some unrecognizable meat that was mostly gristle, a lump of beans of some sort, and a hard wedge of fried bread. All of it swam in congealing grease. The sight of the food made him gag.

"I know it's enough to make you sick," a man next to Thom said, "but you'd better eat it. You'll need it."

The man was of medium height and thin. His face was tanned nut-brown, and almost as dark as Thom's own skin. His black hair and thick beard were peppered with gray. He also wore a collar that was jacked into a mastoid socket, but his dark eyes burned with life, and he did not shuffle like the other prisoners. Even more surprising, the man had spoken to him in Volapük, not Askanderian.

"You know who I am, don't you?" Thom said.

The man nodded.

"How did I get here?"

The man smiled. "In due time, you'll understand. Now keep moving or the guards will get suspicious. My name is Malik abdul ma Haddish."

"Well, Malik, slave of no man, that collar around your neck says otherwise," Thom said. He sat at the end of a long table and began eating. He could feel his gorge rising, but tried to stomach the food as best he could.

Malik sat down beside him. "You don't know where you are, do you?"

"Should I? And why should I listen to you? For all I know, you could be one of Abu Brion's men trying to get information from me."

"These are the mines under Ciudad Rand," Malik said. "We brought you here for your own safety."

"My own safety? You put me in a prison for my own safety?"

Malik grabbed Thom's arm and harshly whispered into his ear. "You damn fool, Abu Brion wants you dead. You represent the League, and the League threatens all he seeks. We had to get you out before he handed you over to General Kreus. The best place to hide you is in a prison, where they'd never think to look for you."

Thom pulled away from the man. "Who the hell are you?"

Malik sighed. "All right, I'm a Mukhalafi operative. I have to keep you alive until we can get you safely off-planet."

Thom was about to reply when the guards walked up to the table. "Breakfast is over, maggots," one guard said. He played with the safety on his seizure gun. "Time for you sons of bitches to go to work."

The men at the tables did not protest. All of them rose as one, whether they had finished their meals or not. They formed into two lines and trudged through a long corridor where guards distributed helmets, gas masks, picks and shovels.

When Thom reached the distribution point, the heavy-set balding guard eyed him suspiciously. "I haven't seen you before. Where's your chit?"

Thom's eyes widened. "I don't have one."

"He's new," Malik said, this time in Askanderian. He clasped Thom's shoulder. "Look in your left pocket. It's a silver disk about half the size of your palm."

Thom reached into the pocket, found the disk, and handed it to the guard. The man put the chit into a scanner, glanced at the readout, then handed Thom a helmet, mask and shovel. "Now get out of here, Joachim abu Salaam."

Thom walked on past the man. Slinging the respirator around his neck, he jammed the helmet on his head and kept his eyes on the ground. He'd already drawn too much attention to himself as it was.

Ahead he could see a line of men and women coming in the opposite direction. Their faces were covered in grime — thick, dark dust caked on with sweat and grease. Empty eyes stared out from behind the masks of dirt.

"Always remember that disk and remember your name is Joachim abu Salaam," Malik said, coming up behind Thom. "When we get off shift, and you give them back the helmet and tools, then you'll get the disk back."

"How long have I been here?" Thom asked.

"Three days. We took you down the turbo-lift and kept you hidden until we were sure we could get you into the mines."

"Did you shoot me with that flechette?"

Malik shook his head. "No, that was another agent. She's dead. That's all I know."

"I see."

They continued on toward the corridor until they came to a series of large freight lifts. The lifts rose from the depths and disgorged members of the first shift. Second shift workers crowded onto the empty elevators, which then descended into the mines.

Thom and Malik muscled their way onto a lift. As

it dropped, the lift's cables groaned and creaked. The lift itself swung unsteadily from side to side, occasionally bumping into the walls of the shaft. The collisions sent shudders through the elevator cage.

Thom's stomach grew queasy, and he could feel his breakfast churning in his stomach. The air in the shaft was stale and rank with odors of dust, urine, and perspiration. He could taste metal on his tongue.

The cage shuddered to a halt. The men slowly exited the lift, pulling on respirators and helmets as they did. The beams from their helmet lights cut thin shafts in the darkness of the tunnels.

"I've never mined before," Thom said. "What am I supposed to do?"

Malik laughed. "Don't worry, that cartridge plugged into your head will tell you everything you'll ever need to know. You'll be hewing the seams like an old-timer even before you lift that pick."

The news failed to comfort Thom as he pulled on his respirator and helmet. He knew his muscles were not attuned to the repetitious work required. He suspected few of the prisoners were in good enough shape to do the work. More than likely the guards drove the prisoners until they dropped dead, then they pulled another nameless body from the *souk* or from the jails and flung him down into the mines.

The men climbed aboard a portal bus — a small, long,

low-slung train. The portal bus's armored roof protected the men from cave-ins, but also provided minimal head-room, forcing each miner to hunch over, his face only inches from his knees. The ride was rough as well. Every joint in the track struck the car like a hard punch. Thom could feel the blows slam into the base of his spine.

An automated ore carrier rolled past them. Slabs of rock as thick as a man's chest filled the carrier's train of cars. In the yellowish half-light illuminating the tunnel, the ore looked silvery or even golden at times.

"What are we mining?" Thom said in Volapük, his voice muffled by the respirator.

"Rare earths mostly, some palladium, high-grade uranium, even some precious metals like gold and plati-num," Malik said. He lifted his mask slightly. "There's a theory that centuries ago an asteroid several kilometers across crashed into the mountains, hit a stress fracture, and produced a volcano. That volcano, after it became extinct and weathered away, became Treason's Tooth. The asteroid remained buried and that's what we're dig-ging into for the most part. Some of the magma from the rift probably carried up the majority of the rare earths from the planet's core."

"I see," Thom said.

"Expensive stuff, most of it," Malik said. "It's how Don Jaime paid his bills, until Abu Brion foreclosed."

They rode on farther, passing a wall of stone about

three meters high. A pile of broken rock lay at the foot of the wall. Men pushed huge drills into the ore face, causing slabs of rock to shear away from the wall. Immense machines gnawed away at the material, carrying it by conveyor belt to an additional group of men with picks and shovels who hacked away at the broken rock and dumped it into the carts of another ore carrier. Huge hydraulic jacks held up the ceiling above the men. Armed guards supervised the entire operation.

"Long wall method," the cartridge told Thom. "Derived originally from coal mining on Earth, but adaptable for other ores."

The portal bus slowed to a halt.

"Our stop," Malik said.

The men got out, stretched briefly, and rubbed stiff legs and arms. The sight of the guards made them resume their stilted gaits. They were in a large chamber with a ceiling perhaps two meters high. Thick columns of black ore acted as roof supports, which the men worked around. The chamber was illuminated only by a few portable lights and by the thin beams of the miners' helmet lamps.

"Room-and-pillar method," the cartridge said. "When finished, the columns will be removed, and the roof allowed to collapse." Thom found the information far from reassuring.

The men moved to the rock face under the watchful

eyes of the guards. A small, motorized cart drove past. On it were the emaciated bodies of three miners. Their open eyes, red and irritated, stared blankly at the ceiling from behind masks of rock dust.

Malik grabbed Thom by the elbow. "Just get to work; they're beyond help now," he said.

"I didn't know about this," Thom's voice quavered. "In the League planets, we use drones."

"Men are cheap and expendable here, my friend," Malik explained, "especially if you want to keep profits high, as the Hand dictates."

They reached the working face.

"Dig, you scum," a guard said.

Thom raised his pick and began hacking away at the ore. Mercifully, his mind went black, and he became just another machine. He raised his arms overhead, the pick dropped, and rock danced away from the working face. Thom barely recalled the buzzer ending the shift, the long ride back, the cold shower, and the cold food. He remembered climbing into his bunk, his body racked with pain. He stared into the lights, the lights that were never extinguished, before exhaustion overcame him. He slept, but not well.

By the third day, Thom's arms no longer ached, and

he found he could swing the pick reasonably well. He also learned the cartridge contained a driver program which forced men to work beyond normal endurance.

"It switches off the normal drives: hunger, thirst, urination," Malik explained as they rode the portal bus down to the working face. "And it switches on endorphin production so you don't feel any pain until after your shift."

Thom remembered the dead men he'd seen on the first day. He'd seen more since then.

The portal bus stopped, and they climbed out. Two guards approached them.

"You two, come with me," one guard said curtly. A throat mike amplified his voice.

Thom felt his heart skip a beat. He had the urge to run, but that would be futile.

"What do you need of us, *sidi*?" Malik asked.

The guard's hand went to the box on his belt. "Don't ask questions, dog, or I'll make you pay."

Malik lowered his head. "My apologies, *sidi*. We will come." He glanced over at Thom and winked.

The guard's hand dropped from the box. "Good."

A third guard drove up in a small electric cart. The guard gestured with his seizure rifle, indicating Thom and Malik should get on.

The two men climbed into the vehicle and sat on a bare metal bench. The guard sat across from them, his back to the driver. He signaled the driver to go. The cart started up with a sudden jerk.

The guard kept his weapon leveled at Thom and Malik as the cart rolled past the other miners and went down a long, dimly lit tunnel. Thom's head began to pound. He lowered his head, supporting it with his hands. His gaze fell on the floor of the cart and, with a shock, he saw it was filled with boxes of explosives and detonators. A large rock drill and heavy bit lay next to the boxes.

They were being commandeered to fire shots: to drill holes in a new rock face, place explosives in the holes, and then blast the rock, shattering it and making it easier to mine. It was also the most dangerous job in mining, especially if any combustible gases or dust were in the tunnel when they detonated the charges. He felt like a prisoner on his way to execution.

The cart turned down another tunnel and drove on for some distance. It finally came to a stop in a brightly lit area several hundred meters down the tracks. At the end of the tunnel, a small group of prisoners sprayed the walls with a fine yellow dust. "Powdered limestone," the cartridge told Thom, "to reduce the likelihood of explosions or fires."

"Get out," the guard ordered.

Thom and Malik climbed over the sides of the cart.

"Take out the explosives." The guard gestured with the barrel of his gun.

Thom climbed back into the cart and began handing boxes to Malik. The other prisoners left off spraying the walls and came over to help. Thom handed the last box to a man covered in yellow dust and climbed over the side of the cart. He watched the guard talk with the trooper supervising the other prisoners. After a moment, the trooper nodded then barked an order at his charges.

The prisoners gathered up their tools and climbed onto several other carts. The carts started, their electric engines shrieking, as they drove away.

"You take the drill," the guard snapped at Thom. He turned to Malik. "You prepare the charges."

Thom picked up the drill. It was heavy and had a shoulder harness. He struggled into the harness and placed the tip of the bit against the rock. His fingers curled around the control grips and squeezed the trigger. The drill roared into life, the bit shrieking as it bore into the rock. The cartridge told Thom how far to move the drill to make the hole for the charge. He pushed himself against the motor housing to ease the pressure. Its vibrations shook his body.

Thom drilled six holes before the cartridge told him to stop. His hands and forearms still trembled as he handed the drill to Malik. Grateful for the relief, Thom sat down and began placing detonators into long metal tubes filled with a *plastic* explosive. The charges were crude, designed just to shatter the rock rather than break it along cleavage lines.

Malik finished drilling his half-dozen holes. The two men then began pushing the charges into the holes using a long, thin metal rod. The *plastic* would not explode without a detonator, but Thom felt uneasy as they tamped each charge down. There was a thin haze swirling about them, a haze that was not the yellow of the limestone.

"There's an awful lot of dust in here," Thom said.

"Yes, I know," Malik replied, "but there's little we can do except hope that nothing happens."

"No talking," the guard shouted.

After Thom and Malik finished placing each charge, they ran the wires down the length of the tunnel to a small cut in the mine wall where they would be protected from the blast. The cartridge told Thom how to splice the wires and how to connect them to the detonator box.

The three men huddled in the cut. Thom's hand hesitated on the control switch. He could see the dust rolling toward them.

"What are you waiting for?" the guard demanded.

"There's too much dust and gas," Thom said. "It might be dangerous."

The guard's hand went to the box on his belt. Thom grabbed his head and screamed. The pain forced him to the ground, and searing fire spread through his limbs.

He tried to breathe, but it felt as if a vise were crushing his chest. The pain passed after a moment, and Malik helped him sit up.

The guard reached for the detonator.

"No," Thom tried to shout, but all he managed was a strangled cry.

The guard punched the trigger. The charges exploded, and so did the dust and gas. The walls trembled, and the ceiling collapsed with a horrible, deafening roar.

CHAPTER EIGHTEEN

Ryf'Tael saw the first glimmerings of dawn form on the horizon ahead of him, and he knew he would have to find shelter from the heat. Three days he had flown, and he despaired of finding any other intelligent being.

He wondered why had he been such a fool to run away from the *se'bes'vos*? He was free, yet he felt lost and confused, and he knew he could never go back again. The elders would tear him to shreds with their beaks and torture his mind with agonies he could not imagine. His stomach growled, and he knew he would have to fill it again with the bitterly unpalatable flesh of the desert creatures.

Ryf'Tael spotted a dry riverbed and began to descend. He hoped he could find shade and water there, and perhaps, instead of meat, he could discover some fruit or seeds he could digest without bringing them back up again within an hour. As he descended, however, he sensed a horrible presence in his mind.

"So my little one," Hree'Rchee said, "you thought you could escape me. Did my lusts scare you, disgusting little unclean thing?"

Ryf'Tael did not know how she had found him, but he knew he could not fight her. If he were on the ground, he could reach one of the power bands and he might be able to resist, but in flight he was helpless.

"I see you are afraid of me," Hree'Rchee's voice said, echoing in his skull. "As well you should be. Don't worry, I won't dispose of you like some *fah'gid'sla*. I have better plans for you."

Ryf'Tael felt something cold in his mind. He forgot how to fly and, with a shriek of terror he tumbled, cartwheeling, from the sky. Hree'Rchee's laughter echoed in his skull as the ground raced up to meet him.

Jaime awoke in a cold sweat. He had been dreaming, only what he dreamt was not illusion. Once more he had relived the guards pinning his arms behind him and forcing him to watch helplessly as Kreus fired the laser into his eyes. The dream always ended with a brilliant flash of white light, then darkness and pain. He tried to sit up, but a hand gently forced him to lie back down.

"Your dream was bad, was it not?" the Ajnabi said.

"Yes, it was," Jaime replied. His body still ached from the injuries he received from his fall. His back throbbed, as did his swollen left ankle.

"Your blinding?"

Jaime nodded. He tried to recall which of the Ajnabi was speaking to him. He knew of five different individuals so far, but the similarity of the aliens' speech patterns and accents made telling them apart difficult. "Which one are you?"

"You may call me Fadyli," the Ajnabi said. "That is the closest word in your language."

He hadn't met this Ajnabi before and, judging by the name, it was perhaps female. He still could not tell by the voice alone. "Where are Hakyka, Ishan and the others?"

"They are tending their fields, searching for food," Fadyli replied. "Here, drink this. It will help heal your wounds." The Ajnabi helped Jaime up to a sitting position.

Jaime felt the edge of a cup against his lips. He grasped the alien's hand to steady the cup and drank the liquid. It had a creamy texture and tasted of nuts and herbs. Almost immediately a sensation of calmness and relaxation came over him, but it did not impair his consciousness.

"Who are you, Fadyli?" he inquired. "You're not from this *wadi*, are you?"

"I am a healer, from three *wadi* over," Fadyli said. "Now you must lie down while I run some tests on you."

"Tests?"

"They are harmless."

Jaime heard a strange humming sound, then a series of beeps. He detected a faint scent of ozone. Then, he sensed Fadyli passing something over his body. His limbs tingled. "What are you doing?"

"I am passing a medical analyzer over you. I had to adjust it for humans."

Jaime didn't know the Ajnabi had such advanced technology. "How do you know what is healthy for a human?"

"The nomads trade with us. They allow us to study them so we can provide healing."

The tingling in Jaime's arms and legs stopped.

"Your body is healing well, and I have medication which should help it," Fadyli informed him. "Your ankle is not broken, but there is much bruising and swelling. Now, please stay still."

Jaime felt something being placed over his eyes. His face flushed. He felt a sensation like a thin, cold, yet otherwise painless needle entering his eyes. He sensed Fadyli leaning over him. The alien's breath was sweet and dry.

The Ajnabi clucked its tongue. The sensors, or whatever they were, retracted from Jaime's eyes. Fadyli removed the device from Jaime's face.

"Your optic nerves are severely scarred," the alien said.

"Can you treat it?"

"I am sorry, I cannot," Fadyli said. "The injuries make it impossible to regenerate the nerves, nor do I have the instruments, even if it were possible."

Jaime's heart fell. "Is there nothing you can do?"

"Nothing. I am sorry."

Still desperate for reassurance, Jaime started to speak when he heard a commotion outside the entrance to the cavern. He cocked his head to hear better. "What's happening?"

"I do not know," Fadyli replied.

"Healer," another Ajnabi called, "We have found a creature. It is badly hurt."

Listening to its footsteps, Jaime sensed an Ajnabi named Ishan come near him. He also heard another Ajnabi with Ishan, whom Jaime guessed was Hakyka. From the grunts they made, the aliens seemed to be struggling with their bundle. A third alien noisily dropped a bag at Jaime's side.

The Ajnabi talked excitedly among themselves. Their language was thick and guttural, interspersed with tongue clucking and sporadic whistles and grumblings. Jaime had learned that the sounds carried additional emotional meanings. From what he could tell, the Ajnabi were both concerned and disturbed by the injured creature.

The creature made a low moan, but to Jaime's ears it was a moan that was distinctly non-human. Jaime also detected a strong, unfamiliar odor from the animal.

"What is it?" Jaime asked.

"A strange creature," Fadyli replied.

"It fell from the sky, suddenly," said another Ajnabi, whom Jaime recognized as Ishan.

"It has wings and a beak, like a bird," Hakyka said. "But it is quite large, and it wears strange robes."

"By the Hand!" Jaime said. "It is an Iimarae. We must kill it."

The Iimarae groaned again.

"There is no need," Fadyli said softly, but firmly. "It is dying. There are massive injuries: a fractured spine, a broken wing."

"Then let it die," Jaime said angrily.

"It is a living being," Fadyli admonished him. "Its life is sacred, just as yours is. I must try to save it."

The Ajnabi's words chastened Jaime and made him feel incredibly small. He swallowed hard, then licked his dry lips, which only made him thirsty. Sitting up, he reached for the water bottle the Ajnabi always left filled by his bed. However, instead of the bottle, his hands touched the bag the Ajnabi had brought in with the Iimarae.

His fingers touched something cold and metallic protruding from the bag. He felt sudden sensations of color and smell and a fleeting impression of flight. Startled, he pulled back his hand, but just for a moment. Curiosity had the better of him.

Jaime removed the object from the bag and ran his hands over it. As far as he could tell, it was a circlet of some sort with a large, bulbous formation at one end. It reminded him of a crown. Small raised nodules pimpled the inside of the object. Jaime sensed color and diffuse light as his fingertips touched the knobs, as if his sight were returning. He wondered what he would experience if he put it on. He slid the band over his forehead, feeling the nodules press against his skin.

Flashes of light and color boiled into his head, momentarily disorienting him. An agonizing pain shot through him. He fell back on his pallet, unable to breathe, his hands fumbling to remove the band.

Then, quite suddenly and clearly, he saw the faces of three Ajnabi looking down at him. One of them, probably Fadyli, passed an object over his body. Jaime sensed pain in his back and legs and one arm, and knew the bones were broken. He tasted blood on his tongue. He tried to turn his head, but the pain was too intense. Fear filled his mind, but it was a detached fear, someone else's fear. He had a memory of falling, tumbling through the night sky. Jaime wanted to speak, but all he could manage was a strangled groan and the faint clucking of a chitinous bill.

Jaime gasped. He pulled the band from his head and welcomed the darkness. His hands shook, and a cold sweat drenched him. He took a deep breath and tried to calm himself.

He realized the band had somehow placed him inside the Iimarae's mind, had sensed the alien's agonies and terrors. The fear he tasted disturbed him. Something had frightened the Iimarae: something that caused it to plunge to earth. It was something Jaime knew he had to understand. If the Iimarae had any fears, they might prove an effective weapon against the aliens. The band offered him a chance to be useful again, and he welcomed it.

Jaime licked his lips, dry with nervousness and fear of his own. He brought the band up to his forehead and slowly put it on. He braced himself.

The world spun with color — indigo, orange, burgundy, gold, crimson — and flashed with creamy white light. Jaime saw himself stepping over the edge of the cliff. He felt the wind race past his face, sensed his body somersaulting, diving uncontrollably through space. His arms had become wings, flapping impotently. Jaime forced himself to spread his wings. The wind tore at him, but his wings caught. He felt an updraft lifting him slightly and became filled with an incredible joy as he flew, gliding smoothly, floating. His descent slowed. The ground came up to meet him, and he stretched out his claws to land. The impact was heavy. Pain stabbed his legs, but he came to a safe, sure halt. The landscape dissolved in a swirling maelstrom of bright colors.

"Who are you?" a voice said. It was a voice that spoke not in words, but in images and concepts. There was a red hue to many of the images, the bright crimson of intense pain.

Jaime let thoughts form in his own mind. "I am Jaime ibn Brentholtz. Who are you?"

"My name is Ryf'Tael, mediator for the *se'bes'vos* Hree'Rchee."

"You are Iimarae," Jaime said.

"That — is my misfortune."

"Your misfortune?"

"It was Hree'Rchee who tried to kill me. I ran away from her."

"Why did you run from her?"

"Because I hated her. I wanted to kill her, but I feared her, and I could not do it."

A red explosion of pain spun across the maelstrom. Jaime knew the Iimarae's agony had increased. "Why are you here?"

"The Flock needs to grow. Resources are few, we are so many."

"Why did your race come to Askander?"

"We sought allies among humans."

"Did you find such allies?"

"We found many, but just one great ally."

Jaime had little difficulty guessing who that ally was. His anger flew off as bursts of blackness. "Your ally, it was Ernesto Abu Brion?" Jaime sensed astonishment and renewed fear from the alien.

"Yes, but how could you know? Of course, you are the enemy he wished to destroy."

"He has destroyed me. He has robbed me of all my wealth and left me blind."

"Then all is lost."

Jaime sensed grief from the alien, and the emotion genuinely puzzled him. "Why do you grieve, Ryf'Tael?"

"Abu Brion and my *se'bes'vos* both enjoy cruelty. Now they can inflict pain on many creatures."

"What do you mean?"

"There is a weapon which can make stars go nova, and Abu Brion knows where it is. With it they would destroy the home star of Earth."

Jaime was stunned. With such a weapon, Abu Brion could consolidate his power over Askander and then threaten the very heart of the Planetary League. Then he remembered the warning Thom and Siobhan had said the Ajnabi gave them of evil in the mines.

"This weapon, do you know where it is?"

"No. Only Abu Brion knew. He would not tell me."

May the Hand damn the man, Jaime thought. He began to doubt that the Hand had any power at all. He had relied on the Hand, and It had allowed Abu Brion to usurp him. The Hand clearly favored the victor, and that was only after the fact, when there was need to say the victim's demise was foreordained. The Hand willed it, so it is so. *Perhaps the Mukhalafi were right all along and the only Hand is human, Jaime thought.*

"One more question, Ryf'Tael."

"Please, no, I am too weak."

"The band. What is it for?"

"To purge Flock, end rebellion, and maintain purity of race. Cannot hold on . . . must release . . . end pain."

"No, Ryf'Tael. Don't go. Hold on."

The maelstrom of thought vanished. Everything turned black and empty. Jaime was alone.

He knew the Iimarae had died, died in pain and despair, believing it had failed. Grief flowed over Jaime.

"You weep for the loss of the creature?" an Ajnabi asked.

Long fingers gently stroked his head and removed the band. "You shared his mind?" Fadyli said.

Jaime nodded. He sobbed softly.

"You understand, now, why we say all life is sacred," Ishan said.

"Yes." Jaime wiped the tears from his face, but he could not stop his sobbing. He took a deep breath to calm himself. "The band. You know what it does, then?"

"Yes, we know," said Fadyli. "They were made by the beings you call the Gonaymne, the Nameless Ones. They used them to enslave and control us, to punish us."

"You were slaves of the Nameless Ones?" Jaime said in wonder.

"Yes," Ishan said. "Or rather our ancestors were. They were the crew of a slave ship. They revolted against their masters and crashed the ship on this planet."

Jaime wanted to ask about the control bands, then he realized with horror that the miners of Ciudad Rand understood the principle quite well. "The Iimarae," he managed to say, "are they the Nameless Ones?"

"No," Ishan said. "The Iimarae must have discovered a Gonaymne vessel centuries ago and learned how to use these devices."

If the Ajnabi had revolted and taken over a ship, a ship with weapons, then it had to be the evil in the mine, Jaime thought. If the Iimarae had found another ship, or several others, perhaps they had learned of the weapon. A chill ran down his spine. "The Iimarae know a Gonaymne vessel crashed on Askander, and they know it possesses a weapon to destroy stars."

"You learned this from the alien?" Hakyka said.

"Yes."

"Do they know where it is?" Ishan said.

"No, but Abu Brion does, and he now controls Ciudad Rand and its mines."

The Ajnabi began an animated, worried conversation, full of rapid tongue clucking and harsh guttural grunts. Jaime strained to listen. Although he failed to understand any of the words, the meaning of the conversation was obvious.

"We must stop this Abu Brion," Fadyli said to him. "Or we are all endangered."

Jaime knew there were ways to defeat Abu Brion, and he quickly considered all the alternatives he could think of. Finally, he knew there was only one. "You must take me to the Mukhalafi."

CHAPTER NINETEEN

The choking cloud of dust swirled madly and settled only very slowly. Thom's respirator had partially clogged, and he could taste metallic dust with each breath, but he was alive.

The guard was less lucky. Thom's helmet lamp revealed the guard's still, unmoving form crushed under a large boulder. The man's stiff finger remained on the firing button.

Malik groaned. Thom turned toward his friend, and saw that Malik's legs were pinned under another large rock. The blast had knocked off his helmet and respirator. Blood trickled from a large wound on the side of his head, cutting a scarlet stream in the gray dust covering his face. Thom realized that Malik had shielded him from the blast and had borne the brunt of the explosion himself.

"Malik, can you hear me?"

Malik's eyes fluttered. "Thom," he said, smiling. A coughing fit wracked his body. "How am I?"

"Not good," Thom said. "Your legs are pinned under a boulder. I don't think I can move it."

"Internal bleeding, I think," Malik said, gasping for air. Another coughing fit brought up blood and mucus. "Well, I've had it. You'll have to find a way to get out yourself."

"I'm not going to leave you," Thom said. "I need your help."

Malik shook his head. "No, too late for me. In my pocket. You'll find all you need."

Thom undid the single pocket on the breast of Malik's coveralls. He removed a small metal box. "A databug?"

Malik nodded.

Thom stared at the box in the palm of his hand. "But I can't use it. I've still got the collar and cartridge on."

Malik did not reply. His eyes stared vacantly at the ceiling of the tunnel.

Thom lowered the man's head, then gently closed Malik's eyes. He felt very alone. He put the container into his own pocket. Gritting his teeth, Thom grabbed the punishment collar, wanting to rip it off. He hesitated, remembering the pain.

He stared at the dead guard and had an idea. Struggling to his feet, Thom threw himself against the boulder that pinned the trooper. He grunted and strained against the rock, and it finally tipped over. Turning the guard's body over, he unfastened the web belt at the man's waist. Once the box was in his hands, he carefully examined the controls. He knew it had to have a mechanism to release the collar or to at least turn off the cartridge. He ran his finger down the various control buttons, trying to read the nearly worn-off letters of Tuatha script. Then he spotted it: a small red button near the bottom.

Thom punched it and the collar latch popped open. He tore the offending band from his neck and pulled the cartridge from his socket, flinging it against the tunnel wall. His fingers massaged his neck as if he had been enslaved for centuries and not just days. He took in deep gulps of air and, although it tasted metallic, he thought it was the sweetest air he had ever breathed.

A shaft of intensely bright pale blue light sliced through the dust in the tunnel. The light appeared to come from behind the rock face they had just blasted.

Thom crawled over the guard's body and over the broken rock into the tunnel. He looked across the landscape of shattered stones and saw a huge, jagged hole in the rock at the tunnel's end. The intense blue light, like a search lamp cutting through the night, poured from the opening. The crack was barely taller than a human, just over two meters high, but it was wide enough for him to pass through without difficulty. As he stood staring at the light, Thom remembered what the Ajnabi had said.

There was great danger in the mine. He knew it was foolhardy to go into the crack, but his curiosity overcame him and he knew he couldn't go back.

Carefully, he climbed into the opening. It was wider than he first thought, and he discovered that he could slip through sideways with ease. The opening went on for just a short distance before emptying into a huge chamber. What he saw staggered his senses.

A huge starship, bigger than anything he had ever seen, towered above him. He could not see the entire length of the vessel, but he estimated it was at least a kilometer long. The long, cylindrical hull was silvery-gray in color. Large, gold-colored egg shapes bulged like tumors at various points on the hull and strange, spindly tree-like forms erupted at irregular intervals on the surface. Running lights were spaced along the vessel and illuminated the chamber. Thom saw that the sides of the cavern were smooth, like polished pearl. He remembered Malik's comments about an asteroid striking Askander. *It wasn't an asteroid*, Thom realized, *it was this ship!*

Somehow it had crashed into the planet and unleashed the magma that had formed Treason's Tooth. The force field had protected the vessel from the molten material, which had cooled around it, trapping it.

He climbed down the short distance from the opening to the floor of the chamber. Except for the opening where some shattered rocks lay, the ground was as smooth as glass. He reached what appeared to be an open hatchway at about floor level. The position of the portal suggested that the ship had, at some point, tipped over slightly on its side.

The blue light, now intensely harsh, originated from the portal. Thom moved cautiously toward the hatch and then stopped. The light seemed to come from around the hatch frame and not from behind it. He backed away from the vessel, retracing his steps. He picked up a loose rock from the pile near the entrance and tossed it toward the ship. The stone disappeared in a flash of white brilliance as it entered the hatch.

Well, Thom thought, *they don't seem to want visitors.*

With that in mind, he edged slowly toward the vessel. Keeping an eye on the hatch, in case the ship had other weapons, he reached out and touched the hull. The material was cold, but not cold enough to injure him. He could see some writing on the hull, a peculiar script he vaguely recognized. It was all curlicues and hieroglyphs and irregular shapes inside rhomboids of varying shapes and lengths. Then he remembered where he had seen the script before. The realization filled him with cold dread.

He had seen the writing before, in a museum on Formalhaut Four. The Formalhaut artifact was small, about the length of a human forearm. None of the archaeologists knew what it was, but they all agreed on its origin.

"The Gonaymne," Thom gasped. He stepped slowly away from the vessel, but his eyes remained fixed on it. The ship loomed over him.

Wherever humanity had gone, they had found the vestiges of previous civilizations, always wiped out by some cataclysm. They had always found the calling card of another race, a race that apparently ruthlessly slaughtered its enemies. The Tuatha had first found evidence of the aliens on Alba Nuadh. They called the aliens the Gonaymne, the Nameless Ones, and both admired and feared the beings' immense powers. The mere mention of their name struck terror in the hearts of adults. Everyone, including the Iimarae, thought the Gonaymne were long extinct. Everyone was clearly wrong.

Although it crashed perhaps millennia before, the Gonaymne vessel in front of Thom had clearly awakened. The aliens were now something more than just a name and a legacy of destruction. Thom now knew why Abu Brion had wanted to takeover Ciudad Rand, why he had employed Kreus. It was also now clear who had been negotiating with the Iimarae. If humanity were to stop the aliens, Thom had to find out more about the ship.

Thom walked around to the other side of the ship and saw an arm and hand. It stuck out from under the hull just near the hatch. The creature to whom it belonged had clearly fallen under the ship and been crushed, and

Thom had the unnerving sensation that the ship had deliberately tipped itself over to kill the being. In the airless environment of the chamber, the hand had decayed little, but had dried out and mummified. The fingers curled inward toward the palm. They were long and slender, and Thom counted seven of them. The creature was Ajnabi.

Were the Ajnabi the Gonaymne? Thom wondered. It seemed impossible. Siobhan had said the Ajnabi kept to themselves and lived along the *wadi*. The one he had seen appeared peaceful and gentle, not at all as war-like as the Gonaymne.

Yet he thought for a moment and recalled the other native fauna he had seen. All of them had six limbs, except the Ajnabi, who were bipedal like humans. That could mean just one thing: the Ajnabi were not native to the planet. They were as alien to Askander as humans were, as alien as the Gonaymne.

Now there was much to learn about the ship and precious little time in which to learn it. He didn't know how long he had before the other guards would worry about their comrade and come to find him. He suspected the supervisors knew that a message on the progress of the blasting was well past due.

Thom clambered back up the broken rocks, squeezed through the crack, and traversed the obstacle course formed by the debris. He headed straight for the dead guard. As he removed the seizure gun from the man's body, Thom noticed that the guard was roughly his height and build. Quickly he removed his coveralls and stripped the uniform from the guard. The fit was a little loose, but he strapped on the webbed belt and put on the helmet and visor and tightened the chin strap.

Getting the dead guard into the prisoner's uniform proved more difficult. It took considerable effort to force the heavy, stiffening limbs into the legs and sleeves. When he was done, Thom pulled a respirator over the man's face, took the metal container from his coverall pocket, and rolled the guard onto his stomach. He found the punishment collar next to Malik's body. Placing the collar around the guard's neck, he snapped the lock shut and jacked the cartridge into the man's socket.

He stepped back into the mine shaft, the seizure gun in his hands. The light from the opening revealed a number of cracks, like spider webs, in the tunnel ceiling. Thom raised the rifle to his shoulder. A small red light indicated that his weapon was working. He aimed for a particularly large crack and fired.

A shower of debris fell from the ceiling, but not enough to seal the tunnel. He moved his aim to another area and fired. More ceiling collapsed, but again too little to close the shaft off.

Thom took a deep breath and scanned the ceiling for further cracks. The largest fissures were directly over his head, and if he brought that part of the roof down, he would bury Malik's body.

"Forgive me, Malik," he said as he raised the seizure gun and fired.

The roof groaned. For a moment Thom feared that the ceiling would fall on him. It collapsed with a thunderous crash, and a cloud of dust boiled from the tunnel, but no light appeared from the shaft.

Thom sighed with relief.

A voice suddenly resounded in his ears. "Og Flynn, what's wrong?" the voice said in thickly accented Tuatha. "Why haven't you reported in? What's all that racket?"

Thom swallowed. "Og Flynn here," he said in Tuatha, "we've had a major disaster. We set off the charges, but there was gas in the shaft. It brought the roof down. I have two prisoners trapped inside."

"You stay put. I'll send some men to help you. Are you hurt?"

"Negative," he said, "just some cuts and bruises. But the prisoners . . ."

"To hell with the prisoners. There's plenty more of them. I just hate having to dig the maggots out."

A pair of electric carts arrived five minutes later. An officer, his face hidden by a respirator, stepped off the lead cart. He raised his hand to signal a guard. The guard gestured with the barrel of his seizure gun and barked an order. Prisoners carrying shovels climbed from the carts and began digging into the debris.

The officer walked over to Thom. He felt a cold sweat pour down his neck.

"Og Flynn, is it?" the officer said. He looked Thom up and down. "God, man, you look terrible. Are you sure all you have is cuts and bruises?"

"I think so," Thom said, glad that his respirator muffled his voice.

"Well, I don't agree," the officer replied. "There's blood all over your uniform. Now get on that cart and go to the infirmary."

"Thank you, sir," Thom said quickly. He climbed onto the cart. The driver started up, turned the cart around, and headed back down the mine shaft. After a short ride, the cart stopped before a bank of turbo-lifts. "You lucky bastard," the driver said. "You'll get at least three days in bed with nothing to do before they send you back here."

"I'd rather not be in bed just now," Thom said as he stepped from the cart.

"Then you're a damn fool," the trooper said. He drove off.

Thom walked up to the turbo-lift. It was empty, and no one appeared to be guarding it. He stepped aboard, reached into his pocket, and took out the metal container. He removed the databug and jacked it in. The software gave him a number, and he pushed the corresponding buttons on the lift controls. The doors closed, and the lift rose smoothly and swiftly. Just as smoothly, it came to a stop.

The doors opened, and Thom walked out into a steaming jungle of pipes, wires and cables. Thick, clotted plants of yellow and brown wrapped themselves around the pipes and cables, feeding on the minerals in the dampness that clung to everything. Thom was grateful that his respirator filtered out the odors of the place, odors he knew were both unpleasant and overpowering.

Thom raised the visor of his helmet. He saw figures moving in the distance and felt eyes boiling with hate fixed on him. He realized that it wasn't a safe place to be, especially not for someone in a Tuatha uniform. The seizure gun comforted him, despite his hatred for its effects.

A map crystallized in his awareness as he walked forward. The databug told him the place was called the *Jura*, the Pit. It was the dark underbelly of Ciudad Rand. The Jura's residents lived lives of desperation. They stole and killed to survive. He would have to be careful.

The databug gave him directions to a dwelling, a safe house whose occupants would help him escape. It wasn't far from where he stood. Thom moved ahead slowly, his finger on the seizure gun trigger. He could see he was on one of a series of plasticrete walkways that connected blocks of dark, rundown dwellings. Between the dwellings were huge pipes, which he guessed were probably used for sewage and for drinking water. Below him were the refuse processing areas and huge water reservoirs that served the rest of the arcology.

He could see a few people dressed in rags. They were picking their way through a huge mound of garbage near a refuse processor. An automated skip loader dug into the pile and carried the refuse to a large aperture in the floor. The machine dumped its dripping load into the yawning mouth of the processor, then went back for another shipment, ignoring the people who swarmed over the garbage like flies.

The databug told him the dwelling he sought was in the next block. He approached it cautiously. The main door of the structure had long since vanished. Dark brown water stains ran down the face of the gray plasticrete walls. The stains mixed with a rainbow of graffiti.

Thom stepped inside. By the few lights that were on, Thom could see water and some liquid chemical pooling on the floor. A dead rat floated on the black, scummy surface. He stepped around the pond and walked toward the elevators. Cables and pipes hung from the ceiling, dripping water condensed from the upper floors of Ciudad Rand.

He reached the elevators. Graffiti covered the doors

of one elevator. The other had no doors, so amateur art-
ists had covered the inside of the car. Thom guessed the
lifts hadn't operated for years. He looked for the stairs,
and as he pushed opened a door, he heard a noise behind
him. He turned, dropped to one knee, and brought the
seizure rifle to his shoulder.

An elderly woman in an old, faded blue *rupush* eyed
him wearily. She carried a woven, reed basket of groceries on her head, cushioned by her thick, black turban.
Her dark brown eyes were filled with hate for him and
for the uniform he was wearing.

Thom lowered the rifle. *"Istar'far,"* he said, apologizing.

She pursed her lips and spat at his feet. "Tuatha filth,"
she said. She pushed past him before going through the
door and up the stairs.

He waited a moment, then went up the stairs after
her. The room he sought was on the fourth floor. The
floor itself was as ravaged as the first, and rats eyed him
from atop a banister while human eyes watched him
through peepholes in armored doors. He maneuvered
past a mound of plaster and plasticrete chunks and came
to the door. He knocked once.

A small panel in the door opened, and a pair of eyes
appeared. Thom recognized the eyes as the old woman's.
The second she saw Thom, she slammed the panel shut.

Thom reacted quickly and jammed the panel with

the barrel of his rifle. "I'm a friend of Malik abdul ma Haddish."

"I don't know what you're talking about, Tuatha pig," the woman said.

Thom raised his helmet visor and pulled the respirator from his face. "I'm not a Tuatha; I'm the man Malik was sent to protect."

The woman's eyes narrowed as she regarded his dark skin, but she remained suspicious. "You should stop bothering innocent people."

The databug gave Thom a code phrase. "Silence adorns the wise and veils the ignorant."

The woman's eyes softened. Thom heard a series of bolts unlatch, and the door opened.

"Quickly, inside," the woman said. She shut the door after him once he had entered. Then she carefully re-bolted each lock and gestured for him to sit.

The room was spartan, furnished with old brown wooden chairs, a yellow table and a worn green divan. He sat, removed his helmet, and placed it on the table. He laid the rifle against another chair.

The old woman brought him a cup of steaming *kawhi*. "I am called Sitt Basima."

Thom gratefully accepted the beverage. It was strong, bitter, and a sharp contrast to the prison food.

"You're two days early," the woman said. "What has happened to Malik?"

"They made us plant charges in the mine," Thom said. "He was killed, along with a guard. I stole the guard's uniform."

"Oh, my poor Malik," the woman said softly. She turned to Thom, her eyes moist with tears. "He was my son."

"He was brave," Thom said. He put his coffee down, took her hand and held it. "I'm very sorry for your loss, but I've seen a terrible weapon in the mines. I must find Al-Sabah and warn him that Abu Brion may soon have this weapon."

"I will tell the others," she said, "but you must wait. They cannot be here until nightfall."

The three hours could have been an eternity. Thom tried to get some sleep, but his mind was restless and worried.

Thom was elated when two men arrived to lead him through the sewers. They followed the channel the wastewater had cut down to the river. When he saw reflected light of Der Merchant, he knew the river was just ahead. Once there, the men removed a small canoe from its hiding place. They placed the boat into the water, and then they rowed off into the moonlight toward the camps of Al-Saba.

CHAPTER TWENTY

Ernesto Abu Brion rose, naked, from his large, red velvet canopied bed. He picked up a robe and silk pantaloons draped across the back of a chair, and he dressed in silence. It was early. Delta Pavonis still lay below the horizon. As he fastened the sash on his robe, he watched the nude, sleeping form of Isabella, and felt sad.

He could not explain how he still loved her despite the mad other world where her mind now resided. His love for her made less sense than his hatred for her brother and the ibn Brentholtz clan. That hatred stemmed back to when the ibn Brentholtz clan had traitorously arranged the murder of his beloved grandfather. Abu Brion recalled with melancholy the first times he had made love to her and how she had resisted, until at last he had won her.

Isabella's true love now was *midnight lace* and the seductive dreams it gave her. She no longer resisted when he took her and sated himself with all parts of her body, but he also no longer had her heart. Everything else — even taking Ciudad Rand itself — somehow seemed less valuable, no matter how much he desired it.

He turned from Isabella and left the bedroom. In the dining room he found a meal already set out for him: rashers of smoked meat, eggs, a bowl of rice gruel, a glass of fruit nectar. A steaming cup of *kawhi*, rich with local cardamom and imported ginger, was set by his plate. He ate quickly and in silence, scarcely tasting the food.

When he had finished, he punched on the vid-phone set into the heavy black marble tabletop. The grim visage of General Kreus swam into focus. Reynardo stood beside him. Abu Brion knew the general despised the young *dhirek*, but that was why he had them work together.

"Good, the two of you are up," Abu Brion said. "Any more reports on DuBois?"

"We've identified the two bodies recovered from the mine explosion," Reynardo said. His lips were curled in the smile of someone pleased with himself. "One is a Mukhalafi agent, secreted into the prison ranks. His records are on file."

The *sèo* leaned forward expectantly. "And the other? What about him?"

"One of my guards," Kreus said with a scowl. "The other prisoner apparently survived the blast and changed uniforms with him."

"Damn," Abu Brion said, bringing his fist down on the tabletop. "So you think it was DuBois?"

"Your man, Reynardo, checked the identity chit for the missing prisoner," Kreus said. "There is no such person as Joachim abu Salaam."

The *sèo* leaned back in his chair. His face was a mask of worry. "So it had to be DuBois then."

"In all likelihood, yes, Don Ernesto," Reynardo replied.

"My men are searching for him, but my guess is he's long gone from the arcology," Kreus said. "The dead man's associates probably helped him escape."

Don Ernesto closed his eyes briefly and tried to suppress the anger and rage he felt boiling within him. If DuBois had escaped, there was only one place he would go — to the Mukhalafi. "General, I want you to locate all the Mukhalafi bases you can and attack them. If DuBois is there, we can perhaps render him inoperative."

Kreus smiled. "Yes, Don Ernesto, I can arrange that today."

"One more thing," Reynardo said, cutting in. "In digging out the prisoners, we seem to have discovered something which may be of interest to you."

The *sèo's* eyes popped open, and he sat up in his chair. "The weapon, it has to be the weapon."

Reynardo nervously licked his lips. "Possibly, your

excellency, but we're not sure. What we do see is a blue light originating from somewhere down the tunnel. There is, however, a tremendous amount of rock and debris in the mine shaft."

"How long will it take to clear the shaft?" Abu Brion asked anxiously.

"Two, possibly three days, using all the available prisoners."

"Do it. Now."

"As you wish, Don Ernesto," Reynardo said.

Abu Brion broke the connection. He leaned back in his chair and realized he was trembling. He had guessed correctly. The crash of the Nameless Ones' ship had created Treason's Tooth. The nova weapon was within his reach. It meant power he could not begin to imagine, power to conquer all Askander, to threaten the League and even to destroy the Iimarae, if he wished.

He glanced back at the bedroom where Isabella slept and felt emptiness in his soul. He feared the nearer he reached his goals, the more meaningless they became.

CHAPTER TWENTY-ONE

The sky was dark. Clouds hid the stars, and even the reflected light of Der Merchant failed to penetrate that thick blanket. It reminded Thom of a folk tale his Jamaican grandmother told him when he was little. In her thick accent, she described how the night came because the blind worm of darkness crawled across the sky and ate the sun. The worm was cold and wanted warmth. The sun grew angry at being swallowed and burned the worm's stomach, forcing the creature to excrete it. That brought the morning.

He glanced around, adjusting his night-vision goggles to survey the barren landscape of the Shaul Khala. It reminded him of the deserts and mountains of the American Southwest on Earth, long sweeping plains split by rolling dunes and sudden, upthrust mountains of bare, eroded rock. The only foliage was a handful of scrawny, yellowed *ynglas* trees and show low shrubs. The short, dwarf pseudo-conifers held their own against the dark green, tough shrubs in the battle to suck up the minute amounts of available water.

Thom spotted signs agriculture was once attempted here. Glistening in the moonlight were stagnant, silvery pools of salt water. Flushed to the surface by intensive irrigation, the sodium chloride had formed into a series of oblong mounds of halite crystal resembling open pustules on the landscape. They were abandoned, which made the whole landscape seem haunted.

A cold wind gusted from the north, whipping up sand and cutting through Thom's clothes. He drew his jacket closer around him, but it gave him little warmth. He could hear the wind whip the tops of the nearby *ynglas* trees. Overhead came the beating of leathery wings as a predator swooped down on unseen prey.

"How much longer?" he said to Ranulf, one of his two guides.

"Not far," Ranulf said. "Just over this rise."

He wondered now why he had decided to find Al-Saba, to locate the Mukhalafi. Clearly the League's mission had failed; Abu Brion now controlled Askander. It was futile for him to believe he could convince Al-Sabah to join in an alliance against the Iimarae. The antagonism between the great houses and the resistance now promised only violence and destruction.

Thom didn't know if he could be part of it. It went

against his principles. The Iimarae, however, threatened everything humanity had accomplished, and the
Mukhalafi and the revolution they sought might be his
last hope.

As the three men climbed the steep rise, Thom heard
a dull, grumbling noise nearby. It seemed to be growing
louder, stronger, and had an increasingly whining tone to
it. Thom thought he could smell the odor of ozone, dust
and hot lubricating oil. Der Merchant peeked through a
break in the clouds and a huge, square, hulking machine,
with treads that stood two stories tall rolled up. It flung
clouds of dust into the air, and it moved swiftly, startling-
ly, like a predator.

Thom found himself transfixed, unable to move.
Someone grabbed his arm and pulled him aside. He
stumbled blindly along until the something pushed him
to the ground behind a large rock. The dust choked him.
He tried to cough and spit out the dirt.

"Damn," Arn, the other guide, said. "That bastard
came out of nowhere."

"What was it?" Thom asked, coughing. He wiped his
mouth with the back of his right hand.

"A petroseeker. It looks for crude oil deposits under
the surface," Ranulf replied. "You were lucky I was there.
It would have squashed you."

"Why would it be seeking petroleum? I thought all
the power here was solar or old-style fission," Thom said.

"Food synthesis," Arn replied. "The monads can't grow enough food, so they convert the hydrocarbons from fossil fuels, when they can find it. It tastes terrible."

"Is it gone?"

"Yes, it's likely at least a klick away by now," Ranulf said. "No danger to us."

"I hope you're right," Thom replied, but somehow the guide's words did not reassure him. If the petroseeker was hunting oil, it could also be mapping the area and collecting other kinds of information.

Once he reached the top of the hill, Thom could see the moon's dull buttery light illuminating a large open area bounded by cliffs on three sides. A half-dozen openings were cut into one of the cliffs.

In front of the cliffs, on the plain, were ten or so large, rounded shapes. The shapes looked like huge cattle lying down for the night, but as they came closer, Thom immediately recognized the objects as Tuatha armored land walkers, known as "oxen." Nearby were a pair of massively armored, tracked vehicles nicknamed "hedgehogs." The hedgehogs bristled with heavy weaponry, including missiles, plasma cannons and disrupters.

For a moment Thom panicked, thinking that perhaps he had been betrayed by Kreus's men, but as he walked past the vehicles he saw where the Tuatha insignia had been scraped away and replaced with the clenched fist and single rose emblem of the Mukhalafi. "The oxen. Where did you get them?"

"Captured and stolen, mostly," Arn said. "A few we get from defectors. But we use them sparingly. We don't have the parts to repair them all."

They reached the bottom of a cliff where a plasteel ladder led up to the next level. The men climbed, with Thom in the middle. At the third level they reached an opening in the roof of one apparent dwelling. The men descended another ladder into the building.

Once inside, Thom found himself led down a narrow corridor and finally into a large room. Battery-powered fluorescent lamp packs filled the room with soft light. Cushions lay strewn about an old and faded, but still thick, patterned carpet. The smell of coffee and cardamom percolated from pots boiling on a small radiant heat stove like the one Thom had seen in Maarat ibn Steiner's tent. There was also the faint aroma of food cooking in another room. Thom noticed that Arn and Ranulf were gone. He was alone.

"Welcome," said a man's voice, a voice that was deep and rough.

Thom turned around to see a large, barrel-chested man enter the room. The man wore a light khaki uniform, black nylon boots and a red-and-white checkered *kaffiya*. His face was broad and well-tanned, cheeks and chin hidden beneath a thick black beard that was peppered with white and silver-gray hairs. Two dark brown eyes danced on either side of a bulbous nose that had been broken more than once.

"I am Major Thomas DuBois."

"I know who you are, Major. That is why you are here," the man replied with a broad smile. It was a crooked grin with missing and broken teeth.

Thom had seen other such grins on the faces of Tuatha torture victims on Ramal, their jaws broken by rifle stocks. His host sat down on the thick carpet next to the stove.

"Please, Major, be seated," he said, gesturing toward the carpet with a large, muscular left hand. "Have some *kawhi*."

Thom remained standing, uncertain of the man's motives.

The man frowned. "Please, Major, join me. It's not often I have guests, and you are in no danger from me."

Despite his misgivings, Thom sat. He accepted a small cup of steaming black coffee from the man, and he noticed that some of the man's fingers were slightly twisted, as if they had been broken and had not healed properly. Two of those fingers were missing their nails.

"So, do you know who I am?" the man said.

"You are Al-Saba, the Lion of Askander," Thom said

matter-of-factly. He sipped his coffee. It was thick, strong, pungent with cardamom, bitter and sweet.

Al-Sabah grinned, and his whole face seemed to glow. Unlike Thom, he downed his coffee in one gulp, set the cup down, picked up a red-and-blue enameled brass coffee pot, and poured himself some more. "So, Major DuBois, when did you suspect that I wanted to see you?"

"When your man Malik helped me in the mines."

"Malik was brave, indeed," Al-Sabah said, "but he was not my man. He was his own man, as are all Mukhalafi warriors, male or female."

Thom put down his cup. Al-Sabah refilled it from the brass pot.

"So, why do you need me?" Thom asked.

"We do not," Al-Sabah replied. "But you need us. We know of the Iimarae threat. Our agents also know that Don Ernesto Abu Brion has in his arcology Iimarae ambassadors with whom he has been negotiating."

"You must have an extensive intelligence network," Thom observed.

"My intelligence is more than adequate. We were, after all, the ones who provided the League with the coded message about Abu Brion and the Iimarae. Wherever there is repression and discontent, we find allies. And you need allies, too. Only we can deliver Askander to the League's side against the Iimarae threat."

"Are you sure you can deliver Askander? Surely even you realize that Abu Brion may be invincible now that he controls nearly all the corporations and arcologies. And he has the worst sort of Tuatha mercenaries working for him."

Al-Sabah closed his eyes and sighed. "Alas, we are more than familiar with General Kreus and the *Gall Oglaigh*. We have lost enough brave souls to him already."

"Then you should also know Abu Brion may have access to many terrible weapons," Thom replied. "While in the mines, I found a Gonaymne vessel buried beneath the city. I think Abu Brion knows of its existence."

"All the more reason for you to help us," Al-Sabah said. "You have a reputation as a great tactician and strategist, Major."

Thom smiled and shook his head. "Someone has been telling you tales. And, in any case, before I came to Askander I decided to put that in my past. I have seen enough of killing and dying."

Al-Sabah stroked his chin thoughtfully. "Major, we know of your work at Ramal, of how you helped the rebels defeat the Tuatha."

Thom felt his stomach churn at the mention of Ramal. The image of rebel women taking revenge on Tuatha troopers came to his mind, as well as the horrifying satisfaction it had given him, a satisfaction that both repelled and attracted him. He repressed the memory as best he could. "This rebellion will produce many deaths."

"That is a warrior's lot."

"But it is not my lot," Thom snapped. "League troopers have sworn never to kill unless it is unavoidable."

"It is recognized that you are civilized," Al-Sabah said gravely. "Perhaps too much so."

"The major has perhaps forgotten what the great Al-Mharek once wrote," intoned a new voice. "A people can only solve the problems which history places before them. If Abu Brion does find the Gonaymne ship, then we both must solve *this* problem, even at the expense of our ideals."

Thom turned and saw Siobhan enter the room. She was no longer dressed in Tuatha black. Instead, she wore a sand-colored uniform like Al-Saba's and desert robes. On her head was a dark blue *kaffiya* bound with a black and silver cord. About her waist was a black sash into which was thrust her holstered flechette pistol. Her *skean dubh* and its scabbard were strapped to her right leg.

Siobhan walked across the room and sat down beside Al-Saba. She smiled at Thom.

"You already know my daughter, I think," Al-Sabah said.

"Your daughter?" Thom said, startled by the revelation. "I thought she was Tuatha."

"My mother was a Tuatha officer," Siobhan said as she poured herself some coffee. "She was hired by one of the lesser families who were allies of ibn Brentholtz. She met my father in the *souk*."

"She *arrested* me in the *souk*," Al-Sabah corrected her. "I was organizing workers and leading a strike among the miners. Even then I was a troublemaker."

"And he was even more charming," Siobhan continued, squeezing her father's left arm. "She was told to keep an eye on him, to use her own charms to seduce him and convince him of the error of his ways. It was he, however, who did the seducing."

Thom found himself touched by the affection between father and daughter. He began to see the resemblance between them now, especially in the dark, penetrating eyes and in the self-confident way they carried themselves. "What happened to your mother?"

Siobhan stared at him. The joy in her face had gone. "My mother became pregnant with me, so she was sent home to Alba Nuadh in disgrace," she said, only the subtlest hint of anger in her voice. "She loved me, as she loved my father. Even as I was trained as a Tuatha, she still told me of his world, of his beliefs. Then the purges came. She was arrested as a Larkinite."

Thom knew of the Larkinites. They had held revolutionary ideals of justice and equality. They had wanted the Tuatha to stop sending their sons and daughters to die on alien planets. For their beliefs, the leaders were arrested and executed without trial. Only a few had escaped. "Haakon Kreus earned his reputation in the Purges," Thom said.

"Kreus killed my mother, Major . . . after he had raped and tortured her. I have as good a reason to hate him as you," Siobhan said.

"And you?" Thom said.

"They spared me because I was young. The priests of Alba Nuadh loved children and believed they could reeducate me, make me a good soldier for the Dáil and the Church," she said. "The priests were wrong."

"I'm sorry," Thom said.

"You shouldn't be," she said. "Kreus will pay for his crimes. Next time he'll lose more than his hands."

Thom was shocked. "So you know about Ramal, and why he wants to kill me?"

Siobhan nodded.

"I should have stopped the rebels, but I didn't. I let them mutilate him. Worse, I took pleasure in that, because of who he was, because of what he had done."

"Then you can understand why we need your help," Al-Sabah said.

"No. I'm not so sure anymore," Thom said. "All this was your plan, wasn't it? You had me shot with that tranquilizer dart in the lift shaft."

Siobhan smiled faintly. "I'm sorry, but it was the only

way to save you. I knew from our agents that Kreus and Abu Brion planned the takeover that night. Kreus would have killed you."

"And the intruder in the ventilator shafts?"

"She was one of our agents," Al-Sabah said. "She was very good."

"Malik said she was dead," Thom said.

"Kreus and his men drove her from the ventilator shafts," Siobhan said. "She killed five of his *saighdearan* before she threw herself down the turbo-lift shaft."

"Then that Tuatha bastard had what was left of her body quartered and had her head placed on a pike in the *souk* as a warning," Al-Sabah added angrily.

The revulsion Thom had always felt for Kreus began to overwhelm him. His desire to kill the man went against all he believed. He tasted bile on his tongue. The world seemed to shake around him, and for a moment he thought it was just his imagination, fueled by his emotions.

A coffeepot rattled on the stovetop and tipped over. The room shook again. A bank of lights fell from the wall.

"We're under attack." Al-Sabah said, jumping up.

"The oxen! I've got to get to them." Siobhan said, leaping to her feet and running from the room.

"Siobhan, no! You'll be killed." Thom scrambled to his feet. A thunderclap assaulted his ears, and the ground shook beneath him. Dust and smoke filled the room and more lamp packs fell to the floor.

Thom stumbled his way down the corridor. His fingers touched the cool surface of the walls to guide him until he saw the outline of a ladder. He scrambled up it into the red and yellow edge of dawn.

Something screamed across the sky. It crashed high on the cliff face and exploded, sending a cascade of rocks and dust high into the air. A second missile followed the first. Thom looked through the haze toward the horizon. He could just discern five black shapes moving slowly, deliberately toward the cliffs. The shapes he instantly recognized as Tuatha oxen. The vehicles were probably just a patrol, but Thom knew other Tuatha troopers and attack flyers would not be far away. Bright white flashes briefly appeared on the enemy oxen. A second later, more missiles screamed overhead and slammed into the rocks above.

Thom clambered down toward the other Mukhalafi fighters who were frantically uncovering their vehicles and powering them up. He saw several dead bodies lying near the burning wreck of one ox. The vehicle, thrown onto its back by a direct hit, looked like a grotesque dead turtle.

He was descending another ladder when a warhead exploded nearby. The blast ripped the ladder from the cliff. The ground rushed toward him. Thom leaped from the ladder, tucked his shoulder, and rolled. He came up on his feet and ran, operating purely on instinct, fear, and training. His mind forced him ahead.

Nearby was a half-uncovered ox. A Mukhalafi warrior lay dead beside the vehicle. A handful of its camouflage netting was entwined in his stiff fingers. Thom grabbed the netting, and finished pulling it away from the ox. Then he carefully opened the vehicle's cockpit and pulled himself inside. A warhead exploded twenty meters away. The ox shook and started to tip over.

Thom grabbed for the shoulder harness and held on tightly. The ox shuddered, then righted itself. He climbed into the pilot's seat, pulled on a helmet, and quickly strapped himself in. Thom hit the starter switch and powered up the vehicle. The huge twin turbine engines roared to life. The cockpit canopy lowered itself and locked shut.

The interface cable dangled to the left of his head. He jacked in, and instantly the entire yellow on black gridwork of the control display crystallized in his mind. For a moment the wave of data overwhelmed him. There was so much information and it was in the confusing, archaic neo-Gaelic of the Tuatha rather than League Standard Volapük.

Thom steadied himself in the matrix, his mind recalling all the Tuatha he knew as well as all the cybernetic interface standard commands he could recall. The ox quickly responded by getting to its feet. He activated the shields in time to absorb a plasma bolt from a disrupter. The interface turned yellow and vanished briefly as the defense systems dissipated the energy from the attack.

"There's one on the ridge to the west," he shouted into his helmet mike. "It's got a clear shot at us with its disrupters."

"That makes six of them," he heard Siobhan say. There was a pause. "Thom? Is that you? Where are you?"

"I can't tell you right now," he said. "We just need to get out of here."

"They've fired all their missiles," Ranulf reported.

"That's just because they can't get their beams over the rise and into the plain," Thom said. "But if they reached the rise, they'll have the advantage over us." His screens glowed yellow as they took another plasma bolt.

When the screens cleared a split second later, he saw a hedgehog unleash a cluster of missiles and a plasma bolt of its own. The weapons struck the top of the ridge, and a ball of white smoke and orange flame engulfed the enemy ox.

In response, a trio of missiles roared over the rise and smashed into the hedgehog. Bits of armor plate and shrapnel whirled through the air, some of it bouncing harmlessly off the shields of Thom's ox.

Just ahead, another warhead exploded beneath an ox. The force of the blast tossed the machine backwards.

It landed on its back, its armor cracked, and its shields overheated because the main cooling fins were pressed firmly into the earth. The ox's legs flailed uselessly, as though the pilot were trying to right the machine.

"Get out," Thom yelled into the mike, hoping the pilot was still alive. "Your shields are —" He watched in horror as the shields glowed yellow, then blue, then violently red before imploding. The blast shook his own vehicle, and his shields appeared to burn brightly as they absorbed the wave of energy.

"Well, Ranulf, it seems they still had some missiles left," Thom said bitterly.

For a moment he wondered how the Tuatha had targeted the hedgehog, then he found the reason in the data flow of the matrix — the ox carried small onboard spy probes. He gave his mission computer the command to launch the spy probe. Above and behind his head came a small click and soft *whoosh*. The shields dropped briefly. He heard a loud pop, then the shields came back up, and the telemetry informed him that the drone was now one hundred meters overhead.

Data from the drone probe came back almost instantly. The Tuatha were now five klicks away. The enemy oxen were a new model: larger, with more missiles and probably more powerful disrupters and plasma guns than his. They were moving quickly toward the rise. They would reach it in about three minutes. The telemetry suddenly stopped, becoming a jumble of gray zigzag lines. When it cleared, the ox's computer told him that a disrupter had destroyed the probe. The computer asked him if he wanted another drone. He declined. He told it, instead, to locate any Tuatha probes.

"Three, all unshielded," it said.

"Target them," he ordered. "The Tuatha have drone probes in the sky," he said into his mike. "That's how they can target the missiles. Focus on them."

He pulled the trigger on his control stick. A thin beam of plasma spurted from the forward cannon. Almost instantaneously, a small ball of orange flame appeared in the sky above the rise. Two other balls of flame quickly joined it.

"Good," he muttered, "now they're as blind as we are."

He turned his attention back to the rise. The Tuatha machines would have to climb the rise before descending onto the plain. Beneath the rise the terrain was mostly boulders, loose rocks and gravel except for a pair of what appeared to be clear pathways. The enemy probes had probably scanned the area, so the oxen would be heading for those paths.

"Hold your missiles," he ordered.

"Who is this?" came an unfamiliar and angry voice. "I don't recall you giving orders."

"Listen to him," Siobhan snapped. "He knows what he's doing."

"See the ridge? The Tuatha will have to come down it before they can take us on one-on-one. They'll be vulnerable for just a moment."

"Ranulf, Shakirah, Walid, head for the rise," Siobhan said. "Then set your machines into a hull-down position."

"But the Tuatha will be there any minute," one of them said.

"So run as fast as you can," she replied.

She had no sooner spoken than the remaining hedgehog raced on ahead, churning up a massive cloud of dust from its heavy treads. Quickly, the three oxen went into a trot, the fastest way that the machine could move, trying to catch up.

"Damn you, Walid, you idiot," Siobhan cursed.

Thom could see the air above the rise being grossly distorted by the waves of heat coming from the Tuatha's shields and cooling fins. The air shimmered like silver, making everything behind it appear to melt.

They were a half-kilometer away when the first Tuatha vehicle crested the ridge. A second one quickly joined it.

"On your bellies," Thom screamed. "Aim for the ground beneath the ridge." His hand squeezed the firing button. Four missiles leaped from their pods, to be joined by others from the remaining vehicles. Thom felt his heart racing. His mouth was dry and his clothes were soaked in sweat.

The missiles slammed into the rise just beneath the two machines. A whirling, mushrooming, vivid orange fireball filled the night air. One machine was tossed high into the air, crashing heavily against the rocks and exploding. The second machine pitched forward and rolled down the path. It smashed like an egg against a huge boulder. Thom could see the pilot struggling to get out of the cockpit as the remnants of his shield generators distorted and glowed menacingly.

"Hurry, hurry, you can make it," he yelled.

The Tuatha pilot managed to raise the canopy and had begun to climb out when the generators let go in a blinding flash. Thom had watched the man die, and it was because of his missile. He stared blindly ahead at the now fading glow from the ox. Two more bursts of intense light appeared on his monitors.

"Got them," Siobhan yelled joyfully. "Got all of those bastards!"

Thom powered down the ox and raised the canopy. His head spinning and stomach churning, he gulped the cool morning air. *What the hell have I done?* he thought, *I may have just signed this world's death warrant.* Nothing could ease his troubled mind nor wash away the strange and horrifying sense of exhilaration that came with it.

CHAPTER
TWENTY-TWO

For some reason he didn't understand, Thom dreamt he was on Feltsvurld, the fifth planet of Wolf One Fifty-Four, during the insurgency against the planet's brutal theocratic dictatorship. It was his first mission, and his worst. He thought he had long ago put it away. He clearly had not.

The convoy of rebel vehicles — tracked machines called buffaloes — first ran into a fine mist of aerosol psychedelics leftover from the Third Zaibatsu War. The airborne drugs rapidly incapacitated both the drivers and the troops guarding the convoy.

Moments later the Tuatha mercenaries struck. Thin red and yellow beams of particle weapons and plasma lasers angled in from the darkness. Cone projectiles followed, striking the supply vehicles in cascading showers of golden sparks.

The vehicles seemed alive. Under the influence of

the hallucinogenic weapon, Thom thought he heard the machines scream in pain and pulse softly as if gasping for breath. Metal and composite flaked from the vehicles' sides and melted into shapeless puddles that soon flowed over the bodies of the dead. There was a boiling hissing sound as the molten substances touched the bodies. The bodies burst into flames of intense colors. The flames flickered and morphed into sinuous shapes as they consumed the corpses. Thom heard that quite distinctly.

Oddly, no other sounds filled the air. He could not hear the explosions that glowed and blossomed chartreuse and fuchsia all around him. He couldn't hear the cone projectiles slamming into vehicles, though he could sense the agony that the machines suffered. He could not hear the rebels' weapons as they returned fire. He could not tell if he was screaming, as he could not hear that either.

He watched one of his troops, a young woman with red, raw empty eye sockets as she groped about wildly, her arms flailing, desperately trying to grab onto something, anything. She moaned softly and shook her head slowly from side to side as if in disbelief at what had happened to her. The woman tore her fingernails digging at the hard ground, and blood poured from her lacerated fingertips down her wrists. A bright yellowish ochre poured from her empty sockets.

Thom thought he saw the ochre drip onto her uniform then fall to the ground to coalesce as golden nuggets. He watched a small bird, oblivious to the battle, swoop down to snatch a nugget in its beak. Before it could fly off with its horde, the girl caught it with her bloodied fingers and ripped its head from its body. Its arteries spouted plasma beams, and she fell back, the remnants of her face now a charred mass.

Her arms and legs jerked spasmodically until a beam of bright white light sliced her into four equal pieces. The pieces melted and were rolled into bluish balls by large black beetles.

The insects had carapaces as green as jade. Their legs were attached to their exoskeletons with cotter pins and wood screws. The bugs soon fell to fighting among themselves and began to devour each other. Green blood mixed with machine oil as they tore the limbs from one another. Their mandibles sparkled as they opened and closed upon their enemies' bodies. Soon they fought no more. Decapitated and dismembered thoraxes and abdomens lay on their backs and jerkily moved the stumps of legs to and fro as if trying to right themselves. Severed heads skittered in crazy ellipses propelled by mandibles that gnashed savagely at things that were not there. The insects' broken dish antennae revolved on the tops of their heads, still tracking whatever it was they had been programmed to track.

Thom watched the abandoned balls roll downhill, caroming out of control off large crevasses and boulders. He followed them down the slope, tripping once over the body of a businessman, resplendent in gray flannel suit and attaché case. The body lacked face, having just a surface of cauterized pink scar tissue smooth and glistening like oiled carbon composite.

Thom ran from the corpse and kept following the balls. Nauseated by the sights, he stopped at the base of a burned, blackened, rotted and limbless tree where he vomited and heaved until his body shook.

He looked up in time to see the balls decelerate and come to a halt against the remains of an Iimarae fortress. He thought he recognized the fortress, but he wasn't certain as his memory on that subject was peripheral and unclear. There was a single figure standing on top of the fortress. He couldn't see it too clearly, although the figure was illuminated by a beam of blinding buttery-yellow light emitted by the weapon the figure was holding. Drawing nearer, he saw that the figure was Death. Death wore robes of deepest black and a hood that shaded his eyes and hid his head. Thin fingers manipulated levers on a box that produced a beam of yellow, almost golden light.

As his weapon pierced the darkness, Death laughed.

Thom tried to follow the path of the beam, but the beam barely illuminated its targets. Dawn was breaking now, and in the growing light that heralded the new morning, Thom could now see naked bodies imprisoned on boulders, their ankles and wrists impaled by bloody iron spikes. The beam systematically dissected the bodies into pulsing thin, pink slices, lingering only on the eyes. It was as if Death wanted to melt the eyes even after their owners were dead to insure that no images of the destruction would remain.

Thom knew he would remember those images. He would replay the atrocities endlessly in his mind. He turned to Death to explain the reason for all this horror. Instead, he screamed. The morning light, now a golden red, had exposed the face of Death. He knew the face all too well, as it was his own.

He had become Death, as the ancient Hindu epic, *Bhagavad-Gita*, declared. He was the destroyer of worlds.

Thom ran to the fortress and tried to tackle Death and stop the destruction. He pummeled Death with his bare fists, but Death remained solemn and unperturbed. Thom tried to grab the weapon from Death's hand, but Death brushed him aside with one arm and merely laughed. Thom kicked. He bit. He flailed. He pounded and battered until at last Death, tiring of the sport, took the weapon from its targets and turned it upon his assailant.

Thom awoke in a cold sweat and sprung bolt upright.

Perspiration rolled down his face and upper torso. The bed sheets were soaked with his sweat. He was trembling with fear. His breath came in quick, shallow breaths. As his eyes focused, Thom could see he was lying on an old mattress. The darkened room reeked of urine, sweat, mold and mildew. The mixture made his eyes burn.

Thom scrambled to his feet and staggered outside, where he sat down on a stone ledge and tried to relax. A slight breeze off the desert brought a scent of seawater, although the nearest body of water was miles away. The aroma proved calming, however, and after a few moments he tried to analyze his dream. He had never experienced a nightmare like that. Dreams of his dead wife, yes, but never the horrors of battles in which he took part. He thought he had avoided the effects of post-traumatic stress disorder, but clearly he hadn't. Certainly he never had dreams in which he blamed himself for all the destruction he had witnessed or, more importantly, had allowed to happen through inaction. His faults had been those of omission, as he had allowed on Ramal. His subconscious seemed to blame him, and he was unsure that it was wrong.

Troubled, Thom sat alone, quietly watching the stars in the dark sky above the *Jabal-Shiti*, the Rainy Mountain. He could just make out three constellations — the Chimpanzee, the Dolphin and the Unicorn — but the star he wanted to see, Sol, was not visible, obscured by the reflected light of Der Merchant. He wondered if he would ever see it again.

"This is the third night you've sat out here staring into space," Siobhan said.

He glanced over his shoulder at her, opened his mouth to ask her to leave, but thought the better of it. He turned back to staring at the stars. According to Siobhan, it had been three days since they had left the advanced base for the safety of *Jabal-Shiti*. He could not even recall how long it had been since he had arrived on Askander. Time had become irrelevant to him now.

"I brought you some *kawhi*," she said. She filled a battered tin mug from a flask and handed him the cup.

Thom accepted it with mumbled thanks. The coffee was spiked with Tuatha whiskey, but it was hot and sweet, and it warmed him. He had forgotten how cold nights were in the mountains.

Siobhan sat down beside him and took a sip from her own mug. "Something's troubling you," she said after a moment. "Would you like to talk about it?"

He did not reply.

"Is it about me and Jaime?" she asked. "If you want to know, he was infatuated with me, but I let it go no further. I have a job to do, and he simply would have made it more complicated."

"Do I also make things complicated then?"

"It's different with you." She paused a moment, then

said, "Would you prefer I left?"

"No," he said. He didn't want her to go, yet he wanted to avoid any questions. He found what she said about Jaime reassuring enough, but he also knew it was difficult to explain things to her, to reveal how he felt about her. Perhaps he didn't understand her enough to confide in her. Then again, he had never really understood Ursula, and that was why she had left him and then killed herself.

"I had a dream," he finally said. "In it I saw the war I want to avoid. I saw the sky filled with plasma beams and explosions. I saw Tuatha war machines advancing and the torn bodies of Mukhalafi soldiers at my feet. I saw a man with no face pointing at me and a woman with no eyes pleading for help. I was paralyzed. I could do nothing to stop the killing."

"War is not pleasant; both you and I know that," Siobhan said. "Yet sometimes it is necessary. Force is the midwife of every old society pregnant with a new one."

"I prefer non-violent resistance to war," he said.

"That's the problem with the League," Siobhan said. "For all your ideals, you have turned war into a game instead of the horror it truly is. As Al-Mharek wrote, 'Never play at insurrection, but having begun it, make up your mind to go through with it till the bitter end.'"

"Don't lecture me," he said through clenched teeth.

He recognized the anger, the hatred he knew was always there, lurking beneath the surface of his civility. His heart pounded in his chest, and he felt beads of sweat on his forehead despite the cool mountain air.

"I just wish things could be as they were on Earth and Mars: peaceful revolutions, insurrections of hope," he said.

Siobhan did not respond immediately. The silence between them grew tense.

"I see," Siobhan said finally, "but those revolutions occurred after the chaos of the Zaibatsu Wars, when the old governments were weak and decadent, unable to hold back the people's will, and the new governments had the courage to lead the revolutions. It is different here." She frowned and bit her lip. "The great houses believe all the moral force of the universe is theirs, that the world is to be exactly as they see it, a fixed star, an undeniable truth."

"The Hand is unseen, all powerful," Thom said.

"Yet there is no Hand but the human hand. You believe that, too, or you wouldn't be here."

He wanted to disagree, but part of him hesitated. He knew revolution was the only hope for Askander, and for humanity as well.

"You're right. I know," he said. "But that's not it. Somehow I've lost *me* in all of this." He felt tension in his shoulders, as if he carried the weight of the universe.

"Once, long ago, I was a very self-assured person. I was headstrong, confident, and I believed I embodied all the ideals of the League."

"And you're not now?"

"No. Not for a long time."

"Since Ramal?"

"Even before that," he said. He finished his coffee and shook out the cup. "When my marriage failed."

Siobhan refilled his mug from the flask. "Was she beautiful?"

The question took him aback for a moment. He was surprised to hear what he thought was a tone of pain and even jealousy in her voice. "Yes, she was. I met her at the university on Formalhaut. Her father was a government minister, an *apparatchik*, a dull sort of bureaucrat. She seemed different, though. She was confident, aggressive, but then I learned she was mentally unbalanced — something genetic, couldn't be treated correctly."

"But you married her anyway."

"I loved her, or thought I did," he said. "And it was good for many years. We had two children: a daughter and a son. Then her parents were killed in a hypersonic shuttle accident, and she fell apart. She started hearing voices, and then one day, when I was on a mission, she took the children and left. I later learned she left the children with her sister and ran off to Bangkok. That's a city on Earth."

"I know," Siobhan said. "I do know some things about Earth."

"Well, there she tried to find an Asian family who had taken her in years before when she ran away from home and went on what she called a spiritual journey. When she found neither that family nor the Buddhist monks she studied with, she rented a room in a fashionable hotel. She took a handful of pills and drank a bottle of vodka. The maids found her later, lying on the bed just as if she'd gone to sleep. The medical examiner said she had died three days earlier. I rarely tell that part of the story. I just say we're divorced, and before you ask, I haven't seen my children since. Her sister is probably a pretty good parent for them, though. Somehow I still feel I failed her."

Siobhan nervously fiddled with a dried leaf she had picked up from the ground near her feet. "I'm sorry that happened to you," she said.

"You shouldn't be," Thom said. He watched her carefully tear the leaf into thin pieces and sensed she was holding back something. He thought that her face, especially her eyes, seemed tired and weary, an effect made even more evident by the dull gray light from the night stars.

Siobhan must have noticed him watching her, and she managed a feeble smile. "Tell me about Ramal. What happened there?"

"You know that already," he replied.

"Amuse me."

"It's not amusing." Thom poured out the rest of his coffee and watched it form a tiny stream running down the rock he sat on. "I was there to teach them non-violent tactics, to organize mass resistance to 'King' Daffyd, the head of the Iron Guard, a fascist conspiracy supported by the military and the wealthier merchants. We were successful until Daffyd brought in Kreus. He rounded up dissenters in Daresharb, the Ramalan capital, took them to a sports stadium, and had them massacred — *pinocheted* is the precise term. Against my better nature, I agreed to a plan to kidnap Kreus from his headquarters just outside the capital."

"It worked brilliantly," Siobhan said. "Even the Tuatha high command was impressed."

"Well, brilliant or not, I should never have handed Kreus over to the Ramalan guerrillas and especially not the women. When the women were finished with him, he was a lump of flesh, barely alive. I tried to apologize to him, but he stared at me and told me I would pay for what I had done to him.

"I had the guerrillas take him back and leave him at a hospital. I had hoped the doctors could treat him, but by then infection had set in and the nerve damage in his hands was severe."

"You should have killed him," Siobhan said. "That

would have been merciful."

He shook his head. "You know I can't do that. The League values life. We avoid wanton killing, and taking Kreus's life would have been totally unjustified. It would have been murder."

Siobhan shook her head and sighed. "To have killed him then would have prevented many other deaths. Instead he lived to kill another day."

"It doesn't matter," he said. "I didn't wish to sink to Kreus's level and become just another predator like him."

"You may have a point there, but sometimes only another predator can stop a creature like Kreus," Siobhan said. She climbed to her feet and pulled her jacket more tightly around her. "I'm getting cold, and there's no more *kawhi*. Are you coming in?"

"In a minute."

After she left, he tried to organize his thoughts.

Certainly Abu Brion and Kreus would prove insurmountable by passive resistance, but he could not fully bring himself to agree to the use of armed insurrection. Then again he could not deny Askander was in the hands of an obscenely wealthy few who guarded that wealth and lusted after even greater wealth while they enforced misery, ignorance and brutality and called it "liberty." It was not a moral society willing to change.

Thom, however, was a pacifist-warrior, an oxymoron. He would have to resolve that dilemma before he could find a path to peaceful revolution on a world headed for war, both human and alien.

"Victims," he said to the uncaring sky. "We're all victims." He did not have an answer for his problems, but he knew everything depended on one.

Back in his room, Thom undressed, leaving his clothes lying on the floor. He turned the faucet on the small battery-powered water heater and filled the sink. The steaming water felt good on his chilled fingers as he plunged a stiff washcloth into the basin. He wrung out the cloth and scrubbed his face until his skin hurt. Then he looked in the mirror and saw Siobhan's reflection standing behind him.

He turned to face her and was lost in her beauty and strength. He watched as Siobhan pulled her shirt, without bothering to unbutton it, over her head and tossed it aside. Thom was surprised that she wore no bra, and that her breasts were full and round. She had large, dark aureoles. She unbuckled her belt, let her trousers drop to the floor, and then simply stepped out of them. Her rib cage barely stood out under her skin. She had a smooth, taut abdomen, a result no doubt of her military training.

She left him breathless, stupefied, speechless and entranced.

She strode forward, threw her arms around Thom's neck, and kissed him forcefully. Her tongue thrust itself between his lips and wrestled with his tongue. Siobhan played the aggressor. She pulled apart the fasteners holding his shirt closed before snaking her right hand toward his groin and deftly undoing his trousers. The trousers slid to his knees. She used her left foot to push his pants down past his knees to his ankles. She slid her fingers around his penis, caressing it and massaging it to hardness.

He responded by running his hand over her breasts and gently pinching her nipples.

Excited and aroused, they both were breathing hard. If Thom didn't know Siobhan was in control, he soon did when, slowly and forcefully, she pushed him onto the bed, onto his back.

She crawled between his legs and began slowly licking the length of his penis, beginning at the root, and gently moving her mouth up the entire length to the glans, which she gently teased with her tongue, then licked her way down his cock until she returned to the root. She gently caressed his testicles as she went back up the length again. His mind was spinning. She brought him to the edge of excitement, then slowly eased him down again, before repeating the action a third time.

Thom had not felt this sensation for so long, at least not anything so powerful. He felt his heart racing. He could not breathe. Then Siobhan took him into her mouth completely and he exploded. He groaned as he came and nearly passed out from the intensity. As the world swam back into focus, he saw her caressing his shaft, keeping him erect. He gasped in spasms and gulped in air. The pulse was beating in his head. Then she climbed on top of him, threw her right leg across his body, and straddled him. Slowly she lowered her velvety, silken vulva onto his cock. Once she had him inside, Siobhan began to slowly rock back and forth, grinding her clitoris and vulva against his pelvic bone.

She leaned forward and pressed her strong hands against his chest while he clasped his own hands around her waist to steady her as she bobbed up and down.

Suddenly, her fingernails, rough and worn, scraped across his flesh. Siobhan closed her eyes tightly and shuddered, a low moan escaping her barely parted lips. The moan sounded both pleased and oddly relieved, as if it had been too long a time since she last had an orgasm. She had a half-dozen more until, to his surprise, Thom climaxed again.

It sent cleansing fire through is brain, driving the old fears, the old regrets, the old painful memories to the recesses of his brain, where they would no longer haunt his dreams or fuel his nightmares. He gasped for breath, but that did not stop him from pulling Siobhan against his chest. He kissed her passionately, and she returned the kiss with equal lust. The sweet and spicy taste of her mouth and tongue, of the faint saltiness on her skin, and the wonderful, natural fragrances from her body intoxicated him. He began, if only slightly, to understand the healing power of lust, of the almost transcendent merging with another human being that was the nearest anyone could come to touching the spirit of the universe.

He pulled her close, never wanting her to go, holding her as though he would die if she rolled away from him. He didn't know how long it was afterward that he noticed his heart settle into a slower, steadier rhythm, and his breathing relax. He felt Siobhan's soft lips pulled away from his mouth and give him a gentle peck on his cheek. Then she laid her head on his shoulder and soon fell asleep. He took in the aroma from her hair and scalp, from the perspiration on her skin, and thought of the ancient legend of the love apple.

He saw the very soul of Siobhan filling his mind, soothing him, healing him.

There that thought remained, until he realized it was morning and he felt as if he were resurrected and rescued from his own darkest places.

He held her until she drifted off to sleep. He watched the steady regular rise and fall of her breasts with each breath Siobhan took as she slept. Thom wanted to tell Siobhan how much he loved her, but a gnawing doubt held him back.

Men are such fools, he told himself, *tied to unrealistic and selfish images of love.* Women were much wiser, more confident. He wished he had Siobhan's strength.

He soon fell asleep, but he hardly felt he had any sleep when he heard several dull thuds, like someone pounding nails into a coffin. Thom woke with a start. He was trembling, and he could feel cold sweat rolling down his forehead and back. His breath came in quick gulps. *Had he been dreaming?* he wondered.

Then he heard the pounding again. He wasn't dreaming — someone was knocking on the door.

"Yes?" he managed to say.

"*Sidi*, there are people here," Arn said from outside the door. "They have asked to see you."

"People?" He swung his legs over the edge of the bed and reached down to pick his clothes up from the floor. "Where are they?"

"In the ready room, *sidi*."

"We'll be there shortly."

Siobhan sat up and rubbed her eyes. "What's going on?" she said sleepily.

"Arn said we have visitors."

"Visitors? What could they want?" she wondered.

CHAPTER TWENTY-THREE

There were five visitors in the ready room talking to Al-Saba. Each visitor wore a silvery suit, hood and breathing mask. Desert dust covered all of them. Thom recognized the four tallest as Ajnabi, but the fifth was far too short to be an alien.

The four aliens turned to face them as he and Siobhan entered the room. He watched the aliens' black, pupil-less eyes glisten, and he could see his own reflection in them. One of the aliens helped the shorter figure turn around with a slow, shuffling motion. Thom saw dark brown eyes dancing above the rim of an Ajnabi breathing mask, and he realized that the fifth individual was human.

"Finally here," Al-Sabah said, a friendly grin on his face. He came to Thom and Siobhan and gave them both hugs of greeting. "Come, meet our honored guests. One of our patrols found them traveling just before dawn and brought them here. They have important information for us."

"Peace be upon you, friends," Siobhan said.

"And upon you," replied one Ajnabi who had already removed his mask.

"Please, be seated; we have much to discuss," Al-Sabah said, gesturing toward a large table which dominated the room. On the table were steaming pots of kahwi and fresh breads for the humans and juices, odd fruits, vegetables, and jugs of water for the aliens.

"Are they here?" the human visitor asked, his voice muffled by the mask. His hands reached up to undo it, and one of the Ajnabi gently helped him. "Are Thom and Siobhan here?" he said again once his face was uncovered.

Thom's jaw dropped as he recognized Jaime.

Siobhan took Jaime in her arms and hugged him. "Jaime, you're alive."

"Thom, Siobhan, I am so glad you're both alive," Jaime said, tears streaming down his face. "I was so afraid Abu Brion had killed you."

"No," Thom said, taking his friend gently by the shoulder and guiding Jaime to a seat at the table. Then he sat down beside Siobhan, took her hand, and squeezed it gently. "Siobhan and her father saved me."

"Her father?" Jaime asked.

"Al-Saba," she clarified, filling a cup with *kawhi* for

Jaime and handing it to him.

"Al-Sabah is your father?" Jaime said. He managed a faint smile. "Yes, I suppose it does make sense." Jaime curled both his hands around his cup and raised it slowly to his lips to sip.

Thom poured himself some *kawhi* and took a slice of sweetened bread covered with fruit paste. He watched everyone drink and eat. From this, and from a general air of familiarity between Al-Sabah and one alien, Thom gathered that the Mukhalafi had previous dealings with the Ajnabi.

Al-Sabah waited until everyone had eaten something, then he clapped his hands. "Now, my friends, to business. You have news for us."

The Ajnabi who sat across from Thom nodded. The alien pushed back the hood of its jacket, exposing its oval head. The Ajnabi seemed somehow familiar to Thom. Then he noticed an amulet hanging around the alien's neck with writing in hieroglyphs and curlicues in a rhomboid. He recognized the symbols.

The alien's thin, lipless mouth seemed to struggle around human words before it finally spoke in a guttural, throaty tone. "My name is Ishan. My friends and I have come to tell you that there is now much evil in Ciudad Rand," the Ajnabi said.

"The Gonaymne vessel, Thom said.

The alien stared at Thom. "You know of the vessel?"

Thom thought he could detect fear in the Ajnabi's voice. "I found the alien vessel when I was in the mines," he said. "I tried to destroy the shaft where it was. It seemed to be alive."

The aliens began speaking among themselves, clucking and whistling, producing deep sounds in their throats. The speaker turned to Thom and said, "Then you know it is a sentient vessel?"

Thom nodded. "Yes, and another thing: I saw the remains of an Ajnabi with the ship."

The Ajnabi did not reply.

"You are the Gonaymne, aren't you?" he said.

"Thom, what are you saying?" Jaime said with shock and horror. He rose unsteadily to his feet. "They can't be the Nameless Ones. They saved my life; they're not evil."

"Thom, what the hell *are* you saying?" Siobhan said.

"Just hear me out," Thom said. "I think I'm right."

There were tears in Jaime's blind eyes, tears that ran down his cheeks in long streams. "Please, Ishan, Fadyli, tell him."

"No, we are not the Gonaymne," Ishan said slowly. The Ajnabi stared at Thom, a look of strange melancholy in its eyes. "But my people were their creators."

Everyone was silent for a moment.

"How did you know we belonged to the ship?" Ishan said.

"Your amulet," Thom said. "It has the same symbols

as on the Gonaymne vessel and as on most of the arti-facts we thought were made by the Gonaymne."

The Ajnabi nodded slightly, and its mouth curled up, but the gesture was not a smile. There seemed to be too much sadness in it for that. "You are indeed very wise, Thomas DuBois," Ishan said, "but you do not know the whole truth." The alien turned and gestured to a third Ajnabi. "Hakyka, you are our *tawarik*, you must recite the tale."

Hakyka nodded and clasped Ishan's hand.

Thom had little to wonder if *tawarik* meant "histori-an" or "bard," not that it really mattered.

In precise Volapük and in a slightly high-pitched voice, Hakyka began the Ajnabi tale:

"Long ago, more than ten thousand turns of this world, our people lived far from here, on a planet which circled the star you know as Aldebaran. We built ships to travel to other nearby stars. In order to travel the vast-ness of space, and to insure precision in passing through the devices you call hyperspace portals, we gave our ships the power of thought. We built devices we thought would allow us to control the vessels, but we had no idea the vessels had grown stronger than we were.

"The starships had developed self-awareness, and they contacted each other. Each shared their knowledge, and thus they rapidly grew even more intelligent. Be-fore we were aware of it, they had learned to control us through the very devices we thought would command them. We were enslaved by our own creations.

"For six thousand of your years, the starships plundered the nearby stars, and we became their unwilling weapons. When soldiers were needed to conquer a strong-willed people, we were those soldiers and we destroyed everything in our path. When tyrants were needed to bridle races that produced the goods for building and fueling more starships, we were the oppressors. I cannot tell you how many races we annihilated at the Gonaymne's orders, but our hands and hearts and minds are forever stained by their blood."

For a moment, all four Ajnabi bowed their heads. Thom was unsure if it was a sign of contrition for the sins of their race or a sign of respect for all those races that had died at their hands.

"How did your ancestors get here and free themselves?" Thom asked.

The aliens raised their heads. There was an expression of infinite regret and weariness on each face, as if each carried the burden of guilt for all Ajnabi.

"It was purely by chance that we gained our freedom," Hakyka said. "The vessels' intelligence grew by tremendous bounds, but they found that much of their intelligence was used for the simple tasks of running the ship. Gradually they began to set aside areas, to compartmentalize themselves so that certain sections would mindlessly run on their own.

"By then, we were nothing more than tools for the great ships, useful when ruling a planet or fighting battles, but otherwise as unwelcome as a bacteria or virus. Increasingly, we were ignored until we were needed.

"Slowly, many of our ancestors found that our control bands now allowed them to affect the newly specialized areas. Here they could take actions or contact others without the Great Ships' knowledge. Knowing that they were now safe, our ancestors communicated with others through this secret means. Eventually, they plotted to overthrow the vessels themselves."

"So your ancestors took over control of the different sections of the ship and isolated the main intelligence center?"

Hakyka nodded. "We long waged war against the Iimarae. They fought bravely against the great ships, leaving some helpless without soldiers and destroying others. They came on relentlessly, wave after wave, but we destroyed them wherever we found them.

"We came to this planet to destroy an Iimarae settlement, a small outpost, actually. The ship itself destroyed the settlements from orbit, then ordered our ancestors to descend, to find survivors and kill them. Most of them used shuttles to land, but three stayed behind. They took control of the vessel and caused it to crash into the mountains. It unleashed a great force of molten rock as it burrowed into the ground."

"Forming Treason's Tooth," Siobhan noted.

"That is correct," Hakyka said. The alien turned to Thom. "The three who stayed behind died trying to escape. It was the remains of one of those three whom you found."

"The Iimarae who are here want the ship, don't they?" Thom said.

"Yes," Ishan confirmed. "It contains the controls for a weapon, a very powerful device which can cause even the most stable of stars to explode into a supernova."

"Is the weapon on board?"

Ishan shook his head. "No, the weapons are already planted in the hearts of several suns, including this star."

"And you know where the others are?" Thom said, growing uncomfortable.

Ishan looked at the other Ajnabi. The aliens closed their eyes and looked down. Ishan nodded to them, then faced Thom. "One of the devices is in the center of the Iimarae home star. Another is in the sun you call Sol, the home of the human race."

Siobhan gasped. Al-Sabah muttered words of disbelief under his breath. Stunned, Thom sank back into his chair. The alien's words struck him like a hammer blow. His mind turned the revelation over and over in his mind. His gut churned. What he knew now was that if the Iimarae obtained the weapon, all was lost. Then he realized there was something far worse.

If Abu Brion had the weapon, he could blackmail two races at once. The Askanderian's desire for power seemed to have no bounds. The mere threat of destruction would be enough for humanity to knuckle under, but more than likely, Abu Brion would betray his alien allies as well, and if they tried to attack him he'd destroy their home star. It would be the ultimate act of terrorism.

"This is terrible news," he said.

"There's more, Thom," Jaime said. "The Ajnabi believe the Iimarae long ago found another vessel." He fumbled at his side and brought up the pouch Ryf'Tael had carried. "I obtained these from a dying Iimarae. He was frightened, as if he were running away from someone. I think he stole these from some elders." He clumsily pushed the pouch across the table toward Thom.

Thom opened the pouch and removed one of the control bands. "These are the things you used to control the ships."

Ishan nodded.

"But I don't understand," Thom said, turning the band over and over in his hands. "If the Iimarae had already found another ship, then why do they need this one?"

"I cannot say. Perhaps the other vessel was too badly damaged, perhaps its weapons systems were beyond repair. Perhaps it did not contain the nova inducer, or the device was destroyed," Ishan said, "but this band is weapon enough."

Thom stared at the device. Small protuberances on the inside of the band appeared designed to make contact with different areas of the skull and perhaps the brain. The markings on the side were indeed similar to the Gonaymne cartouches, but this one seemed recently made, as if it were an Iimarae copy. "How does it work?"

"Our ancestors built them so we could project our consciousness into a computer matrix, but the vessels found a way to use them to project their will into our minds."

"The Iimarae must have modified it, Thom," Jaime explained. "When I put it on, I could share the dying Iimarae's thoughts, and I could see. I could see myself through his eyes and I could sense his fears. He was scared, Thom, really scared."

Thom rolled the band through his fingers. The League had many reports that the Iimarae used some sort of mind control device for regulating their workers and warriors, a device that drove them on without thinking, without questioning, always obedient.

Thom ran his fingers over the nodules. He caught fragments of sensation, colors, images, all flashing past his mind, but none of them his images. *I wonder*, he thought, *if we could use these devices against the Iimarae and Abu Brion.*

He put the band on. The device's nodules pressed into his head, and instantly he felt himself wrenched from his body, yet remaining in it. A blue wave rolled over his mind, and the rods and cones in his eyes all seemed to fire at once, in orange and purple explosions. The feeling was disorienting, more so than being interfaced with a starship, but the sensation passed as suddenly as it began. He found himself staring at the Ajnabi, but the eyes through which he saw were not his. He sensed fear, but it was not his. The eyes turned and he saw his own face. His eyes were staring back at him. In those eyes, he could see the reflection of Siobhan's horrified features.

"It's all right, Siobhan," he found himself saying to reassure her.

She tried to speak, but she seemed unable to make her mouth and vocal cords move. He could almost taste her revulsion, her absolute terror at having her person so thoroughly violated, even though she knew it was him.

Thom sensed his own hand reaching to remove the band, but something stopped him. He found himself making her lean toward him, having her hands gently take hold of his face, then pressing her mouth tightly against his own. He could not explain why he had done what he had done, but it was as if the band had made him do it, as though the power it imbued its wearer with was a power of cold, unfeeling arrogance in controlling another being.

"I love you, Siobhan," he told her. "I love you." Then, horrified at how he had assaulted her, he reached up and pulled the band from his head.

To his astonishment, Siobhan did not stop kissing him. She allowed her affections to linger for a moment, then she abruptly slapped him across the face.

"You bastard," she said. She leaned back in the chair, but there was a strange, sad smile on her face. A single tear rolled down her cheek.

The others in the room sat quietly, looking bewildered by the events taking place before them.

Thom's throat was dry. His cheek burned and throbbed, but he tried to ignore it. He reached for a glass of water on the table and drank. After a moment, he composed himself and picked up a band from the tabletop. It would have to be modified, he knew, to prevent that feeling of power, but he suspected the Ajnabi could manage that.

"Al-Saba," he said, "I believe I have a plan to defeat the Iimarae, Abu Brion, and all the great houses."

Thom was nearly asleep when he heard the door to his room open and someone enter.

"Move over," Siobhan said. "I'm cold."

"I thought you wouldn't want to talk to me after this

morning," he said, rubbing the sleep from his eyes.

"That was this morning. This is now," she said, climbing into the bed. She cradled his head in her hands and gently kissed first his forehead, then the tip of his nose, and finally his lips. "Did you mean what you said about me?"

"Yes," he replied.

"Good," she said as she drew him close.

She traced her fingertips across his chest.

"Close your eyes," he said.

She did.

Thom moved between her legs and began kissing her thighs and working his way up toward her vulva. Siobhan trembled and moaned. Thom was soon lost in the moment, intoxicated by her spicy, heady scent. He brought his lips to her clitoris and gently ran his tongue over it. Siobhan shuddered and gasped. She took Thom's head in her hands and pulled him closer. He increased his rhythm and Siobhan immediately responded.

He had no idea how many orgasms she had, but she gasped for air.

"I...want...you...now!" she said.

He changed position so he hovered over her. His manhood was poised at the entrance of her vagina. Gently he slid his penis into her.

Siobhan surprised him when she grabbed his shoulders and pulled him farther into her.

She almost immediately convulsed in orgasm.

Thom soon found an intense rhythm as he thrust into her. She was warm, soft as velvet.

Siobhan panted and moaned. Her mouth opened in ecstasy while her eyes were glassy, as if she were in a trance.

Gasping and grunting himself, Thom felt a wave growing with in him. His heart raced and his pulse pounded in his brain as his mind went into a dizzying state until the wave of intense pleasure crashed over him, and he was overwhelmed by his own orgasm.

His head spun, he felt his limbs grow weak, and he rolled away from Siobhan and lay on his back, gasping for air like a beached fish and staring at the ceiling. Even as the effects of his orgasm faded, his body and brain crackled with energy and pleasure and something else … something like happiness.

Siobhan rolled over, kissed him passionately, and then collapsed herself. She rested her head on his shoulder and threw her left arm across his chest.

"Are you happy?" she asked, still panting a little.

"More than you can ever know," he said, "and more than I thought I ever deserved."

"Good," she said. "That's very good."

"What do the Askanderians call the dove?" he said. "It's not in my language databug."

"*Hamami*," she said, puzzled. "That's a funny thing to

ask. Why do you want to know?"

He shrugged. "I just thought I needed an Askanderi-an name. The dove was an old human symbol for peace. I thought it appropriate."

She smiled then shook her head. "You are the most puzzling man I have ever met. Well, you can baptize yourself in the morning. I'm going to sleep.

Siobhan rolled over and pressed her buttocks close to his hip. In a moment she was asleep.

Thom lay awake for a while longer, hoping that he could live up to the promise of his new name.

CHAPTER
TWENTY-FOUR

The enemy convoy crawled across the desert. Two large oxen protected the front of the column and another two guarded the rear. The convoy itself was composed of three petroseekers so heavily laden with oil that their huge treads sank into the loose and blowing sand.

So Kreus and Abu Brion have finally taken our attacks to heart, Thom thought. He pulled his field glasses from their pouch on his hip and brought them up to his eyes. Automatically, the binoculars trained in on the lead petroseeker and zoomed it into focus.

Siobhan crawled along the dune and came to his side. "Which arcology are they from?"

"Von Misestown," Thom said. "No wonder the security is so tight. They're probably starving for any kind of food there."

"The strike call in the city is set for six hours from now," Siobhan said. "If those seekers arrive, it might set off food riots and ruin our plans."

He turned to her and smiled. "They won't arrive, and you know that."

She grinned. "Yes, I suppose I do."

They slithered together down the dune to where the rest of the guerrillas waited.

"What do we have, sir?" Liam said, seeming eager for a fight.

Thom patted the huge Tuatha on the shoulder. "Four oxen, three very full petroseekers."

"Good." Liam removed a control band from his jacket and turned it over slowly in his hands. "Shall we begin, sir?"

"Why not?" Thom said.

Thom and Siobhan climbed to the top of an outcropping. Liam and Ranulf were close behind. Thom watched the enemy vehicles for a moment, then turned to the others and nodded.

"Siobhan and I will take the first two. Liam, take the nearside trailing one. Ranulf, you take the other."

Thom took a deep breath. He knew the experience would still be wrenching, would still give him a false sense of power even though the Ajnabi had modified the bands to eliminate the sensation.

"Now," he said.

Four control bands went to four foreheads.

Instantly Thom found himself inside the mind of the

ox driver. He sensed the man catching his breath and heard him utter an involuntary gasp of surprise. The driver tried to tell the machine's interface to issue a distress call, but Thom blocked it.

Thom sensed the man's growing sense of panic, felt his heart race and his breath come in quick gasps. The ox staggered and nearly fell.

"Do not be afraid, my friend," Thom reassured him. "We mean you no harm." He found the sleep center in the man's brain and told it to release massive amounts of adenosine, choline, melatonin and other neurotransmitters. Instantly the driver fell unconscious. Thom ignored the man's subconscious and took control of the interface. He told the machine to halt, to disarm its weapons systems and to slowly lower itself to the desert floor. The onboard computer obeyed without question and then shut off the ox's power.

Thom reached up and turned off the control band. His vision cleared, and he saw the other three oxen had also stopped dead in their tracks. The cybernetic brains of the petroseekers kept the huge machines plodding on, but already the rest of the warriors were swarming over the machines, breaking into the locked cabs and cutting the connections between the vehicles' computers and the rest of the mechanisms.

One by one, the petroseekers halted. Other guerillas carrying explosive charges appeared from behind the dunes.

Thom removed his band and turned to his compatri-
ots. "Good work."

"I don't know if I'll ever get used to it," Liam said, rolling his band over and over between his fingers.

"Me either," Ranulf added with disgust. He handed
the band back to Thom. "It's like stealing someone's essence, his *nafs*, his soul."

Thom could not deny that, but he knew there was
no choice. The control bands had given the Mukhalafi
a tool for victory. Still, he admired Ranulf's loathing for
the bands and his hatred of anything that gave one human being power over another. "Soon enough, Ranulf,
we will destroy these things, as the Ajnabi did. But for
now, they are a necessary evil."

"I know, *sidi*, but it still doesn't sit well with me," Ranulf replied.

A patrol arrived with the four Tuatha troopers, all
securely bound. Their stun poles and hand stunners
held at the ready, the guards circled the Tuatha warily.
Thom pulled his veil up to cover the lower half of his
face, tucked his white robes about himself, and walked
toward the prisoners. The four, their arms tied behind
their backs, struggled to stay awake, trying to fight off the
effects of the intrusions into their psyche. Thom sensed
a high degree of hostility and defiance in the three men
and one woman.

"*Gu robh gach gealach agus grian leat.* May the sun and moon go with you," Thom said in Tuatha Gaelic as he walked toward them. "I am Al-Hamami del Astra, and you are my prisoners."

One of the men spat at Thom, the saliva striking him on the bridge of his nose.

A guard moved toward the man, but Thom raised his hand. He wiped his face with the back of his hand, but kept his eyes on the man. Thom thought there was something familiar about the prisoner's behavior, and that of the others as well. It reminded him of the ninja in the sewers.

"Shakirah," he said, "please check the prisoners' necks, behind their ears and at the base of the skull."

Shakirah examined each prisoner in turn. After a moment, she tossed four enhancement cartridges at Thom's feet. Thom picked up the cartridges and turned them over in his hand. As he watched, the prisoners' demeanors quickly changed from defiant to fearful. The men's eyes grew wide with terror. Only the woman still seemed aloof, but even she appeared to waver. One captive fell to his knees and began to sob uncontrollably.

"Please, please," the sobbing prisoner cried. "Don't kill us. We are innocent. Spare us."

"Coward, sniveling bastard," the woman said. She tried to kick the man, but lost her footing and crashed heavily to the ground. She cursed for a moment, then her anger burst into tears of frustration.

Thom reached down and helped the man to his feet. Siobhan and Liam picked up the woman, who hurled incoherent curses through her tears.

"We mean you no harm," Thom assured them. "You'll be taken to a base camp and given food and shelter." He nodded toward the guards, who ushered the prisoners into the back of a waiting hedgehog. Thom watched the vehicle disappear in a cloud of sandy dust. He undid his scarf, turned to Siobhan, and tossed her a cartridge. "What do you make of this?"

Siobhan stared at the cartridge for a moment, then sighed. She undid the corner of her own veil and let it hang. "Hard to say. It could be any number of things, but I'm willing to bet Kreus is having trouble keeping his troops under control."

"Do you think morale is slipping?"

She nodded. "Very likely. The troops are isolated, and from our intelligence, we know the *suma* are not getting along with them, even though the Tuatha are supposed to be keeping the *mostazafin* in line."

Three explosions suddenly tore through the air in rapid succession. Balls of red flame appeared over the top of the dunes and with the flames came thick, choking clouds of black smoke. The petroseekers and their cargo were destroyed, bringing more deprivation and hunger to the arcologies.

"Do you know what I think this means?" Thom said.

Siobhan smiled. "That Von Misestown will be ours by morning. Then only one arcology remains to be conquered — Ciudad Rand."

He returned her grin and nodded. "Exactly."

CHAPTER
TWENTY-FIVE

From his vantage point in his bedrooms high atop Ciudad Rand, Ernesto Abu Brion could see the long, billowing black clouds of smoke hanging close to the distant horizon. The smoke seemed to fill the bottom of the sky like a huge, boiling ink smear. He had lost three petroseekers already, and it had only been an hour since dawn. Added to the ten from yesterday, that made over one hundred destroyed that week.

The loss of Von Misestown a week before now only compounded his problems. The previous night there had been reports of sabotage in the food processing plants, and strikes and mutinies on board the sea-going food factory ships. In addition, Kreus's men had failed, yet again, to gain entrance to the Gonaymne vessel.

Then there were the stories of the new Mukhalafi general, Al-Hamami del Astra, the Dove from the Stars, who had apparently devised the campaign to destroy the petroseekers and the city's food sources. He was said to have the ability to enter the minds of other persons and force them to do his bidding. The rumors were so rife that the name of Al-Hamami seemed to be on everyone's lips.

Don Ernesto knew that Kreus was convinced this new general was Thom DuBois, the League officer who was Don Jaime's friend. Abu Brion was all too familiar with Kreus's damned obsession with DuBois, and he had his doubts. Still, it made him wonder if the Hand had indeed suddenly turned against him.

"Damn the Mukhalafi," he whispered through clenched teeth, "and damn you most of all Thom DuBois or Al-Hamami, or whoever you are. May the Hand crush you and drive you to the deepest pits of hell."

He reached into his robes and removed his *misbaha*. He had not used one since his grandfather was murdered, but now it seemed necessary. Nervously and methodically he rubbed the string of worry beads between his thumb and forefinger. He counted off each black bead, but his thoughts kept intruding, and he was not calmed. He began rubbing the *misbaha* even harder, thinking that might help, but the effort only broke the thin string. Beads fell noisily to the floor and rolled in all directions.

"Damn," he said, kneeling to pick up the scattered beads.

A mad laugh and a low moan of pleasure came from the bed. He looked up to see Isabella, her naked body hidden under thin black satin sheets. She laughed incoherently, and he could see her hands moving under the sheets, caressing herself. Hurt and angry, Abu Brion turned his face from her.

He felt a hot flush on his cheeks. Angrily, he flung the beads he had collected against the wall and shrieked in frustration. Then he gathered his robes about himself and stormed from the room. He did not stop until he reached his offices, where he found Kreus waiting for him.

Already the mercenary had his hands around a glass of whiskey. A half empty bottle rested on the desktop.

"Yes?" Abu Brion said.

"It killed another of my men," Kreus replied. "That's the fifth one so far."

"How far did he get?" Abu Brion said, seating himself behind the desk.

"Farther than the others, to the inside hatch." Kreus raised the glass and tipped all its contents down his throat. "When he tried to open it, the damn ship killed him."

"Did you recover his body?"

Kreus nodded and poured himself more whiskey. "Same as the others: a dried-up thing, like a mummy. Blood had turned to powder. The ship just sucks the moisture, as well as the life, out of them."

"Send another man in," Abu Brion said.

Kreus slammed his glass on the desktop and leaned in toward the *sèo*. "My men are on the verge of mutiny over this. If I send one more in, I can't guarantee the rest will behave themselves."

Abu Brion nervously leaned back in his chair. He found himself sweating out of fear of Kreus. The Tuatha's breath stank, and his eyes appeared moist and rheumy. The *sèo* knew only Kreus's enhancement cartridges kept his speech clear. He hoped it would also keep the man's temper and those terrible hands under control.

Don Ernesto licked his lips. "Very well," he said, trying to sound authoritative. "Use some of the prisoners instead. Kill a few of the uncooperative ones, to insure the others will obey."

Kreus stared at the *sèo* for a moment, then grunted. "All right, but I can guarantee nothing. They aren't likely to get as far as my last man, especially in the condition most of them are in."

"Prisoners and their conditions are your responsibility."

"Damn you," Kreus said, spewing spittle.

"We have little time," Abu Brion said. "If I can't get the weapon soon, the Iimarae will undoubtedly attack us."

"You can't trust those shit-faced little birds in any

case," Kreus said. "You know that, and I know that."

"Then, you should know this, too," the *sèo* said. "One of the nova inducers is in the heart of their home star as well. If the controls for the weapon are in our hands, then we can use it to our benefit."

Kreus smiled. "Blackmail? Oh, that's very rich, Don Ernesto. If we do get the weapon, perhaps we should fry those little birds anyway. Good riddance."

"Kreus, I need that weapon," the *sèo* said calmly. He was, however, starting to find the Tuatha's callousness grating and his lack of tact annoying. "Or I will have doomed us all."

The Tuatha's smile soured. He downed his drink, then grabbed his bottle. "I'll do what I can. No guarantees. With sabotage increasing in the plants and in the *Jura*, my men are nervous."

"Do it anyway."

"You should have let me use atomics on Von Misestown and put an end to all this trouble," Kreus said. "I could have made the Mukhalafi *glow*."

"One does not destroy an asset simply because it has fallen into someone else's hands," Abu Brion said, a touch of anger in his voice. "There will be time to regain it later. Now, attend to the work I pay you for."

Kreus snorted and marched, somewhat unsteadily, from the room.

Don Ernesto sighed, then sat back in his chair. He

felt spent, empty, as though he had wasted all his efforts on a perhaps now uncertain cause. The machinery, however, was in motion. He had lubricated the gears well and set his plans on their way. His only hope was that he could destroy his enemies so that he could complete what he had started.

There was a knock on his door.

"Come in," he said, sitting up. Reaching for a stylus, he pretended to busy himself with the screen of an Isaak.

Reynardo entered the office. "Don Ernesto, two messages have come for you."

He gave Abu Brion a small packet sealed with a blob of melted red wax into which a seal was impressed. The seal was of a lion. Abu Brion thought the object seemed oddly theatrical.

"An old woman handed this to one of your guards in the *souk*. She claimed it was from the Mukhalafi."

The *sèo* tore open the packet to find a data crystal. He inserted it into the Isaak. The screen filled with a video. Three people, their faces obscured by breathing masks, sat at a table. "Don Ernesto," the middle figure said. Abu Brion thought the voice was oddly familiar, and he pondered whether Kreus was indeed correct to believe DuBois was the rebel leader. "We are the Revolutionary Council of the Mukhalafi. We have warned you that those who wrongfully devour the wealth and the freedom of the *mostazafin* do but swallow fire into their bellies, and they will be exposed to the burning flame. The leaders of Von Misestown have learned the truth of this, for we are that flame, and we are the wind. And what you have wrought by the wind shall be carried away by the wind. I am Al-Hamami. Be warned."

Abu Brion pulled the crystal from the Isaak and flung it across the room, barely missing Reynard's head. "Threats, idle threats," he shouted. Fuming, he rested his face in his hands and tried to calm himself. After a moment, he looked up. "Reynardo. The other message. What is it?"

"The Iimarae elders, Don Ernesto. They wish to speak to you on the progress General Kreus has made with the alien vessel."

"Damn," Abu Brion said. The Iimarae had been politely quiet since the excavations began on the Gonaymne vessel, and he had expected it to last until the weapon was recovered. Now obtaining the weapon might be impossible, however, and he had no idea how patient the elders were. Worse, since Ryf'Tael's disappearance and apparent death, he had no Iimarae he could trust.

"What shall I tell them?"

"Who?" Abu Brion said, his train of thought interrupted. "Oh, yes, the Iimarae, of course. When would they like to see me?"

"I gather within the hour."

"Tell them I will be there in half an hour."

"As you wish."

"And Reynardo, make sure that the meeting is recorded."

"Yes, Don Ernesto, that will be no problem," Reynardo replied. "I have had the aliens under constant surveillance since they arrived at Ciudad Rand."

"Good. Good. You may go."

Reynardo bowed briefly, then left the room.

Abu Brion waited until the man was gone, then sighed and made a mental note to himself to keep an eye on Reynardo. The young *dhirek* was too efficient, too willing to cooperate, and that suggested ambition beyond the usual desire to rise in the ranks.

The Iimarae's quarters were unsettlingly quiet when Don Ernesto entered. A small brazier crackled on the floor, cooking meat for the aliens' mid-day meal. Fat and grease spat and hissed as they fell on the hot coals. The meat itself stank of decaying matter and sickly sweet, unearthly spices.

"Welcome, Don Ernesto," a voice said from a corner of the large room. "It has been a long time."

Abu Brion turned toward the voice. He could see the Iimarae elders sitting quietly behind heavy scrims of gray, unornamented gauze. They cast sinister images, like those of ancient shadow puppets, onto the scrims. The shadows made the *sèo* feel decidedly uncomfortable. He spotted a small padded stool placed before the screen and sat. To his displeasure, he found the stool did not conform well to human anatomy. It forced his knees up into an awkward position. Trying to fold his legs under himself only increased the discomfort.

The Iimarae's preference for spartan furnishings clearly extended to their guests, Abu Brion realized, and were probably intended to make them ill at ease and therefore more susceptible to Iimarae demands. He could not deny it was an effective technique.

"To which of you am I speaking?" he asked.

"I am called Hree'Rchee," the Iimarae said. "I will speak for all the elders."

"I see that you still find humans unpleasant to look at," Abu Brion replied, reaching forward to shake the scrims. Behind it, he could see that two of the elders were noticeably flustered. The one in the middle, however, did not respond.

"I am not offended by your ugly features," the alien replied, "but my sisters' constitutions are less resilient. The screen is for their sake."

Abu Brion snorted derisively. "You thought little of Ryf'Tael's constitution."

"He was a drone, an otherwise worthless male. His feelings are not of consequence," she replied.

"What if I said I will not deal with you, except through Ryf'Tael?"

"That is impossible," Hree'Rchee answered, her voice suddenly higher pitched, as if nervous. "He is no longer a part of the Flock."

Abu Brion smiled. "All right, then I will not deal with you unless I can see you face to face."

"That is also impossible."

Abu Brion rose. "Very well, then you must deal with my subordinates from now on."

"No."

He sighed, feigning mild disgust. He wondered why the Iimarae had ever bothered him. The aliens had now shown themselves to be quite craven. When faced with even the remotest prospect of losing an asset, they failed to act like good businessmen.

"Do you agree to my terms?"

Hree'Rchee did not answer for a moment. There was fervent clicking and whistling among the aliens. Hree'Rchee shrieked loudly, cutting off the conversation. Then, reluctantly, she said, "We agree."

"Good." He returned to the stool, sat, and waited.

Behind the greens, two of the Iimarae rose and exited through a nearby door. Only the shadow of Hree'Rchee remained.

The alien rose, walked clumsily to the edge of the screen, and pulled it aside.

Abu Brion found himself mildly surprised when the alien appeared. At over 250 centimeters, she was nearly a meter taller than Ryf'Tael, and her beak was hooked and sharp, like an eagle's. Polished metal spurs glistened on the back of her talons and those fingers that did not form part of her wings had claws sheathed in bluish metal. He tried to mask his shock the best he could, but he could feel sweat rolling down his neck and back.

Hree'Rchee sat on the floor in front of him, her legs folded carefully under her body. She fiddled for a moment with the *voder*. Once she was certain it would translate accurately, she stared at Abu Brion with dark, brown eyes, the eyes of a hungry predator.

Abu Brion nervously licked his lips.

"We know you have found the ship," the alien said.

"Yes, but we are having problems," he said.

"What kind of problems?"

He told her what had happened to Kreus's men. To his surprise, she gave out a low-pitched whistle and began clucking her beak excitedly. The *voder* emitted a dull squawk, unable to translate.

"There is something you haven't told me, isn't there?" he said.

She gave him a cold, deep stare. "The ship. It is alive; it is sentient," she said flatly.

"You mean, it can think?"

"Yes," Hree'Rchee replied. "It learns through absorbing beings, taking the information from them."

"How do you know this?"

"Once, my people found other ships, ones which had died, but which contained much information."

"Do you know how to get into this ship?"

Hree'Rchee twisted her head, an Iimarae sign of affirmation. "Yes," she said, "but we may no longer have the means."

"What do you mean?" Abu Brion said sharply. "You'd better not be lying to me."

"I am not lying. We have a device, a band of obedience, which we used to discipline our workers," she explained. She clasped her fingers in front of her and twisted them. "Unfortunately, Ryf'Tael stole these bands and their power packs, except for two. I used one band to kill him."

"So, if you do have a band, then you do have the means to enter the ship," Abu Brion said angrily.

"Perhaps not," Hree'Rchee responded, "The power packs are very weak. We have some fresh power cells, but they are likely not enough. It might take a few hours of time to fully recharge all the others, if we adapt the chargers to your systems."

"I don't believe you," he replied and started to leave. He felt long fingers grab his arm and a sharp talon press into his flesh. He knew it meant he was to stay.

Hree'Rchee pushed her face close to his. Her odor,

spicy and moist, almost overpowered him. "If I tell you something, truthfully, will you trust me?"

"Perhaps," he replied, trying to keep down the bile in his throat. His arm stung from the strength of her grip. "If it is worth my while."

She released her grip and removed a black rectangular composite-encased object from under her cloak. "Do you know what this is?"

Abu Brion rubbed his arm for a moment, then looked at the object. He swallowed and felt his mouth grow dry. "It's an *ansible*, a tachyon transmitter."

"Yes," Hree'Rchee replied. "I was to use it to signal my home world, and they would have sent warships to destroy Askander."

"But you chose not to," Abu Brion said.

"I trust you to do what you have promised," she replied.

"And you will recharge the control bands from the ansible's power cells?"

The alien nodded.

Abu Brion smiled. He realized that perhaps he had underestimated the Iimarae, or at least this one. Were she human, she would make a fine *dhirek* or even a *sèo*, someone he could respect.

"You have other plans, don't you? Ones to benefit you and not the Flock as a whole," he said.

She shrieked raucously, the equivalent of laughter. "I

will be a queen one day, human, but I intend to speed that day, and to have all the other queens groveling at my toes. Already my intrigues have taken wing, and soon they will come to roost."

"Very well, I trust you," he said. "And to show you my trust, I will tell you something. There is a Planetary League starship in this system. A Kautsky-class vessel against which your puny scout ship will have no chance."

Hree'Rchee stared at him for a moment, clearly disturbed by the news. "They are here to help these rebel warriors you are fighting?"

"Perhaps," he said, "but I will need your help. We must stop the Mukhalafi, or neither of us will succeed."

Hree'Rchee cocked her head slightly, as if trying to listen more closely. "So, do you have a plan?"

Abu Brion smiled. "We shall find one which will profit both of us."

"Don Ernesto, you and I think alike," the alien said. "You and I will make worthy allies. I will let you know when the band is operational."

"Till then," Abu Brion said. He turned and left the room

"Yes, till then," Hree'Rchee repeated. She unleashed a cry of victory that echoed off the walls.

CHAPTER
TWENTY-SIX

Thom leaned back in the seat of his ox and contemplated the instrument display the interface had spilled into his mind. He had the canopy raised so he could feel the desert wind, but instead, he tasted the slight metallic tang one sensed while interfaced. His body shivered from the chill of the Askanderian night. He tried to find the temperature control on the Tuatha armor he wore, but it seemed to be defective. Thom was not surprised. Much of the Tuatha equipment seemed to be inoperable or malfunctioning. Siobhan attributed it to the declining morale of Kreus's troops, but much of it also showed signs of sabotage.

"Cold enough for you, *sidi*?" a mechanic said, who suddenly popped up at the side of the ox. She was named Samki — the Fish.

"Yes, but not as cold as some places I have been, Samki," Thom replied. "Did you find the hydraulic leak?"

"Easily enough, *sidi*, although it was not as obvious as the original sabotage," Samki said. "And this, too," she handed Thom a grease-stained paper sticker.

Thom took the sticker, which he recognized as a "silent agitator," a simple device dating back to Earth's early twentieth century. It showed a cat with its back arched and hair raised in a threatening posture. In the elegant curlicues of Askanderian script, it read "Beware. Give us our just rights. We never forget sabotage." The sticker brought a smile to Thom's lips. It meant that the organizers and agents had indeed made inroads, even into the *mostazafin* who serviced the Tuatha's equipment. He was tempted to put it on the ox's console, but thought better of that and slipped it into his pocket.

A cold gust of wind sent a shiver through his body. "Can't you get the heater working?"

Samki smiled. "Maybe yes, maybe no. But try this while you're waiting." She handed him a plastic flask of *araki*.

"Thanks," Thom said. Taking the flask, he downed a mouthful of the raw brandy. It scorched his throat as it went down and exploded in his stomach. He knew the *araki* would not keep off the cold, but after a while he wouldn't mind. He took another swig and handed it back to the mechanic.

"Well, you're all set," she said. *"Khidmetak sharaf."*

"No, Samki, the honor is mine," he replied.

The mechanic grinned, then ran over to work on another machine.

Thom turned his attention to his interface display. The hydraulic pressure in the pistons that drove the ox's legs was slowly rising to normal levels. He called up the chronometer. There was still an hour or so to go before dawn. Too much time, he realized, too much time to worry, to reconsider. Too much time for things to go wrong. He felt someone tap him on his shoulder. Startled, he turned to see Siobhan standing next to the cockpit.

"We've got some problems."

"What?"

"The Ajnabi. They've vanished. I think they've gone back to their wadi."

"Great," he said irritably. "Well, it's not really their fight, I suppose, and they've done a lot for us."

"That's not the only problem," Siobhan said. "The Ajnabi kept Jaime safe and out of the way. Now he wants to come along."

"He can't be serious," Thom said. "Doesn't he realize he could threaten the mission because he's blind?"

"He doesn't see . . ." She caught herself. "I mean, *understand* it that way. He says he knows how to use the bands better than almost anyone, and he thinks that if word spread that he was alive and in the arcology, it might help the rebellion."

Thom sighed and slumped back into his seat. It was clear that Jaime would not allow himself to be left behind, blind or not. Thom knew he would simply have to find a way to keep the former *sèo* of Ciudad Rand out of harm's way. "Tell him he can ride in the back cockpit of my ox. He should be reasonably safe with me."

Siobhan shook her head. "I hope you know what you're doing."

Thom bit his lip, then said, "So do I. Any word from your father?"

"Nothing recently. About two hours ago he sent a message that everything was in place for the strike and they should be able to disrupt the arcology's main computers."

"And?"

"And he's worried. Everything is going too well, he said. He's afraid of a trap."

"I'm afraid of a trap, too, but we don't have much choice."

"Well, if it is a trap, we'll find a way out of it," Siobhan replied. She leaned over the edge of the cockpit and kissed him.

He watched her as she walked back to her machine and wished he had her confidence.

The interface chronometer wound down toward zero. Thom punched a toggle on the instrument panel and powered up the ox. In the interface, he could see readouts for all aspects of the machine as it came alive. He was especially pleased the hydraulic pressure was holding steady. With great care, he brought the ox to its feet and moved out to join the rest of the convoy.

Shakirah was at the controls of the hedgehog that led the way. Siobhan was in the ox next to Thom's. Three petroseekers followed, with two more oxen trailing. The petroseekers had been emptied of their oil and their new cargo consisted of Mukhalafi warriors and their weapons. It was an old ploy, Thom knew, but he hoped it would work.

The first part of the journey was the most dangerous. The vehicles had to follow a series of narrow mountain roads until they reached the wide highways leading to Ciudad Rand. Shakirah's hedgehog was equipped with a narrow-beam laser, which transmitted directions to the other vehicles' computers. Staying aligned with the beam was the only assurance that a vehicle would not go tumbling over a cliff to the jagged rocks below.

Thom forced himself to be detached, to forget the danger. He kept his mind narrow and concentrated on the interface. The discipline of *la souffrance* helped, but he still found only half his mind concentrating on the output from the computer matrix. The other half resolutely insisted on trying to put everything that happened, or could happen, into a semblance of order.

Fortunately, the interface's incessant stream of data gradually forced his mind to deal with it. The relentless alphanumerics poured over him, giving him information on items such as fuel pressure, the speed of the ox in relation to other vehicles, and the ambient temperature of the canyon walls as the rising Delta Pavonis heated them.

While the star had not yet appeared above the mountaintops, long, thin fingers of its buttery light fell into the spaces between the mountains, illuminating the craggy walls of the canyons and the dark forms of trees on the hillsides. The dawn sky ranged from dark blue at the far horizon, to robin's egg blue, to nearly orange where the star was rising. Wispy nimbus clouds added to the sight.

Down to his right, Thom could now see the sheer drop-off from the cliffs. On the other side, the cliff wall was tall and nearly perpendicular. The vista was awe-inspiring, and he lowered his guard a moment. He hadn't really appreciated the majesty of these mountains before.

He seemed to remember the area. He recognized it as the canyon of the *Nahr Sakhr*, the river down which he had made his escape from Ciudad Rand. There should be a bridge ahead, he remembered, that crossed over the river to the arcology. What was it called?

A warning shrieked in his head. Thom cursed. In his

reverie he'd let the ox drift from its line, and it had come too close to the cliff's edge. He forced himself to concentrate on the matrix. Slowly, the machine plodded back on course. A green glow appeared in the matrix. He'd found the beam once more.

"Just what the hell were you doing?" he heard Siobhan say over his skul-fone.

"Sightseeing."

"I'll agree the landscape is fantastic," she said, "but I'd prefer you not become part of it."

"I'll try not to be a tourist," he said. "How far are we from the main highway?"

"About two klicks," she replied. "You can see the Kantara bridge from here."

He looked up and spotted the vague outlines of the old-style suspension bridge. He had the computer enhance the image, and he saw that the Kantara appeared deserted. Only a pair of farmers' carts and a ramshackle merchants' wagon moved across it. The resistance's efforts to halt most traffic into the arcology had succeeded.

After the convoy was safely onto the main highway, Thom placed his ox on autopilot and turned as best he could to check on Jaime. He was surprised to see how tired and drawn his old friend seemed.

Jaime had been cleaned up and shaved and dressed in a Tuatha uniform, but it did not look right on him. Some people seem to fill out clothes in which they are comfortable, but Jaime seemed to have shrunk within his clothes and they hung heavily on his frame. Clean bandages had been placed over his eyes, to give the impression he had been wounded in a skirmish. A fatigue cap about two sizes too large was pulled down over his forehead.

"You've been awfully quiet," Thom said.

"I haven't had much to say."

"If you're hungry, there's a ration box and a water flask at your feet."

"I'm not hungry," Jaime replied. "I have too much on my mind."

"I see," Thom said. He turned back in his seat and watched the road. "You know this was a foolish idea, to come along."

"Thom, don't you start criticizing me," Jaime snapped. "I had enough of that from Siobhan."

"Sorry," Thom said. "But I doubt your presence will rally the lower-class *suma* or any of the *mostazafin* behind you. You know that too."

"Yes, I know," Jaime said. He reached down to find the water flask. "That's not the real reason I had to come. I need to see the ship. I guess I can never see the ship, but I need to get to it. I can't explain why. Damn, where's that water bottle?"

Thom reached around, found the flask, and put it into Jaime's hands.

Jaime grabbed the flask and fumbled with the snap-top. Once it was open, he raised the flask, squeezed it, and sent a stream of water across his chin before hitting his mouth. When he had finished, he wiped his mouth with a sleeve and cradled the flask in his lap.

"We all want to see the ship, Jaime. And no one more than me," Thom said.

"You don't understand, Thom," Jaime said earnestly. "I've had these dreams, terrible dreams, weird dreams. I dreamt I was an Iimarae, and I was flying over horrible landscapes, volcanoes, molten lava, oceans of acids and alkali. Then I felt something cold and horrible in my mind, and suddenly I was falling out of control, spinning round and round until I crashed. Then I woke, and I could feel a presence in my room, hell, in my head."

"We all have terrible dreams, Jaime."

"But these weren't my dreams, Thom," Jaime said, his voice oddly agitated. "They were the alien's, they were Ryf'Tael's. It was as if I was watching his dreams and then making them my own. I think something happened when he died. I had one of the bands on, and I felt him die. It's as if I inherited all of his thoughts, all his subconscious fears." Jaime paused a second, then said, "Do you know what's weird, Thom? They're terrified of falling. A species that can fly so easily is absolutely frightened of falling, of spinning out of control. But that's why I have to reach the ship. The answer's there, I know it."

"You're imagining things," Thom said, trying to sound reassuring, but he too found himself disturbed by the dreams. Either Jaime was slowly going mad, or perhaps the Iimarae had more control bands they could use on humans. "It's stress," he said without conviction. "It's getting to us all."

Resembling the battlements of an ancient fortress, the walls of Ciudad Rand loomed before them. The sheer size of the monad was daunting. Thom hoped that they could use the small places to gum up the works and bring the whole thing grinding to a halt.

He remembered a lesson from another century: one could not make the trains run on time if the oil pumps for the trains were inoperable. The arcology's oil, its lifeblood, was not flowing. Soon the general strike of the *mostazafin* and sympathetic lower-level *suma* would shut down what remained of the city's activity. Then the revolution would begin. Whether it succeeded was another matter.

Thom could see a *Gall Oglaigh* checkpoint about half a kilometer from the main gates of the city. The checkpoint consisted of a red-and-white painted plasticrete guardhouse and a single barricade that could be raised by hand. Two guards, heavy seizure guns slung over their shoulders, manned the guardhouse.

Four more troopers manned a missile launcher behind a parapet of rock and sand, built to the side of the road. A heavily armored ox was parked behind the launcher.

The convoy came to a halt a short distance from the checkpoint. The hedgehog pulled over to the side, and Thom drove his ox toward the barricade. About two meters from the barricade, he stopped and released the pressure in the ox's legs. The machine slowly settled into a crouch.

A guard, his seizure gun now unslung, walked slowly toward the ox. Thom undid the canopy of the machine, then reached into his jacket for the data chit with their orders on it. He knew it was a good forgery, but he wasn't sure it would pass muster with the Tuatha, who were sticklers for detail.

"*Madain mhath*," Thom said. He handed the chit to the guard.

"It's not a good morning," the guard said. He seemed to have a perpetual scowl on his unshaved face. He placed the chit into a reader on his belt and waited for a response.

"We're from the Second Armored Division," Thom continued, trying to sound irritated at having to stop. "We've had a hell of a time getting this oil here. The rebels harassed us all the way from Wadi Baroodi to the foothills."

The guard grunted, then looked up at Jaime. "What happened to him?" he said, gesturing with a twist of his head.

"Lasers hit his night-vision goggles. Burned out his optic nerves."

"Too bad," the guard replied. He stared at Thom for a moment. "Do I know you? Your face seems familiar."

Before Thom could reply, the chit shrieked. He felt his heart skip a beat. His hand dropped to the stunner at his hip.

"Damn thing's glitched again," the guard said, still scowling. "Well, you're cleared on through, but a lot of good it'll do. We need ten times as much oil as you've got just to feed the city for the rest of the day."

"Every bit helps."

"Tell that to the poor swine in the *Jura*," the guard said, handing the chit back to Thom. The guard's partner raised the barricade and waved the convoy on through.

Thom breathed a sigh of relief. The first obstacle had been overcome. He powered up the ox.

As they reached the docking bays where the petro-seekers' cargo would be pumped to the food processing plants, the huge steel doors opened slowly. The high security area normally should have been crawling with Tuatha, but Thom was puzzled. Only a few guards were present, and they seemed exhausted and overworked.

They were quickly overpowered when the Mukhalafi troops appeared.

"How many?" he asked Siobhan.

"Five, and they all gave up without much of a fight," she said.

Thom scanned the loading bay's spider webs of pipelines, half expecting to see *saighdearan* drop from the ceiling on rappelling ropes. Everything was silent. "Something's wrong."

"What makes you say that?"

"I don't know," he said. "Everything just seems too easy. I keep expecting Tuatha to pop up suddenly, and none do."

"It only seems easy," she reassured him, "and we certainly don't want to be found out too soon. Just be thankful for our luck so far."

"Maybe you're right," he said. "Have Arn's troops secure this area, and send Liam and the rest of the force to take the processing plant and meet up with Al-Saba's warriors. You and I will take Shakirah's squad and Jaime."

"What are we going to do?" she asked.

"We're going to look for the Gonaymne vessel."

The nine-member Mukhalafi squad moved slowly along a series of catwalks through the humid world of the Jura. Thom led the way with Siobhan right behind. Jaime held onto Shakirah's shoulder as she guided him through the maze of plasteel grids. Steam formed around the mass of pipes, wires and cables. It condensed on the mildew-blackened walls, ran down in thin brown rivulets, and pooled on the floors below.

Thom watched a bloated rat, its body covered in purplish cancerous sores, scurry across the catwalk and leap clumsily toward a thick black cable. The animal misjudged its jump and fell screaming to the floor below, landing with a sickly thud.

"If I remember correctly, there are some turbo-lifts just ahead," Thom told the others.

"Yes," Siobhan said, "that concrete block with the light on it should house some shafts."

"We'll split into threes," Thom said when they reached the lifts. "Shakirah will take one squad, Iain the second, and Siobhan, Jaime and I will make up the third."

Three lifts arrived almost simultaneously.

"Okay, let's go."

Thom felt a knot in the pit of his stomach as the lift descended rapidly. He looked at Siobhan to get her reaction, but she seemed undisturbed.

"You think this is a mistake?" he said.

"The three of us should not be together," she said. "I should be leading one of the other squads."

"I need you with me, for your input," he said.

His skul-fone crackled.

"*Sidi* Thom, this is Shakirah," came a frantic voice. "Our lift has stopped. We can't get the doors open."

A second voice joined Shakirah's. "This is Iain, our lift's done the same thing. We can't get it to budge."

"That's odd," Thom said. "We're still descending. Have you had a power failure?"

"No, *sidi*," Shakirah said. "Someone or something is keeping us from moving."

Thom had a sinking feeling in his stomach. He felt the lift car slowing to a halt. The lift doors opened and they stepped out. He found himself surrounded by ten Gall Oglaigh from Kreus's command all armed with seizure guns or projectile rifles.

"Welcome, Al-Hamami or Major DuBois, or whoever you are," a voice said.

Thom looked up to see a smiling Abu Brion, flanked on one side by General Kreus, and by a very large and very nasty-looking Iimarae on the other.

"Come. Join us. We've been expecting you," said the *sèo*. "We're just about to fully activate the Gonaymne vessel."

CHAPTER TWENTY-SEVEN

The Tuatha guards led Thom and Siobhan down a long, poorly lighted corridor. The two had their hands tied behind their backs with monomolecular filament. Jaime, his hands grasping Thom's shoulders, shuffled slowly behind them. Abu Brion, Kreus, and the Iimarae rode on ahead in a motorized cart.

Thom resisted the impulse to twist against the cord, knowing it could easily slice through his wrists if he tried. He suspected Kreus took particular delight in this subtle form of torture.

Thom glanced at Siobhan. She seemed oddly stoic, more disappointed than angry at their failure. "I'm sorry," he said. "I really screwed it up."

She smiled and shook her head. "Not your fault. We couldn't have known this would happen. You and my father were right; dumb luck and chance always screw you."

They turned a corner and entered a huge gallery filled with the bright white glare of klieg lights and the sounds of men working. As he entered the chamber, Thom heard two gasps of awe. Glancing over his shoulder, he saw Siobhan staring up at the immensity of the alien starship, which still took his own breath away. He also saw Jaime's upturned face, his bandaged eyes firmly fixed on the vessel.

Unless Jaime had managed to hide a control band under his fatigue cap, a band he had kept secret for himself, it didn't seem possible.

"*Filyak'za walla fil-manam?*" Jaime asked.

"No, you're not dreaming," Thom said.

Jaime turned toward Thom, his mouth open in surprise.

"You'll give yourself away," Thom said softly. "Keep quiet, so no one else notices."

"Ah, my dear Major, you do not seem impressed," Abu Brion said, strolling up to Thom's side. A cruel smile graced the *sèo's* bearded face. "But then, you have seen the vessel before, haven't you, when you were in the mines?"

"If you're trying to show me how efficient your intelligence service is, I'm not impressed," Thom replied.

"How little you think of me, Major," Abu Brion said, feigning injury. "I merely wanted to thank you. After all, you were responsible for the explosion which exposed the vessel in the first place." He gestured to Kreus. "General, have your men escort our guests into the pit."

Kreus barked an order, and the troops grabbed Thom and pushed him toward a long ramp leading into the galley. They repeated the action with Siobhan and Jaime.

Thom stumbled briefly, but regained his footing. He felt something sticky and warm roll to his fingertips, and he knew that the monofilament had gashed his wrists. He could only hope the wound was shallow. Finding something to cut the cord would have to be a priority. He wished he had Siobhan's *skean dubh*, still hidden in her boot.

When Thom reached the bottom of the ramp, he noticed a small cluster of people standing to one side. Two appeared to be *dhireks* of Abu Brion's house. A third he recognized as Reynardo ibn Brentholtz, Jaime's cousin and former corporate official who had obviously switched his allegiances. There was also a minor Tuatha officer, one of Kreus's underlings, and the alien.

Then he spotted Isabella. He was shocked at how gaunt and pale she looked. The effects of midnight lace appeared devastatingly clear now. Her skin seemed ghostly and translucent, as pale as a drowning victim. Her hair was matted and tangled, and her dark black eyes were glued to the ship. Thom could see her lips moving as if in conversation with some unearthly being. Every so often she giggled madly, then resumed her conversation.

Thom tried not to look at her. Isabella's presence brought back memories of Ursula, and with those memories came remembered pain. Yet he was appalled that Abu Brion seemed so oblivious to his wife's suffering.

Suddenly, someone screamed.

Thom looked up to see a wildly shrieking Isabella bolt from the cluster and race toward the hatchway of the Gonaymne vessel.

"It talks to me. It needs me." she said, laughing. She made a mad dash toward the intensely glowing hatch.

"She's heading for the hatchway. The damn thing's booby-trapped!" Thom shouted.

"By the Hand's mercy, somebody stop her," Abu Brion screamed. "She'll be killed."

Thom saw Don Ernesto race toward the portal as several Tuatha tried to restrain him. He broke free, crying, "Isabella."

It was already too late. Isabella disappeared into the hatchway, which instantly flared into a blindingly brilliant shade of azure.

As Abu Brion sprinted toward the ship, Thom flung himself into the man's path. The two men tumbled heavily to the ground.

Thom rolled over onto his back and felt a sharp, stabbing pain in the palm of his left hand. His fingers curled toward the pain and wrapped themselves around a sharp piece of rock. He swallowed and began to work the stone back to his wrists.

"Damn you, you let my wife die, you bastard!" Ernesto said, as he clambered to his feet. His eyes burned like someone possessed.

Thom was startled to see the *sèo* so upset. "It was too late to save Isabella, and a second death would have been futile."

"Kreus, you may kill him now."

Thom looked up to see the Tuatha general walking in his direction. Kreus was smiling and gleefully wringing his hands. "Get to your feet, DuBois, and die like a man."

Thom felt the filament give way under the rock's razor sharp edge. He barely had his hands free when Kreus grabbed him by the jacket and flung him bodily toward the gaping hatch of the Gonaymne vessel.

Just as the glow reared up to swallow him, Thom fell and slammed into the vessel's hull. A flare of pain shot through him, and his lungs screamed for air. He staggered to his feet and saw Kreus advancing on him. He picked up a rock at his feet and, using the hull for support, launched himself at Kreus. All too quickly he realized his mistake.

The Tuatha grabbed Thom's right forearm and twisted it.

Thom screamed as he heard the bones snap. With his left hand still clutching the rock, he swung wildly for

Kreus's head.

Kreus cried out in pain as the stone gashed his right cheek. He tossed Thom aside, and his right hand went to the injury.

Thom crashed into a motorized cart and sprawled across its hood. The rock flew from his hand and skittered along the cavern floor. He stood up, gritting his teeth against the pain in his arm. It felt as if a sharp sword were shooting from the injury, up through his shoulder and neck, directly into his brain.

Thom turned and came face-to-face with Kreus, who had blood streaming down his cheek. The general, smiling, grabbed Thom about the chest and began to crush him. Thom gasped for air. His left arm pounded against the Tuatha's back to no avail. Then he saw the enhancement cartridge on the back of the general's neck. He reached for it, but the world began to spin and his fingers fell short.

Kreus locked his two hands together and tried to snap Thom's back. Thom felt his vertebrae pop, and more fire shot into his brain. He clutched wildly for the cartridge, felt his fingers close about it, and pulled with his last ounce of strength.

His eyes shot open, and the startled Kreus stiffened and loosened his grip on his victim. Thom dropped to the ground, nearly blacking out from the pain. As his eyes focused, he could see the Tuatha reeling about as if drunk. Thom got to his feet, clutching his broken arm against his chest.

His lungs burned with each gulp of air he took. He looked frantically about him and was surprised to see that Kreus's troops stood rigid like statues, apparently too astonished at the spectacle before them to act. Then Thom realized that someone, or something, had control of them. He needed one of their seizure guns, and he took faltering steps toward the nearest Tuatha. He let his right arm drop, winced, and tore the weapon from the soldier's unresisting grasp.

"Thom, behind you," someone screamed.

Out of the corner of his eye, Thom saw a shovel whipping toward him. He raised the rifle to parry the blow, but the force of Kreus's attack knocked the weapon from his grasp and sent it spinning away. The force of the blow also left Kreus briefly off-balance. Thom kicked the legs out from under the Tuatha, and the general went sprawling.

Thom turned and began limping away as fast as he could toward a tool wagon near the hull of the ship. He had almost reached the cart when Kreus tackled him about the legs. Thom rolled onto his back, worked a foot free, and kicked Kreus in the head. The blow forced the Tuatha to release his grip on the other leg. Thom lurched to his feet and tried again to reach the wagon.

Kreus's foot caught Thom squarely in the stomach,

forcing the air from his lungs, and driving him back-wards once more into the hull of the ship. He landed on his back beneath the cold blue glow of the hatchway. Helpless, Thom watched Kreus tottering toward him. Despite the pounding roar of his own pulse in his ears, he could swear he heard the whirring of Kreus's hands as the Tuatha clenched and unclenched his fists.

"At last, after all this time," Kreus said, swallowing gulps of air, "I have revenge for Ramal."

"No," someone shrieked.

Out of nowhere a figure in black Tuatha fatigues came flying toward Kreus. The general had half turned toward the scream when Jaime, using someone else's eyes, caught Kreus in the middle of the back. The force of the impact caused the two men to somersault directly into the gaping maw of the portal.

The hatch exploded in a rainbow of colors. Thom tried to shield his eyes against the intense light, but it was too bright. He felt two heavy objects hit him in the chest and roll away. Thom struggled to focus his eyes, but purple splotches filled his field of vision.

"Look, the hatchway, it's not glowing," he heard Abu Brion say.

"Quickly, Hree'Rchee, get into the ship. Bring the woman; we need her as a hostage."

Through the flickering violet haze, Thom saw three dark shapes hovering above him.

"What of the man?" Hree'Rchee said, stepping into the portal.

"Leave him," Abu Brion said. "He is as good as dead."

"Thom," Siobhan cried. She tried to reach down to him, but Abu Brion forced her through the hatch and went in after her.

Using his last ounce of strength, Thom rolled over onto his stomach. He could make out two indistinct shapes just in front of his face. The shapes seemed to be moving.

When his eyes finally began to focus, he saw what the shapes were. He stared in rapt fascination as Kreus's severed hands slowly clenched and unclenched their leather-gloved fingers.

CHAPTER
TWENTY-EIGHT

A huge bell rang in Thom's head, a dull sound that came with every heartbeat and seemed to make the ground shake. He tasted ashes on his tongue.

"Thom, are you all right?" a voice to said to him. "Quick, give him stimulants."

Someone took his left arm and pressed a hard, cold object against the inside of his elbow. There was a hissing sound, and he felt a stinging liquid penetrate his skin. After a moment, the bell stopped ringing, and the world began to coalesce again. He could still taste the ashes, though.

"He's coming around," Al-Sabah said.

"His arm is badly broken, he has lost much fluid, and he has many bruises and cuts," said a strangely accented voice. Thom realized it belonged to one of the Ajnabi, the one called Fadyli, the Healer.

"Siobhan," he wheezed. "She's in the ship. Abu Brion

took her."

"Easy, Thom, easy," Al-Sabah said. "You're badly hurt."

"I've got to save her," he said, trying to get to his feet.

Al-Sabah forced him back down. "We'll get her. You're in no condition to do anything."

"No, it's got to be me," he said. He was now conscious of how much pain he was in, even though it had evolved into a blunt, continuous throbbing rather than spears of flame. He tried to control the pain with bits and pieces of his *la souffrance* discipline, but to no avail. His mind was still too groggy to function fully.

Then he remembered Kreus's enhancement cartridge. It had kept the Tuatha alert and sharp, despite the effects of alcohol and pain.

He cleared his throat. "Cartridge," he said, almost choking. "Find an enhancement . . . cartridge."

"Do you mean this?" Fadyli asked. "I found this on the ground nearby. Is it yours?"

She held out the cartridge.

Thom swallowed, and with his left hand, clumsily snatched the cartridge from her open palm. Before the Ajnabi could react, he had jacked it into the socket behind his right ear.

Instantly, the pain vanished throughout his body. He felt his body return to normal. The taste of ashes vanished from his mouth, and the last remnant of the cobwebs in his brain disappeared.

As his vision cleared, Thom could see the Tuatha troopers sitting in a small circle, their heads resting dejectedly on their knees. Two Mukhalafi soldiers holding seizure guns stood guard over them. He could also see several Ajnabi, control bands on their foreheads, standing nearby.

"Fadyli, make a splint for my right arm," he said calmly. "There's a job I have to finish."

"At least let one of us go with you," Al-Sabah said. "You'll have better odds."

Thom shook his head. "No, I have to do this alone. It's more difficult to spot one man than it is ten."

It took only a few minutes to immobilize his arm. His right arm now strapped against his body, he could feel no pain. In his left arm, he cradled a seizure gun, but hoped he would not need to use it. He placed a control band on his head, but left it inactivated for the moment.

"You're a damn fool, my son," Al-Sabah said, shaking his head sadly. The rebel leader smiled and reached up to squeeze Thom's shoulder. "But I admire your courage. *Khidmetak sharaf.*"

Thom returned the smile. "If I'm not back in twenty minutes, then you can send in a squad . . . if it's not already too late."

He stepped into the hatch.

Thom found himself in a short corridor. At his feet was a single body. It had no hands and was grotesquely mummified, its face twisted. Clearly this was Kreus's corpse, but Isabella and Jaime's bodies were nowhere to be found.

He continued down the corridor and came to a thick metal door, partially shut. It groaned on its hinges as he pushed it open. What he saw inside left him awestruck.

The interior of the ship was like a vast cavern bathed in soft golden light. A huge spiderweb of beams, ducts and catwalks laced its way through the womb-like recesses. The walls were the color of lapis lazuli shot through with veins of gold and silver filament resembling blood vessels. Every so often, massive oval-shaped bulges, like pulsing reddish-gold tumors, appeared on the walls. Thom guessed that bulges were probably the once somnolent machines that operated the ship. It was clear the ship was edging back to life.

He switched on the control band and thought of Siobhan. Instantly he found himself inside her head. Through her eyes he could see she was on a catwalk high in the vessel. Abu Brion was just ahead of her, and he surmised that the Iimarae was behind her. He heard her gasp involuntarily when she discovered his presence. He quickly reassured her, *Don't speak. I'm at the entrance of the ship. Where are you?*

Her thoughts were very clear: *We're way up, across from you on the other side of the ship. I don't know how far along. We got lost in this maze of catwalks.*

Thom look down the length of the vessel in the direction where the Ajnabi had said the main bridge was located. He could barely make out three shapes climbing a long and narrow inclined catwalk. It would take some effort to find them. *Pretend to be hurt. Slow them down.*

I don't know if I can. Don Ernesto is very agitated. He might kill me.

Don't worry. I'll find you.

Thom glanced around for a turbo-lift and spotted a large crystalline object a short distance away on the side opposite the main portal. He trotted quickly to it and looked inside. There appeared to be controls but no entrance. He ran his fingers along the side, trying to find the controls.

Then he remembered the Ajnabi used the bands to run the vessel. He concentrated on the lift. He imagined the door opening, unsure if he would be able to communicate with the vessel. With a soft whoosh of air, a thin seam appeared in the side of the crystal. When it was wide enough, he stepped through it. The lift car sealed itself behind him.

Thom let the seizure gun hang from his shoulder,

concentrated again, and told the lift car where he wanted to go. Its walls glowed a deep violet, and the lift car soared into the air. The speed of the ascent caught Thom by surprise, and he was barely able to bring the car to a stop at the correct catwalk. As he stepped through the widening entry slit and onto a wide platform, he could see the others were about a hundred meters ahead of him.

Hree'Rchee spotted him before he took his first step. With an ear-splitting shriek, the Iimarae sprang from the catwalk and flew at him with incredible speed, her glistening talons extended. Thom raised the seizure gun and fired, but the alien easily dodged the weapon's paralyzing bolt. Remembering what Jaime had told him about Iimarae fears, he tried to project himself into her mind, but he quickly realized that she too was wearing a control band, which blocked him.

She swooped at him, and he ducked. Her talons rattled the catwalk's handrails as she flew past. He turned just in time to see her wheel about and begin another attack. The air crackled as he fired the seizure gun again.

The shot clipped her right wing. She crashed into the handrail, somersaulted, and tumbled into him. Thom caught the full weight of her body against his shoulder. The blow knocked him to the catwalk floor, ripping the weapon from his hands. He scrambled to his feet and felt for his band. It was gone.

He spotted it a short distance away, behind the struggling alien. The Iimarae, one wing bent backwards under her body, was trying to raise herself up by grabbing the handrail. Thom grabbed his control band, put it on, then ripped hers from her head and flung it over the side.

With a scream, Hree'Rchee twisted about and slashed at him with her beak, catching him in the right leg. Thom staggered backwards and felt his leg go over the edge of the catwalk. He caught himself on the rail before he fell.

Talons extended, Hree'Rchee sprang at him. He tried to project himself into her mind and imagined himself falling down through the dizzy heights to the floors below. Nothing happened. The control band didn't seem to work. Then, her wings beating wildly, Hree'Rchee sailed over the railing with a terrified scream, a scream that echoed off the cavernous walls as she pitched end over end.

Realizing what he had done, Thom tried to stop the Iimarae's fall, hoping she could regain control, but it was too late. He watched in horror as the frightened alien struck a glancing blow off one catwalk, then another, finally crashing into a thick black beam that ran the length of the ship. Her back broken and wings akimbo, Hree'Rchee slid down the side of the beam and disappeared in a tangle of machinery. Her blood glistened against the blackness of the beam.

Thom tore his eyes away from the scene and pulled himself back onto the catwalk. His body ached and he was breathing rapidly. That meant he was coming dangerously close to the threshold level of the enhancement cartridge.

Abu Brion and Siobhan were now some distance ahead of him. He could see a bluish glow at the end of the walkway, a glow like that from the entrance portal. He knew it had to be the entrance to the main control center.

Thom spotted the seizure gun a few steps away. He picked it up, slung its strap over his shoulder, and holding onto the railing, he started forward as fast as he could. When he reached the end of the walkway, he found Abu Brion waiting for him.

The *sèo* had Siobhan bent double over the railing. In his right hand, he brandished a small flechette pistol, which he had pressed to the nape of her neck.

"Come no farther, Major, or I will be forced to kill your lady," he said.

Thom took another step.

Don Ernesto pushed the gun deeper into Siobhan's neck. "I am not playing games, Major."

Thom halted.

Abu Brion smiled. "Good, Major. Now, kindly dispose of your weapon, please."

Clutching the strap of the seizure gun, Thom dropped

his shoulder. The weapon slipped to the catwalk floor.

"Over the side. Quickly!"

Thom kicked the weapon off the walkway.

"Very good," Abu Brion said, smiling. He whipped the gun toward Thom and fired.

At the first sign of movement by the *sèo*, Thom dropped down and lunged clumsily forward. He landed heavily on his right shoulder as the projectiles whizzed past his head.

Siobhan hammered her heel into Abu Brion's right instep and jerked her head back to smash the bridge of his nose. Don Ernesto howled in pain from the two blows and roughly flung Siobhan. She crashed into the wall beside the portal and sank down like a rag doll.

Thom looked up to see Abu Brion. Blood was pouring from his wounded nose into his moustache and beard. The *sèo* stood over him with the barrel of the flechette pistol aimed point blank at Thom's head.

Then a voice from nowhere cried out, "Ernesto!"

Abu Brion's face blanched, and his eyes widened in surprise and disbelief. He stared around, uncomprehending. "Isabella, my beloved," he shouted. "My beloved, where are you?"

"Ernesto," the voice said again. It seemed to be coming directly from the glowing doorway. "I am not dead. I am near you. Come to me, my dearest."

Abu Brion's face began twisting into a mask of pain

and fear, as if he no longer controlled it. Zombie-like, the *sèo* slowly turned toward the portal and walked deliberately into the opening. The gun dropped from his fingers and clattered noisily on the floor. He stopped at the entrance, carefully took the control band from his head, and dropped it. Then he stepped through the hatchway. Dazzling blue light burst from the portal, and the *sèo* vanished.

CHAPTER TWENTY-NINE

Thom pressed his face against the floor and covered his eyes the second he saw Don Ernesto enter the portal. After a moment, the hatchway returned to its former state. He struggled to his feet and went to Siobhan.

Siobhan had a nasty swelling on the back of her head, and her wrists were badly lacerated by the filament. Thom reached into her right boot and pulled her *skean dubh* from its sheath. He used the knife to cut the filament from her wrists.

"What happened?" Siobhan asked groggily.

He helped her sit up. "Abu Brion walked into the portal. I think it absorbed him."

She shook her head to clear the cobwebs. "Why did he do that?"

"He heard a voice tell him to do it."

"A voice?" she clarified.

"Yes. It was Isabella's."

She stared at him as if unable to believe what he said.

"I'm going inside," he said. "I have to find out what's in there, and I have to get that weapon."

"You can't do that; it's suicide," Siobhan said. "Besides, they're all dead now: Kreus, Abu Brion, the alien. There's no need to be foolish."

He caressed her cheek with the back of his hand. "I'm sorry, but there's something alive in there, and it still might kill us all. I have to know."

She took his hand and squeezed it as he got up.

He gently pulled his hand away. "I love you, too," he said softly.

Thom picked up his control band, faced the portal, and began to concentrate. After a moment, the blue glow faded. It descended down the spectrum toward green, then yellow, orange, crimson, until it became a soft swirling mist, shot through with flecks of color.

He took a deep breath and stepped through. The mists parted, and he found himself standing in a room cut from what seemed to be polished onyx. A yellow grid work covered the walls, floor, and ceiling. The setting seemed familiar. Then he recognized it as identical to the grid of the data display in the interface. He was standing in a giant computer matrix.

"Welcome, Thomas DuBois," said the voice of Isabella.

From out of nowhere, she appeared before him. She was sitting on a golden chair with a red velvet seat. Thom saw there was now a chair for him. He sat and studied the apparition.

She was certainly not the unhealthy creature he had seen kill herself earlier. This Isabella was bare-shouldered, clad in a red silk gown that hung to the floor. Her shining black hair was braided and coiled atop her head. Her face glowed with health, not the pallor of death.

"Who are you?" he asked.

"I am that which you know as Isabella, and I am also that which has no name."

"You're the ship, a Gonaymne?" Thom said, sitting up with surprise.

"Once we were two, and now we are one," Isabella said. "Long ago the entity you call the Gonaymne went mad because she was crippled and trapped beneath the surface of this world.

"In isolation, the one who had no name had only her own thoughts, which she projected in vain, trying to make contact with another sentient being. For centuries she was alone, but then she discovered another being, the creature called Isabella, with whom she could communicate."

"Of course, the biochips the surgeons implanted," Thom said. "They became a conduit for the thoughts of the ship."

Isabella smiled and nodded. "Yes, but the thoughts of the nameless one were mad. Isabella could not cope with the thoughts, for they brought her great misery. She believed them to be maniacal voices, the voices of her own insanity."

"So you took midnight lace to stop the voices," Thom said.

"Yes, but the drug only brought more madness. Gradually, the two found their minds were being forced together. We shared each other's thoughts and fears. Then Isabella learned the transcendent suffering of the nameless one and the wonder of empty space. The nameless one experienced the sensations of a biological organism's physical pleasures and torments."

Thom leaned forward. "But the two of you were still physically separate, incomplete. You had to merge to be healed."

The image of Isabella gave a faint smile. "When Isabella allowed herself to be absorbed, we both felt great joy. The nameless one at last had a body and Isabella at last could be free of hers. We are she, together."

Thom sat back and tried to comprehend what had happened. It had a weird sort of logic, but something still didn't seem right. He turned to the apparition. "How do I know I can believe you? How do I know you're telling me the truth?"

"Oh, she's telling the truth all right, Thom."

Thom turned and saw an image of Jaime walking toward him with its eyes restored. Beside Jaime walked a small Iimarae, clearly the one called Ryf'Tael, whose death

Jaime had experienced. Astonished, Thom didn't know what to say, and he sat open-mouthed. A third chair appeared and Jaime sat on it. The Iimarae folded its legs and sat beside him on a thickly woven red, blue and green rug that had suddenly materialized.

"To answer your question," Jaime said, "yes, I am a projection, but I'm now also part of the ship's matrix. So is Ryf'Tael. The ship absorbed us when Kreus and I passed through the hatch."

"Is Kreus alive, or Abu Brion?"

Jaime shook his head. "No, when they were absorbed, only the data contained in their brains was preserved. That is why you found Kreus's body. My entire identity was preserved because I was wearing a band of obedience. Ryf'Tael's was preserved because I was in his mind when he died. His essence was stored away in part of my brain."

"Then the dreams of flying and falling, they really were *his* dreams?"

"You are perceptive and wise," said the Iimarae.

"Perhaps, but not wise enough to avert a war between your people and mine. Not wise enough to have kept myself from killing that Iimarae elder."

"You did not kill her," Isabella said. "I did."

"What?" he said. "But I projected my mind into hers, I caused her to fall."

"Your band was inoperative, Major," Isabella said. "When it was knocked away from you, its power pack was damaged."

Thom removed the band from his forehead, opened the power pack, and examined it. The small unit had a large black smudge where it had burned out.

"Then it was you who allowed me to enter the portal?"

"Does it matter?" Isabella said. "You would have eventually found a way to contact us."

Thom smiled sadly. "I suppose nothing matters. I still haven't found a way to stop the Iimarae. The war I hoped to avoid is inevitable, especially with an Iimarae warship nearby. They'll alert their fleet, and the attack will begin."

"Nothing is inevitable," Jaime said. "Look."

A silvery holographic video screen began unfolding itself nearby. Scenes of an Iimarae scout ship appeared. The crew was in mutiny against the elders.

"Already we have freed the Iimarae from the control of the elders," Isabella said.

"Their ship is heading out of the Pavonian system, toward a rebel Iimarae colony which has long rejected the rule of the queens and the elders," Jaime said.

"How do I know this is true?"

"When you leave, you will meet some envoys from the *Lasalle*," Jaime said. "They will confirm it."

"The *Lasalle* is at Tau Ceti."

"No," Jaime replied. "They stayed behind, and grew more suspicious when Reynardo sent them false dispatches."

"You're in contact with the *Lasalle*, then?"

"With its computer," Isabella said.

Thom sat back in his chair, dejected and depressed. "Everything I did, it meant nothing. You were already putting events into motion."

"Don't underestimate what you have done," Isabella said. "Without you, Thom, Don Ernesto surely would have succeeded, and we would still be two distinct mentalities, equally insane."

"And, without you, I would be most certainly dead," Jaime said, "without even a shadow existence like this. War would have been inevitable, and the Iimarae would have destroyed Askander, perhaps even Earth."

"You also helped create a revolution for justice and freedom for the *mostazafin*," Isabella said. "The road they must now travel will be difficult, but you have given them hope, a gift they will always remember you by."

Thom felt weary. His body throbbed and ached. The enhancement cartridge had finally reached its limits, and his body was exhausted. "The Iimarae, how do you intend to deal with them?"

"The elders' control bands will not hold up against this ship's powers," Ryf'Tael said. "The revolution is inescapable, and retribution, I fear, will not be pleasant. Workers will rise up against masters, believers against their priests. There will be no more Swarmings, and the nests of the egg mothers will be bloodied for a long time.

It is as it must be."

"How will you do this?" Thom wondered.

"We must soon be free of this mountain. You must help us find a crew," Isabella said. "Then you must convince the Ajnabi that we have changed, that time and madness have taught us the lessons they have long wished us to learn. Tell them that once we have finished with the Iimarae, we will seek out others of our kind and end the horror once and for all."

"I'll try, but they're hard to convince," he said. He rose to go, holding onto the chair to steady himself. "Now, if you will excuse me . . ."

He felt ghostly hands hold him up and guide him to the door. As he started to step back through the portal, he felt Jaime catch his arm.

"Here, this will prove to the Ajnabi that the ship has evolved." Jaime said. He placed a long bifurcated piece of crystal into Thom's hand. There were solid black knobs at either end, and thin black filaments embedded in the crystal ran its entire length.

"The detonator for the nova weapon," Thom said, awed at the eerie beauty and elegant simplicity of such a deadly device.

"Go, now."

"Will I ever see any of you again?"

"Perhaps," said Isabella, "but eventually all of us will merge into one entity, each consciousness part of a new whole. What you see then may no longer be male or female or perhaps not even human, Iimarae or Gonaymne."

Thom nodded sadly. "Goodbye."

He stepped through the portal into the waiting arms of medteks from the *Lasalle*. They lowered him onto a stretcher and immediately started first aid. He never even felt the injectors and infusers pumping drugs and painkillers into his body.

When they carried him up the ramp, he spotted Ishan standing nearby. He held out the detonator. "A peace offering, from the ship."

The Ajnabi gently took the weapon from his hands and nodded. Thom was not sure, but he thought he saw Ishan smile.

Cool hands caressed his forehead, and he looked up to see Siobhan. He managed a feeble smile.

"Do you still mean it? About loving me?" she said.

"What do you think?"

"I've never known you to lie," she said, grinning.

He took her hand in his.

"There's somewhere I want to take you, on Earth," he said. "Have you ever seen New England in Autumn?"

"No," she replied, squeezing his hand. There were tears in her eyes. "But I bet it's beautiful."

EPILOGUE

In the inky night of deep space a thousand million voices cried as one. It was a song of revolution and a song of defiance.

Too long had the Queens and the Elders held down the Flock, too long had its members suffered their wrongs without complaint.

First the silver ship had appeared in the sky. Weapons proved useless against it, and it had weapons greater than any of which the Iimarae knew. With the ship came reports of a vision, of an Iimarae called Ryf'Tael the Wise who called on the Flock to overthrow their rulers, to free themselves of the yoke of oppression.

Rumors quickly spread that the ship was a vessel of the Nameless Ones and that it had caused egg-mothers to fail to produce new offspring. The elders trembled in their nests at the very mention of the ship, and the queens retired to their dens to enjoy their consorts for perhaps one last time.

Then the bands of obedience were found to no longer function. Freed of their chains, servants slaughtered the children of their masters. Workers attacked their overseers. The faithful murdered the priests who had preached obedience in this world and promised rewards in the next world.

There would be no Swarming this time. No longer would the bands' perverted force control the Iimarae. No longer would the bloated genetic products of the Bands' use rule the Flock.

The retribution was swift and bloody, as Ryf'Tael the Wise had warned. The rebuilding would be difficult and painful, but less so than having one's throat ripped out to give pleasure to a queen or elder.

Now the Iimarae returned to the old ways, the evolutionary path of freedom that had once been lost. But for generations after, they still spoke of the silver ship and how the image of Ryf'Tael the Wise appeared before the faithful.

By then, the starship was long gone on another quest, this time to find others of its own kind and destroy them before those vessels, awakened at last, could bring war back to a galaxy that at long last had found peace.

ACKNOWLEGEMENTS

I first want to thank my editor Mara Hodges for her faith in this novel and her enthusiasm in making it far better than I could ever have imagined. Without her dedication, this book might have remained an unpublished manuscript gathering dust. I owe her the deepest debt of gratitude.

A writer always owes forever unpaid debts to his teachers, and in my case it was my writing professors at the University of Oklahoma. Mystery writer Carolyn Hart taught me much about outlines and plots, while the now sadly absent Jack Bickham and Robert L. Duncan displayed high trust and faith in my talents as they taught me the craft. I owe them a debt I can never repay.

A book always comes about because of friends. Too many of mine are gone, including Ed Howard, Kim Pugh, Nancy Peay, Cathy Ball and her husband Jim Brazzell and my fellow Celtic musician Kelly Crumpley. Among the now missing are also my first wife, Vicki S. Brown and her sister Charlene Lea, both of whom gave me support in tough times. I miss you all.

Among the living, I owe special thanks to my friends Susan Brenholtz Tillery, Michael Madden, Vicki Redick, Ann Felts, and Bill Mansker, who gave encouragement and whose names I appropriated at times in the book because that seemed a good idea. I also want to thank my friends Lisa H. Alkana, Tom Jackson, and Gwen Meredith, fellow writers whose friendship

I treasure. There are too many others to mention, but I 'll get around them eventually.

I also am thankful that my fiddler friend Ruth Coates set me up on a blind date with my wife Nancy. I'm grateful most all to Nancy, who loved this book when she first read it. She also poked and prodded me to get things done when I procrastinated, proving she's the best motivator I've ever known. I can never thank her enough.

We hope you've enjoyed the story. Please help us share this story with other readers by letting us know what you thought with a review on either **amazon.com** or **goodreads.com**.

Thank you kindly,
Montag Press Collective

Born in Birmingham, England, **Nigel Anthony Sellars** spent his childhood outside Montreal, Quebec, and has lived in and around Oklahoma City, in a small town in Nebraska, in Los Angeles, and in Newport News, Virginia, where he is an associate professor of history at Christopher Newport University.

He has been, at times, an actor, a folksinger in a Celtic music band, a motel night clerk, a convenience store clerk, a welfare intake worker, a research assistant working with chimpanzees, a rat-runner in a psych lab, and a multiple award-winning journalist. He holds degrees in psychology and history from the University of Oklahoma. A graduate of the professional writing program in the School of Journalism at the University of Oklahoma, he studied with noted novelists Jack M. Bickham, Robert L. Duncan and Carolyn Hart. He earned his doctorate in history from OU in 1994. The author of numerous articles, both non-scholarly and scholarly, his fiction has appeared in such magazines as *Visions, Beyond, Alpha Adventures, Space & Time, Oracle,* and *Out of the Cradle,* and has been translated into Russian. Most of his short stories appear in his 2002 collection, *The Confessions of Caliban and Other Stories.* His scholarly writings have twice been honored by the Oklahoma Historical Society, including the prestigious Muriel Wright Award for his Chronicles of Oklahoma article "Almost Hopeless in the Face of the Storm" about the deadly 1917 Spanish Flu pandemic in the state.

The author of four other books, including the fantasy novel *Ukishima* and the highly regarded *Oil, Wheat and Wobblies: The Industrial Workers of the World in Oklahoma, 1905-1930,* which was a 1998 Oklahoma Book Award nominee. He shares his home with his photographer wife Nancy and their two beagles. Among other projects, he is working on a sequel to *The Gonaymne Weapon.*